Bluegrass Undercover

A Bluegrass Brothers Novel

Kathleen Brooks

Books by Kathleen Brooks

Bluegrass Series

Bluegrass State of Mind

Risky Shot

Dead Heat

Bluegrass Brothers Series

Bluegrass Undercover

Rising Storm

Secret Santa, A Bluegrass Series Novella

Acquiring Trouble

Relentless Pursuit

Secrets Collide

For Chris, Milo, Marcia and Kathy.
Thanks for all the hard work and support.
And most importantly, to my wonderful readers.

Prologue

He wiped his sweaty hands on his mesh shorts and took a deep breath to calm himself. If he got caught, it would end his high school football career, cost him a chance at a college scholarship, and his parents would be pissed. Those factors were outweighed by the fact that he was a full two tenths of a second slower in the 40 than his backup, and that meant if he didn't pick it up, he'd be riding the bench this season.

The glass doors were looming in front of him as he approached the dealer. His hands left sweaty imprints as he pushed the doors open and tried to casually walk inside. His heart pounded as if it were up to him to make the last-second play to win the big game. He smiled to those he knew, which, thanks to being such a small town, was practically everyone. Did they all know what he was about to do?

The locker room was just ahead of him now. This was it. He put his hand in his pocket and felt for the cash he'd stolen out of his mom's and dad's wallets over the last couple of weeks. He'd had to empty his piggy bank and save up his allowances for a month, but if this worked, it would be worth it. He'd be faster, stronger, and maybe even Mr. Football in Kentucky. A scholarship to a Division I school would make everything perfect. Even his parents couldn't get mad about taking a couple hundred from them if he was going to be on ESPN every Saturday.

"Hey, man."

"What's up?"

"You got the five hundred?"

"Yup."

He pulled out the cash and handed it to him. His eyes darted around the momentarily empty locker room. Someone could walk in at any minute, but his dealer was as calm as could be counting out the cash. Shouldn't he hurry and give him the stuff before the police barged in?

"Here you go kid. Ten units three times a week." He caught the small, black duffle bag and nodded his head toward his dealer before he walked as fast as he could out of there.

He managed to get home before his parents got back from work, but his little sister was already home and would be a problem. If only he had a lock on the door. He moved his desk chair over to his door and shoved it under the doorknob. It would have to work. If Cindy knew he was home, she'd come running in, wanting to play or talk about the gossip going on in cheerleading camp. God, little sisters were a trial.

He placed the duffle on his bed and slowly unzipped it. Inside were a handful of diabetic syringes and a small glass bottle with a black rubber stopper. Pulling off the orange cap on the needle, he slowly poked it through the rubber stopper and measured out ten units. He dropped the bottle back into the bag and pulled down his shorts. He heard the garage door open and knew his parents were home. He had to hurry. Would he feel stronger by tomorrow? Would he be like Spiderman? He envisioned himself as the best football player in the country, shredding defenses and scoring every time the ball was in his hands. He'd be a hero.

He grabbed the skin at his waist between his thumb and middle finger. This was it. The needle met resistance as he pressed it against his skin. It pricked, and he winced as he pushed it through his skin.

His thumb pushed the plunger down, and he watched the drug that would change his life enter his body.

"Honey! Dinner!"

"Coming, Mom."

Chapter One

Annie Blake felt the ocean breeze ruffle her sweat-drenched hair. It was Miami in August. Even being on the beach did nothing to cool her off. She hardly ever went to the beach. Who had time? But, she must admit, the sand did feel good between her toes, and the smell of the salt floating by and the feathered waves of the breeze did relax her.

She looked over the sparkling blue water as far as she could see and took a deep breath. It was going to be a great day. She scanned the beach and saw kids playing, sunbathers in barely there swimsuits, and a thug by one of the beach bars. He was shorter than she, probably around five six to her five seven. His black hair was pulled back into a low ponytail at the base of his neck. His body was shiny with sweat, which made his tattoos sparkle in the sunlight. His jean shorts started at his thighs and ended at his ankles. She had no idea why thugs liked this style of clothing, but it worked for her. It was hard to run with your pants falling down.

A young boy, maybe fifteen, sauntered over to the thug with a cocky attitude. His athletic shorts fell to mid-calf as he hiked them up over plaid boxers. The thug nodded his head to the nearby ice cream cone stand. The kid and the thug walked over, got in line and started talking.

She had been tracking this thug for weeks. He was a drug soldier for Juan Carlos's gang. About six months ago, Annie's team at the

DEA had been notified by an ER doctor of his suspicions of a new drug being pushed to kids, a drug that caused heart attacks in young, athletic boys. Annie investigated and found all the victims were local high school football players ranging in age from fourteen to eighteen.

Then, two weeks ago, she got a call from the same ER doctor. A kid was admitted for collapsing during a friendly football game. She rushed to the ER and interviewed the kid before he went in for heart surgery. She had been told of Diego, the friendly neighborhood drug dealer. She had tracked him to this beach as his primary place of dealing while the kids were out on summer break.

She adjusted her dark pink sarong to make sure the small Sig 9mm Mosquito that was tucked into her pale pink bikini bottoms was hidden from view. The last thing she needed was for someone to see her walking down the beach with a gun. She pulled her long, red hair from the ponytail and shook it out. The guys told her they liked seeing long hair dancing in the breeze, so she went with it. She pushed up her breasts so they were almost spilling out of her triangle top. She was pretty sure Diego wouldn't become suspicious of a big-breasted, beach bimbo.

"Geezus, Blake! You trying to garner attention? You're supposed to be undercover," her earpiece crackled. Annie looked past the ice cream stand to the ice truck parked in the lot. She gave the DEA agents who filled the truck along with surveillance equipment a little wink.

Annie gave one last toss of the hair and started walking across the beach to the ice cream stand. Her voluptuous hips swayed, and her breasts teetered precariously in her top as she banked the intelligence behind her dark green eyes. Diego and the kid had just bought their cones and were now standing to the side of the ice cream stand. She headed right toward them and gave Diego a sultry smile when he looked up and saw her.

"Hey," she bit down seductively on her pouty, lower lip. "I heard you were the man to contact if I wanted to *score*," she winked.

"Dios mio. I would love to help you, but I don't sell what you're looking for."

"But, I was told you were the man. That you could give a girl anything she wants." Annie paused, "Well, how about whatever you're giving the kid. Maybe that can hold me over until I find a real man to give me what I want."

"Oh, lady, you're killing me. This stuff is for athletes. How about you both meet me here tomorrow at two." Diego turned to the kid, "You bring your buddies. Tell them it's five hundred a vial." Annie bit her lip again in a pout and wrapped some of her straight hair around her finger. "And you, hmm," he said to her as he rubbed his crotch, or what she guessed to be his crotch. She couldn't tell where anything was under his baggy shorts. "You meet me here, too. I will get something special for you. Three hundred." He gave one last rub to his crotch and started walking down the beach, holding up his shorts as he went.

"Good job, Blake. We lost sight of the kid. Do you have eyes on him?"

"Yeah, he's with five other boys, ages fifteen to seventeen. Looks like they're going to be playing a little beach football." She lay down on her towel and pulled out her camera. She snapped some photos of the beach and then swung the camera around and got some photos of the boys. She zoomed in on the t-shirt of one of the boys with the name of a local high school football team. Bingo.

"Hey, sexy, how about we put that camera to good use?"

"Get lost, jackass."

"Aw, don't hate the player, hate the game."

She looked up at the muscled beach bum, "How about I hate both. Now get lost, I'm not going to have sex with you now or ever." He looked stunned at the rejection and slowly walked off towards his next victim.

"Ouch, Blake. We thought you were a bitch because you couldn't get laid."

"Bite me."

"With pleasure."

"The boys are leaving." She watched as they started to walk toward a minivan that had just pulled up and honked its horn.

"Copy that. Go home. Same place and time tomorrow."

Annie stood up, rolled up her towel, and stuffed it into her beach bag. She closed her eyes for a second and felt warm rays of the evening sun on her face. She'd have to try to make it to the beach more often.

Annie reached her one-bedroom apartment in twenty minutes. She unlocked the deadbolt and threw her bag down on the chair in the living room. She placed her gun in the safe and walked into the small kitchen that overlooked the living room. The walls were white, as she'd never bothered painting them. This wasn't her home. It was just a place to live.

She opened the freezer and pulled out a Lean Cuisine at random. She tore open the box and tossed it into the microwave. As she walked through the living room, she turned the TV on to the Dolphins' exhibition game and headed for the shower. Tomorrow she'd be one step closer to bringing down this drug ring.

Annie was worried that her gun might not work if she sweated on it anymore. The sun was so hot on her skin that the sweat running down her spine was cascading around her Sig tucked securely in her lavender bikini bottoms.

She saw the kid and his buddies eyeing the ice cream stand and decided it was close enough to the meeting time to head up there. Diego hadn't shown yet, but he could be waiting for them. She tied her hair back into a ponytail and slipped off her flip flops. She needed to be able to run if anything happened.

Annie saw the second the kid recognized her. He ribbed his buddies and they all stared. Maybe she should have worn a one piece. She was meeting with kids after all. But, Diego really liked her bikini so the tiny bikini won out.

"Hola, senorita. Let me take care of these kids and us adults can talk," Diego said, appearing suddenly beside her as he ran his hand slowly down her arm. "Hey, kid. You all got the funds?"

"Yup, twenty-five hundred, just like you asked for." The kid handed a plastic shopping bag over to Diego who in return handed over his own shopping bag.

Annie watched as the kids sauntered off, knowing that part of her team was waiting to follow them. As soon as they had Diego in custody, they'd arrest the kids and scare them and their parents into full confessions and lots of information.

"Why put up with those brats?" she asked as she turned back to Diego, who was ogling her breasts.

"Have to. I specialize in a new product. It's steroids on steroids for young athletes. High school mostly, but our middle school market is picking up."

"Sounds expensive at five hundred a pop. Where do kids get that money?"

"That's the best part. The majority of our clients are middle to upper class. They just take it from their parents and are above suspicion. No one will question the star of the private school football team, and it reduces the risks on our end."

"How?"

"Kids like this have more to lose if they talk. They also aren't used to life on the streets, so the risk of violence is low. It's a win-win for us."

"Do you make the drug yourself? It sounds very interesting."

"No. We import it from up north. Now, enough about them. Let's talk about you. I got you something special."

"Ooh! What did you get me?"

"A nice designer drug that gets you high as a kite but with the sensations of Ecstasy. How about we go back to your place and test it out? If you like it, you can show me your gratitude and I won't even charge you for it." He reached out and grabbed her waist with his hands. He ran them up her ribcage, stopping at her breasts. She counted to ten to try to rein in her temper.

"So, if I have sex with you, you'll waive the three hundred dollar fee? Look at me. I think I'm worth more than three hundred. Throw in two more packages and you have a deal."

"You run a tough bargain, but you look worth it." He pulled out three little pouches from his pocket down by his knee and slipped them into her triangle top.

"Now, let's go party."

"Sure thing, big boy." Annie reached into her bag and brought out her cuffs. "You're under arrest for the sale and distribution of narcotics. You have the right to remain silent. Anything you say may be used against you in…" Annie's head was snapped back by a strong slap to the face. A *slap*? Who slaps these days?

Diego took off down the beach in what could barely be described as a run. It looked more like skipping as his shorts kept falling down, causing him to miss steps while trying to keep the pants up.

"We got him, Annie," she heard in her earpiece.

"No. He's all mine. Go pick up the kids."

"Remember your temper. Take a deep breath. It was just a little slap," the agent chuckled.

"Don't forget the boob grab."

"Really, Annie. Take it easy." But it was too late. She had reached him in just a couple strides. She pushed off the sand with the balls of her feet and launched herself at him. She wrapped her arm around his waist, taking him to the ground as his shorts slipped from their precarious perch on his thighs to his ankles. Annie sat half on top of him trying to secure her cuffs.

"Puta!" Diego grabbed whatever he could, which happened to be her top, and pulled. Her ties dug into her neck as she felt his nails dig into the soft skin above her breast.

He brought his hand up and boxed her ear. Sand burned her eyes as her ear rang. Okay, that was enough. Annie pulled back her right arm, tightened her hand into a fist and brought it down as hard as she could onto the side of his face. She heard the satisfying grunt and watched as his eyes rolled back in his head. She secured his hands in the cuffs and stuffed her breasts back into the tiny bikini top. She'd hear about this for months. Nothing like having her boobs popping out on surveillance to suddenly have every agent in the department wanting to review the footage to "help out."

She looked up and saw the telltale sign of federal agents: cheap suits on a beach. No blending in for these guys coming towards her.

"Blake, you're going to be in deep trouble when Cruz hears about this. This is the fourth guy you've knocked out in three months."

Annie took a deep breath. She knew every set of eyes on the floor was on her now. She looked up at the door belonging to her boss, Special Agent in Charge Manuel Cruz. Show no fear. She raised her hand and knocked on the door before opening it. She was expected, she had been summoned. She hadn't even had time to get dressed before she had been called to his office. There was no dignified way to face your boss in a barely there lavender bikini, but she lived by three rules – one, never show fear, two, never get attached, and three, if all else fails, fake it until you make it.

She stepped up to the large oak desk covered in papers and files and clasped her hands behind her back. "You wanted to see me."

"Jesus, you could have gotten dressed first." Cruz took in her apparel, or lack of apparel, and shook his head. "Here." He threw her a DEA t-shirt and waited until she slipped it on.

"You said it was important, sir."

"I know I did. I have a huge problem. I have a massive drug ring targeting kids, and I am this close to having my ass chewed out by the U.S. Attorney because I have *another* perp beaten up. Luckily, it was caught on camera that he sexually assaulted you and hit you on the head. At least that's the angle we're taking."

"So, what's the problem then?"

"The problem is I can't cover for you anymore. You've had three mandatory cycles of anger management, but I still can't control you.

The problem is you're my best agent, and you know the most about this new drug." Cruz paused and shuffled through some of the papers on his desk until he found the one he was looking for. "Diego spilled his guts as soon as we said we'd let you interrogate him. He doesn't like you very much anymore. It turns out the shipments all originate from a small town called Keeneston, Kentucky." He handed the paper to her.

"I'm being transferred to the Lexington office?" She stared in disbelief at the paper in her hand.

"Yes. You'll be undercover as Annie Hill. I got you a job in Keeneston at the high school so you can keep a close eye on the kids there. If it's being made there, then I'm sure they're using it. You'll be at ground zero and reporting to Special Agent in Charge Vincent Romero. You're his problem now."

"When do I leave?" She stood straighter. She would not show the hurt she was feeling. It was just one more move in her life. It's not like she hadn't done it a dozen times before.

"You're transfer is immediate. Good-bye, Agent Blake."

Chapter Two

Trevor Gaylen didn't want to answer the ringing phone. He knew it was the boss, and he was sure the boss had also heard about the incident in Miami. The boss was going to be pissed and take it out on him. After all, he was in charge of recruitment. He was upper management, and with a nice share of the profits also came the responsibility of having control over middle management.

Miami had sales that were skyrocketing in the last six months. Just last month he'd gotten praise for it, but now some street soldier had messed things up for him. Hopefully, Boss would know he had nothing to do with this and let him live.

"Gaylen," he said into the phone.

"What the hell happened in Miami?" the digitally disguised voice asked. Yup, Boss was pissed.

"I don't know. The reports I'm getting from management is that a soldier sold S2 in front of a DEA agent and then sold her drugs. When she went to arrest him, he clocked her, and then there was something about sexually assaulting her, but no one is really clear on that."

"How much did he know?"

"Management swears he only knew the name of his supplier."

"I don't want to risk it. Order a clean sweep of the Miami franchise. No one left alive. For God's sake and yours, find a stronger manager who knows how to handle his soldiers."

"Done. I have had my eye on someone for expansion, but he'll do well as a new manager. He has a strong cocaine ring that's been running for seven years. He's stable and knows his business."

"Good. Make sure everyone is gone by the end of the night. And, Gaylen?"

"Yes?"

"I don't want any more screw-ups or I will hold you personally responsible, understand?"

"Yes, Boss."

Cade Davies couldn't decide when to teach meiosis in his freshman biology class. He sat at his desk at Keeneston High School and stared at his lesson plan. He ran his fingers through his dark blonde hair and decided to teach it with photosynthesis before he tackled Mendel. Football camp started Monday and he wanted to use these two days to get all his teaching plans for the year ready.

He looked up from his desk when he heard a grunt from his bearded collie Justin, then noticed his friend Will Ashton trying to push the door to his classroom open. Justin liked to lie against doors, and fifty-eight pounds of dog was hard to move. Will pushed harder, and because of Justin's long black and white coat on the slick tiles, Justin slid along the floor like a mop as the door opened.

"Hi, Will. Am I missing a coaches' meeting?"

"Nope. But, I did want to talk to you about the team."

"Sure, what's up?" Cade asked his longtime friend.

Will Ashton had played football at Keeneston High and then went on full scholarship to the University of Kentucky. He was a standout quarterback who got drafted into the NFL and played for years before his father had a heart attack. He left the NFL at the end of the season, as the number one quarterback in the country, in order to run the family thoroughbred farm. He had succeeded at that too, with back-to-back Kentucky Derby winners in his stable. On top of running the farm, he was also the volunteer head football coach at the high school. Having grown up in the same town, they had known each other since they were knee high.

"Well, now that the trial is done, I want to focus on Kenna. You know she is due in six months, and what with recovering from the shooting and all, I just really want to help her out with getting ready for the baby. She's trying to do it all: working full time, helping out with the farm, and getting the nursery ready. I'm telling you she's out of control."

Poor Will. He was frantic over the prospect of having a child. After having his wife shot and then having her as the star witness at the center of a major corruption and murder trial, he didn't want her more than five feet away from him. It didn't matter that McKenna was perfectly capable of taking care of herself.

"So, I am resigning at head coach."

"What? You can't do that."

"I know I will be letting the kids down, Cade. We have a very young, very inexperienced team this year, but I can't give them my full attention. It wouldn't be fair to them. I have talked to Margaret, and as principal she agreed to the new hire already."

"New hire? Who is it?" He watched Will straighten up to his full six feet two inches and smile.

"I'm here to officially offer you the position as head coach."

"Me? But, I'm not qualified. I've only been an assistant for a couple of years and no head coaching experience." Cade was overwhelmed. He had just started getting the hang of being the offensive coordinator, but to take over the whole team...he wasn't ready for this.

"You'll do great," Will said.

Cade looked at his friend and thought he actually meant it. "I guess I have a lot of work to do this weekend." Cade sat back down in his chair and stared at his lesson plans. He now had to finish his lesson plans and figure out a coaching strategy by Monday.

"Don't worry. You'll be fine. Call if you have any problems." Will gave him a thump on the back and headed out the door.

Cade pressed his fingers to the bridge of his nose and sighed. This was a hell of a year to start out as a coach. The whole offensive line was empty because of graduation. The quarterback Austin Colby was good but lazy, and the only wide receiver worth mentioning was Ryan Hall, and he was a freshman! At least he had senior Trey Everett at running back. The defense was small, but they had Corey Bonner coming off an all-state season as linebacker.

To make matters worse, spring practice had been a nightmare. It was like the whole team, except Trey, quit. They were lazy and acted as if they didn't care. This was definitely a rebuilding year.

"Come on, Justin. Let's get home for dinner. It's going to be a very long night." Cade stood up, packed up his folders, and grabbed the team's playbook. Justin jumped up at the mention of food and trotted out of the room ahead of Cade.

Cade dug into the pocket of his jeans for the keys to unlock the doors to his Highlander SUV. Justin leaped into the front seat and pressed his black nose to the window. His pink tongue hung out as the hot sun warmed him up.

"Is your dog wearing a bow in his hair?" Cade turned and saw Principal Margaret Lopez standing behind him, staring at Justin with a goofy little grin on her face.

"The groomer put it in. He can't see without it. His hair falls into his eyes."

"Well, maybe next time ask for another color besides pink. Poor boy, he looks embarrassed."

Cade agreed. Justin did seem embarrassed by the tiny pink bow on top of his head. He kept pawing at it and even growled at himself when he saw it in the mirror. "Well, let me be the first to congratulate you, Coach," Margaret said as she patted him on the back. "I know you'll do a great job."

"I hope so, even though it's a rebuilding year." Might as well make sure everyone knows not to expect miracles.

Keeneston wasn't known as a football powerhouse. It was better known as a rifle club powerhouse. While everyone bled blue for the University of Kentucky basketball and football teams, they just didn't have the population to support a strong program in those major sports at the high school level. Even though they weren't a power house, he hated to disappoint his town. They may not be the best, but they definitely had the most hometown pride. People closed businesses for big games, parades were given for Homecoming, and most of the town showed up to support "their boys" at the football games.

"Will warned me about that. The town will support you, especially with your knowledge and talent. All the kids love you. You just take good care of those boys and do the best you can. Well, I'm off to Bluegrass Airport to pick up our new guidance counselor. I am so glad we finally got that position filled. I was afraid I was going to have to ask you to do it!" she joked.

"Where is the new counselor coming from?"

"Miami. Has a great resume and references. Gosh knows I haven't found anyone I liked so far. She's on a one year probation, and then we'll offer her tenure track if she works out."

"Good. I hope she does. See you Monday for orientation and football camp. Are you planning on giving your normal talk to the team before practice?"

"Yes. But then the new counselor will be coming and getting smaller groups of freshmen throughout the day as their names are called for the smaller orientation groups. If that's okay?"

"Of course it is. See you then."

Cade jumped into the car and rolled the window down for Justin, who enjoyed the wind blowing back his hair as they drove down the country road surrounded by rolling hills, black fences, and hungry cows. It was going to be a very long weekend, and he needed to get home fast to finish up those plans and then pretend he knew what it meant to be a head coach.

Annie walked off the plane and into a small, neat airport. There were no signs in Spanish. There were no lines at a Starbucks. And there were no noisy people yelling the finer points of LeBron James' game. It was so foreign. It made her nervous that everyone she passed smiled as they went on their way. From the plane she saw large tracts of land surrounded by white and black fences. The land was not covered with tall buildings or sprawling apartment complexes. Was there even a downtown? Looking at the artwork on the walls as she waited for her bags, she guessed there was a small one at least with one very tall blue building.

"Miss Hill?" Annie turned and saw a short woman with caramel-color skin and dark brown hair looking at her.

"Yes?"

"I am Margaret Lopez, the principal at Keeneston High. I'm so very glad to meet you."

Annie shook her hand and smiled. She seemed very nice and very matronly, like she would feed you in an instant if you said you were hungry.

"Let me help you with your bags. We're really excited to have you join our staff. We're like a family, so if you need anything, don't hesitate to ask." Margaret picked up some of her bags and led her to a silver minivan.

Annie looked around and couldn't believe there was so much green space everywhere. Colorfully painted horse statues stood nearby, and just off in the distance the real thing ran in pastures surrounded by white fences.

"We're so lucky we found you. I have been interviewing, but no one has been qualified. We start on Monday with new student orientation. We have ten groups of kids scheduled. We'll start at nine in the morning and go until three in the afternoon. We'll show the kids the school, tell them about the services we have and sign them up for their electives. It doesn't give you much time, but I put together a folder for you with information about the school and town. I thought we could meet at seven thirty and I could show you around."

"Thank you. That will be a big help."

"Your principal at your old school, Mr. Cruz, said you were seeking the transfer to be closer to your family. I believe he said they were in Louisville?"

"Yes, I have a cousin in Louisville."

That much was true at least. It didn't matter that she'd never met her or that she didn't even know if her aunt was still alive. She'd been raised in a series of foster homes until she turned eighteen, foster homes filled with fighting and foster parents who only cared about when the next check was coming. Not all homes were like that—she had heard of the good ones, but because she refused to be a victim and fought back when her foster siblings started beating on her and stood up to an abusive foster dad, she got labeled a "bad kid" whom the system couldn't help. The result of being labeled bad was a constant string of houses where the parents were essentially absent or just turned a blind eye to a boy beating up his sister. Annie thanked God every day that she had been able to fight. Some of her foster sisters had not been so lucky. They ended up severely injured, or some ran away never to be heard from again.

When she turned eighteen and graduated from high school with honors, she headed to Florida State University on full scholarship. She majored in chemistry, and upon graduating six years ago, she started working for the DEA after graduating from DEA Training at Quantico. She had been moved from office to office ever since. She had never looked back and had never kept in touch with anyone from her past. As far as she was concerned, her life started when she went to college. No one knew about her before then. It seemed no one cared, no one until Chrystal Sharp.

Chrystal had sent her an email two years ago. In it she told Annie that they were cousins, that she lived in Louisville and was researching the family tree and had tracked her down. She wanted to get in touch, get to know one another, wanted to become family. That all sounded nice, but Annie knew it wasn't the truth. If Chrystal and her mother hadn't cared enough about her when Annie was ten, and her mother went on a weeklong bender that took them from Indianapolis to Orlando where she finally died from an overdose in an alley behind Disney World, then screw them. She had fought and won against staggering odds, and she wasn't about to forgive and forget.

See, what her social worker didn't know was that Annie had heard her on the phone with her aunt while at the hospital. Her mother had just been declared dead and Annie had given the social worker her aunt's name. She heard the social worker begging her aunt to take Annie, but her aunt had refused. She said she wanted nothing to do with her sister or her sister's bastard child.

Now, here she was on her way to yet another home, driving through the beautiful countryside outlined with black and white, four-board wood fences surrounding horse farms with rolling hills, horses grazing, and grass that appeared slightly blue. After all these years, she was just two hours away from the only family she had left, and the only thing she felt was anger.

"I believe you'll find Keeneston very different from Miami. But, I think it's a good thing. I grew up in Keeneston, so if you need anything just let me know."

"Thanks, what is Keeneston like?"

Annie looked out the window, and since they were traveling around ten miles per hour, got to enjoy the scenery that was slowly changing from open fields to houses on big lots filled with old trees. In front of them on the narrow country road was a huge green tractor. Unlike the Kenney Chesney song, she did not find the tractor sexy.

"Well, we're coming up on Main Street. It has everything you need."

Annie tried to see around the tractor but gave up. Within a minute, a picturesque town with its old buildings painted in whites, yellows, and tans came into view. Barrels of pink, purple, yellow and white flowers lined Main Street. Some people stood talking on the corner and waved at Margaret as she drove by. There were little shops that sold antiques, a stately courthouse and more people waving at her.

"That's the Blossom Café. If you ever need something to eat, their food is amazing." Margaret pointed to the restaurant on her right where a thin woman in a flower print dress was sweeping the sidewalk. "That's Daisy Mae Rose. She and her sister Violet run the Café."

As they drove by, Margaret honked the horn, and Daisy raised her arm to shield her eyes from the sun. Her eyes narrowed as she looked into the car and saw Annie. In a split second she called something into the open door of the Café, and people started walking out to stand on the sidewalk. Some had sandwiches in their hands, some just had cold drinks, but they were all looking at her.

"What are they looking at?" Annie asked.

"You." Margaret rolled down Annie's window and leaned over. "This is Annie Hill. She's our new guidance counselor."

Annie felt her eyes go wide as twenty people started saying hello at once. She didn't really know what to do, so she smiled and waved back. It seemed to placate them and they turned to hurry back into the Café.

"We are a small town. There is no hotel, but St. Francis just built a new rectory for Father James, and the Church is renting out the old rectory. I'm sorry, it's very small. Only has one bedroom, but it's clean, cheap and close to the school."

"Sounds good to me."

Annie watched as they drove past a bank, a law office and a boutique before finally turning into St. Francis' parking lot. The church was old, with a beautiful rose window above the old oak front doors. At the far end of the parking lot sat a tiny little house with a statue of the Virgin Mary out front by the steps that led up to the wood porch. An elderly priest with graying hair stood on the porch and smiled at them.

"That's Father James," Margaret said as she got out of the car, "Hello, Father!"

"Hello Margaret. And this must be our new tenant. It's so nice to meet you Miss Hill."

Annie shook the older man's hand and smiled. It wasn't very often she met someone she instantly liked, but Father James was one of them. He was kind of portly, balding on the top of his head and had a smile that made you want to sit down and tell him your whole life story. He could be trouble.

"It's nice to meet you too, Father."

"I put some groceries in the refrigerator for you. There are clean linens on the bed. If you need anything, I'm right across the street on the other side of the church. And, here is your key, young lady."

"Thank you," Annie said, and for once meaning it.

"Well, I better be going too. I have to get dinner on the table for the family. I will see you at the school on Monday."

Annie stood on the old wooden porch and waved good-bye before heading inside to check out her new home…for now. She closed the front door and looked around. It was spotless but sparse. There was a kitchen table for two, the kitchen smaller than the one in Miami, a living room with a TV that was so old it wasn't flat screen, and there was no chance of watching sports in high-def. She made her way to the small bathroom complete with one shower and a tiny pedestal sink. Connected to the bathroom was her bedroom. A twin bed with a homemade quilt filled the room. There were only two other pieces of furniture in the room: a small night table and a chest.

First things first. As soon as her car arrived tomorrow, she would be driving to Lexington for a high-def TV and some microwaveable meals. The groceries were great, but she didn't cook. No one had ever taught her so she never bothered to learn. She walked outside and sat down on the cushioned chair while looking out over the church parking lot. So, this was to be her life now.

Chapter Three

C ade thought the steam coming from his ears was visible. He had never been met with such indifference before. Yes, it was hotter than a billy goat in a pepper patch, but it was August in Kentucky and it's always hot and humid. You just say, "Damn, it's hot," and move on. But his players were lagging. They weren't even trying to run the drills at full speed. Shoot they weren't even running them at half speed. Some of the freshmen were trying and Trey Everett was trying, but that was it.

"Okay. Players with the last names E-H go with Coach Parks for drug testing. First strings get on the field. We're going to try to run a play at full speed." Cade blew his whistle and watched as the starters meandered onto the field.

Center Lee Faust snapped the ball to Austin Colby, the junior quarterback, who handed it off to Trey for a run. Trey blew through the defense and scored. Cade blew his whistle and tried to remember they were just kids.

"Bonner, get over here!" He watched as Corey Bonner sauntered over with a bad attitude written all over his face. "What is the matter with you? This is a simple play and you blew it. You didn't even try to tackle Everett."

Cade watched as all two hundred and twenty-five pounds of Bonner went from cocky teenager to pissed-off teenager.

"What do you know about it? You've never coached before. You can't tell *me* what to do. I'm the only all-state player you got on this team, and I'll do whatever the hell I feel like doing. Now step off." Bonner turned to go back onto the field and Cade snapped.

"Bonner, get your ass back here. You leave when I tell you to. Now, you will stand here, listen to me, fix your attitude or ride the bench all year."

Cade knew when someone was itching for a fight. After four years in special ops you could tell the second someone decided to fight, and by the set of Bonner's shoulders, he had decided in favor of it. Cade watched as Bonner spun around and shoved Cade with all his might. Bonner may outweigh him by fifty pounds, but Cade had stayed in special ops condition. He took the hit but didn't budge.

"See, if you hit lower like you were supposed to, you could have moved me." Cade wasn't given the chance to continue with his lecture. He saw Bonner's hand close in a fist and stood still, waiting for the punch to come so he could deflect it.

"What do you think you are doing?" Cade took his eyes off of Bonner as a red headed woman jumped in between them. Bonner didn't react fast enough and let go with the punch intended for Cade. Cade lunged forward, but the woman had already handled it. She easily blocked the punch with her forearm and grabbed Bonner by the front of his football jersey.

"You want to try that again, kid?" Annie asked him as she got up in his face.

Here Annie was just coming out to get a group of kids for their orientation and she walks in on a fight. Clearly this coach couldn't take care of the matter, so it had been up to her. She looked into the boy's eyes and wasn't surprised to see them dilated and crazed. He was much taller than she was, so it was easy to look at his pulse in his carotid artery. It was pumping feverishly and slightly erratically. His face was beet red and his body clearly agitated. She had just found her first lead. This kid was definitely on S2. Bonner slapped her hands away and took a step back, staring down his coach.

"Yo, this bitch just saved you. Next time you try to chew me out she won't be around to save you."

He turned and headed into the locker room, leaving the field momentarily stunned. Cade was a badass and everyone on the field knew that, except Bonner and this woman apparently. Cade couldn't believe this curvy spitfire thought he couldn't handle a teenager. She had put herself right in the middle of a highly volatile situation with someone two times her size.

"The better question is what do you think you are doing? Do you know how idiotic it was to get in between us?" Cade's hands went to his hips as he stared down into the dark green eyes of the woman in front of him.

"Well, excuse me for saving you from an embarrassing ass beating from a teenager." She mimicked his stance.

Who was this woman? Whoever she was, she was very amusing. Cade smiled as he rocked back on his heels. Confusion clouded those beautiful eyes, and that gave him a bit of pleasure he realized.

"Do you really think he'd beat me up?" Cade asked as his smile grew.

"Yes," she answered without hesitation.

Cade's smile slipped and he felt his ego deflate under her withering stare. She should be an interrogator. He bet she could make any man feel so low that he'd say anything to get back into her good graces. She was beautiful, but in that unassuming way that just made her even more desirable. She was normal height, fit, but not like the actresses Hollywood pushed out. She was strong, curvy, and quite voluptuous. He never understood that old description, but now he did.

"He's a rabid dog. You better take care of him or he'll take your whole team out." Annie quickly lowered her eyes to check him out. He was tall, probably six one. Dark blonde hair slightly longer than a buzz cut. His hazel eyes conveyed that he was not just some dumb jock. And a body, well, he had a body that reminded her it had been almost two years since she had been… oh never mind. She raised her eyes in a span of a blink, but he had noticed. Most men were so caught up in her chest they never noticed when she was surveying the area or even them. But he did, and by the cocky smile on his face, she guessed he knew she liked what she saw. Just as fast as the smile came, it went.

"I just drug tested him this morning, and after what I just saw, I'm pretty sure we both know how that test is going to come out." Cade knew he was about to lose his star defensive player, but why? He had a spectacular season last year, and there was no way he was on drugs then. Why now?

"Test the levels of magnesium. If it's very high, then you know you are probably dealing with S2. It's a new drug on the market for athletes. Have you heard of it?" Annie watched his eyes to see his reaction, but there was none but curiosity.

"No, I haven't. But, Keeneston isn't really known to be on the cutting edge of anything, especially a new drug I haven't heard of before. It's most likely plain old steroids."

"But see, the high levels of magnesium, which is used for the prevention of muscle cramping, is a sign it's not plain steroids. If it shows up high, you'll need to send it out for a chromatography/mass spectrometry reading. It's the only way to test for S2. It will come up looking like steroids, but is masked by heavy doses of probenecid, which prevents excretion of the steroid into the urine."

"I have two questions." Cade watched her become slightly hesitant before she nodded her head for him to continue. "First, who are you? Second, how do you know this?"

"Oh, sorry! I'm Annie Hill, the new guidance counselor. I just came out here to gather some of the freshmen for their orientation."

"Nice to meet you, Ms. Hill. I'm Cade Davies, head coach and also the biology teacher." Cade stuck out his hand and she shook it. "Now, how did you know all of this?"

"I saw it at my old school. One of our kids died from a heart attack after using it. He was sixteen. The school had run a regular urine test and didn't detect it. If they had run the chromatography/mass spectrometry, they would have. It's an expensive test, but if you have a hunch that a player may be taking it, it's the only way to prove it."

"I'll order it for the whole team then." Cade ran his hand through is hair in frustration. These were good boys. What were they doing hooked on drugs? He then turned his attention to her.

"Thanks, but I need to get back to practice. Hurry up with the orientation. We're behind schedule." Cade turned back to the field to see his receiver miss another catch.

"Hey, Coach." Cade turned back to Annie when he heard her call out to him. "Tell your QB he's focusing on his target receiver too soon."

Damn if she wasn't right. But she turned around on her heel, and he watched what could only be described as her mesmerizing backside as she walked away from him. Who was this woman?

Cade tossed a bottle of beer to his older brother Marshall and took a seat on the new couch in his living room. Actually, most everything in the house was new. He had been living with Marshall while his house was being renovated and updated. His brother lived two pastures over, about a mile or so to the south. His parents were another mile to the southwest, and his oldest brother Miles lived about two miles to the west.

His family was very large, six children, and very tight knit. He, Marshall and Miles had gone off after 9/11 and joined the Army Rangers. Two years later they signed up for a classified elite Delta Force. All three of them had made it in after a rigorous test and training period. He had helped in rescue missions of dignitaries that no one had ever known about, or would ever know about. He had rescued, killed, and garnered intelligence for his country for four years before coming home, completing his education and becoming a teacher.

His other brothers were surprised when he chose to teach instead of going into business with one of them. While they were overseas in the Army, Miles had started buying up small tracts of property surrounding his parents' farm. He and Marshall liked the idea, and so they too started buying small tracts whenever they came up for sale. As a result, the Davies family now had a huge spread in Keeneston, where his parents raised vegetables and he and his brothers had a cattle ranch. But, like his brothers, it was just a hobby. Miles was a corporate tycoon who helped small family farmers fight against the big corporations, and Marshall owned his own security firm in Lexington. His younger brother Cy was the black sheep. No one knew what he did, and Cy hadn't felt like telling them yet. He technically had cattle on the farm but was hardly ever around to take care of them. As a result, he shared the profits with his brothers who took care of them for him. His youngest brother Pierce was a graduate student in agriculture at the University of Kentucky. He liked to plant things and watch them grow. Finally, there was his sister Paige who was going to be the first one of the Davies' kids to get married. Her fiancé Cole Parker was a good guy – FBI, but more importantly cared for and loved his sister.

Now Cade's mother had gotten it in her head that all her kids should marry and settle down. She'd even made a wager with the Rose sisters at the Blossom Café about when Paige and Cole would have a baby. Every Sunday night the whole family gathered for dinner, and her mother always had a new "friend" she wanted one of the boys to meet.

"Mom said she has a new friend she wants me to meet," Marshall complained. Marshall slumped on the couch and sighed. He was an inch taller than Cade, and instead of having his dark blonde color, he had the same brown that ran in the family. All the brothers looked similar, the differences being their facial features. They all had hazel eyes, but Cade had sharp angles to his face, giving him an old-fashioned, aristocratic look compared to Marshall's more square face complete with a sharp nose that was slightly crooked.

"Where did this friend come from?"

"A dental hygienist from when she got her teeth cleaned yesterday. Apparently she has a sister..." Cade groaned, so that was why his mother had called him earlier today.

"I think I already got a call about that. Speaking of women, I met the most confusing, frustrating, sexy woman today." Cade took a drink from his beer and slouched back on the couch with his brother.

"Really? Don't tell Mom or she'll reserve the church. So, who is she?" If Cade didn't know his brother so well, he would think by his posture he didn't care, but his eyes were the giveaway. Marshall was dying to know.

"Annie Hill, the new guidance counselor."

"What did she do?"

"She walked right into the middle of a Corey Bonner steroid-induced meltdown. Sent him packing when he threw a punch and then, well, then she told me she was protecting me!"

Marshall choked on his beer, "She said she was protecting you? From a kid?"

"Yup, she said she didn't think I was able to protect myself. I couldn't believe it." Cade shot him a glare as he started laughing. "Stop laughing, Marsh. It, um, gets worse." Cade ran a hand over his face, embarrassed to tell him the rest.

"How could it get worse?" Marshall said between chuckles.

"She identified the problem with my quarterback on the pass plays in under a minute." Cade hung his head as Marshall's chuckles turned into laughter.

Cade took another drink of beer, but he had a feeling that it did not matter how much he drank, Annie Hill had taken up permanent residence in his mind.

Annie tossed her car keys onto the small, worn kitchen table and carried the bag of frozen dinners to the freezer. She needed to hurry and check in with her boss. She should have done it yesterday, but she kept putting it off.

She jammed the meals into the small freezer and dug out her cell phone from the back pocket of her jeans. She scrolled through her emails until she found Special Agent Romero's phone number.

"Romero," her boss barked into the phone.

"Hi, sir, this is Agent Blake checking in."

"About time. Welcome to Kentucky. We need to set up an appointment to meet in person. I think…" Annie about jumped out of the chair when she heard the knock at the door. It must be Father James. She didn't know anyone else.

"I'm sorry, sir. Can you hang on?" She waited until he grunted his approval and went to the door. She opened the door and stood staring at a woman dressed perfectly in black trousers, and a pink button-up blouse accessorized with a casserole dish.

"Hiya! I'm Pam Gilbert, the PTA President," she said as she smiled at Annie and held out the casserole dish. "I wanted to welcome you to town on behalf of all the parents." Annie took the dish in her hands and stared at it. Homemade food? She couldn't remember the last time she had homemade food.

"Thank you, Pam. It's nice to meet you."

"Well, I won't keep you, but if you need anything just give me a shout." Pam gave a little finger wave and went back to her minivan.

"Blake!" Annie shook her head as she watched the minivan with the Dale Junior sticker on the back window, next to the white stick figures of a dad, mom, and two boys, peel out of the church parking lot.

"Sorry, sir. Just meeting the locals." Annie closed the door and headed to put the casserole into the freezer.

"As I was saying, I was hoping we could meet in person on…" Annie pivoted in the small entryway when the doorbell rang. "Was that the doorbell?"

"Yeah, sorry. Hold on for just a sec." Annie balanced the casserole dish on her hip and the phone on her shoulder as she opened the door. She looked out and then down to a trio of white-haired ladies.

"Hello, dear. We're the Rose sisters. I'm Lily Rae. This is my sister Daisy Mae." The leader bobbed her head toward the thin, wiry looking sister with her silver hair pulled back into a tight bun, with a couple pencils poking out of it. Annie realized that she had seen when she had driven past the Café. "And this is Violet Fae." The small, round woman grabbed her around her shoulders and pulled her into a hug that had the casserole dish teetering and the cell phone coming close to getting lost in Violet's puffy cleavage.

"Bless your heart – you are a skinny thing! Thank goodness we brought you some food. You must be starving!" Violet clucked as she looked Annie over.

"Thank you for the food. Someone named Pam just dropped off a casserole. This is all very nice of you."

"Dang it! Pam beat us here. We'll never hear the end of it." Daisy shook her head and shifted the large basket hanging at the crook of her arm.

"But I bet she didn't stay to give her a proper welcome. She had to pick the boys up from soccer practice," Lily pronounced. "We won't run out on you so quickly. Come and sit for a spell and we'll get know one another." The sisters pushed past her and into the small kitchen before Annie could stop them.

"I'm sorry," she said as she trailed after them. "I do not mean to be rude, but I'm on the phone." Annie paused at the kitchen and watched as they looked around.

"That's okay, dear. Give us that casserole and we'll just put the food away. I'm sure you want to finish your call with your…boyfriend?" Lily asked as she reached for the casserole.

"I don't have a boyfriend." Three white heads swiveled around and smiles appeared at once.

"Well, love your heart! It's lucky we stopped by then. We know plenty of men. Now don't be rude and keep that person waiting on the phone. Don't mind us!" Lily put the casserole in the fridge, turned to her sisters and started pulling out covered dishes from the basket. Annie looked down at the phone and cringed.

"Sorry about that. The welcoming committee is here."

"I guessed that. Now about our meeting." The doorbell went off again and her boss dropped the f word.

"I got it, dear!" one of the sisters shouted from the kitchen.

"Go ahead, Romero. But, you may want to make it quick." Annie looked to the door to see a pretty woman her own age with a handsome man who had Fed written all over him. "Sir, do you have anyone else in town?" she whispered, looking away from the couple.

"No, why?"

"A fed just walked in. I would bet my life on it."

"Details."

"Thirty, dark hair, silver eyes, six feet, no visible tats. He's with a woman in her mid to late twenties, brown hair." Annie waited as she heard the keys of Romero's computer tapping as he ran a search.

"I think I got it. Cole Parker. He's the Special Agent in Charge of the FBI's Lexington Office. I heard through the cop-vine he just got engaged. If you need anything and he's nearby, you get him to help. He's the one that just took down that corruption ring out of New York and D.C. Now, before we get interrupted again. Jesus, was that the doorbell again?"

"Yes, sir." Annie was sure she heard the whistle of steam coming out of his ears.

"Meeting, tomorrow, seven in the morning at the office. Got it."

"Yes, sir." The doorbell rang again and Romero hung up while rattling off a string of curse words. They really did have a lot to discuss. Annie tucked away her phone and turned to see her small house filled up and people hanging out on the porch. Who were these people and why where they here?

"Oh, good, you're off the phone. Come meet everyone!" Lily took her hand and dragged her over to the FBI agent and his fiancé. "This is Cole Parker and Paige Davies."

"It's so nice to meet you. I heard all about you and I just had to meet you!"

"Heard about me?" She shot a glance at Cole. Maybe he knew somehow who she was. The look she got back said he didn't, but he was smart enough to figure it out.

"Yes! Marshall told me all about you and my brother. It was so funny that I had to meet the woman who didn't swoon at his feet."

"Sorry. Paige forgets that not everyone knows her family tree. The brother to whom she is referring is Cade Davies. He's the biology teacher and football coach at the high school."

"Oh! The guy that needs to learn self-defense. Yeah, I know who you're talking about. It's nice to meet you both."

"Annie, come meet this young man. He's single too!" Wow, Lily was sure one for subtlety. "This is Ahmed. He's not from here either."

Annie looked at the hard man and cringed. Was everyone here a fed? At least the feds here were hot. Ahmed was shorter than Cole, but was built. His body showed a life dedication to training and she bet she could bounce a quarter off his...well, his everything.

"So, what do you do for a living?"

"I am the head of security for Mo," he said in a heavily accented voice. Middle East somewhere she guessed.

"Mo?"

"The Prince of Rahmi. Well, and now also his fiancée Danielle." He nodded to the couple now talking to Cole and Paige. "So, Miss Lily has put you on the must need to be married list."

"It appears so. Never really wanted to be married. My lifestyle doesn't support it."

"Hmm. Guidance counselors have tough schedules." He gave her a look that said he knew way more than she wanted him too. "If you ever need help...guiding someone, let me know. We single-don't-want-to-be-married people need to stick together." With a quick bow of his head, he turned and headed out the door. Who were these people? She needed to hook up her computer as soon as she had her meeting with her boss, get her new login to the database and run a search on the whole town.

Chapter Four

Cade stared at the papers spread out on his desk in disbelief. He had never felt like hurting a kid, but he sure did now. What were they thinking? Drugs… drugs in Keeneston. It didn't happen. It just didn't happen. But, the evidence was right there in front of him. Not one, not two, but three of his players had tested positive for S2.

They had had an alright practice on Tuesday, and besides Bonner being an ass, practice today went well too, not good, but not as horribly as Monday's. Now, though, he was going to have to get rid of three of the team's best players. The starting wide receiver was out, Bonner was out, and the only offensive lineman with any experience was also out. The team went from a five hundred team to a "we'll be lucky to win a game or two" team. Worse, he was going to have to tell these kids that their dreams of college ball were over because he was left with no other choice but to kick them all off the team.

Cade shoved his long legs out from the desk and paced around his classroom. What would their parents say? He knew they would all be asking to talk to him. He paused by one of the large rectangular windows and looked out into the almost empty parking lot. Corey Bonner and Lee Faust, the starting senior center who also tested positive for S2, were standing by their cars. Cade watched as Bonner shoved Faust and started waving his hands around angrily.

Faust calmly looked at Bonner and said something that made Bonner freeze. Faust was always the one you had to worry about when he was quiet. Cade watched as Bonner pulled out his cell phone and made a call. As soon as he put it away, Cade pushed up the window and leaned out.

"Boys, I need to see you a minute. Come on into the room." Cade didn't wait for them to acknowledge him before closing the window and heading back to his desk.

Cade picked up the drug test reports and put them in his desk drawer as the door to his room opened. He looked up and into the face of Faust who clearly looked guilty and ashamed. Bonner, on the other hand, looked cockier than ever.

"What did you want, Coach?" Bonner asked as he leaned his large body against the wall by the door.

"I wanted to know if you boys had anything to tell me?" Cade folded his arms behind his head and waited. Faust looked like he was about to confess all.

"Yeah," Bonner pushed himself off the wall and walked over to Cade's desk. He put his hands on the top of Cade's textbooks and stared right into his eyes. It was hard for Cade not to break eye contact. He was just so shocked at Bonner's appearance. His eyes were bloodshot, his face flushed. Beads of sweat dotted his brow. "You're not letting me blitz the quarterback enough."

"Is that it?" Cade slowly put his arms down and stood up and walked around the desk to face the boys.

"What kind of question is that? Of course that's it. If there was more, I would have told you." Bonner folded his arms across his wide chest and glared at Cade with such anger it rolled off of him and hit Cade in the face.

"Then, I'm sorry to tell you, you both are off the team for testing positive for S2. Go clean out your lockers immediately." Faust hung his head and nodded once. Before Cade could say anything more Bonner exploded.

"You can't do that! Football is my life. It's my way out of here. I have scholarship offers to some of the best schools in country!" Bonner yelled. The sweat on his brow was now rolling down his cheeks as his face became redder and redder.

"What did you expect, Bonner, you were taking illegal drugs? You knew if you were caught you'd be off the team. Why risk it?"

"You asshole! The drugs were to get me into LSU. I was so close to a scholarship offer and you just ruined it for me!" Bonner took a step toward him and glared pure hatred.

"There is no reason for me to ruin you. You ruined yourself. Now go clean out your locker." Cade stared him down. The situation was so volatile he knew Bonner might snap. A flicker of color appeared behind Bonner, and Cade glanced quickly to see if it was a threat.

That split second was all Bonner needed. He pulled back his right arm, curled his hand into a fist and planted it right on Cade's cheek.

Annie stepped further into Cade's classroom and sighed. Here we go again. Could he not see that he was about to get...punched? Ow. Annie didn't wait to see what happened next. She kicked out her leg and hit Bonner in the back of the knee, sending him falling to the floor. She was afraid Cade might collapse to the floor in dramatics, but when she looked up, she saw that he was staring daggers at her instead.

"You really need to learn self-defense. I can't always be around to save you." Annie knew she was being a smartass, but it was fun to see the way his mouth hung open like that.

"You bitch," Bonner moaned from the ground as he turned towards her. His face was so red Annie gasped. Sweat was pouring off his face. His shirt was damp. She watched in horror as he tried to stand up to grab her arm but fell face down onto the cool, tile floor. She saw a trickle of blood run out of his nose and pool on the floor.

"You, kid... call 9-1-1! He's had a heart attack. Tell them to send the heli." She didn't wait for the kid to pull out his cell before falling to her knees to help Cade turn Bonner over.

"You sure it's a heart attack?" Cade asked her as he felt for a pulse.

She focused her attention to finding the pulse. It was there but fading. His heart was struggling to work. He had stopped breathing, or it was so shallow she couldn't detect it.

"Yes. It's a side effect of S2. We need to start CPR if he's going to have a chance to live." She waited for Cade to start the chest compressions before tilting back Bonner's head, pinching his nose closed and breathing into his mouth.

They continued CPR while Lee stood frozen to the spot, cell phone still in hand. Annie could feel that Bonner's skin had turned clammy. This was not good. She felt for his pulse again and felt it flutter. They needed to hold on a little longer. If they could keep him breathing, the doctors may be able to save him.

Annie was too afraid to check to see if he was breathing on his own or not. But the white tint to his skin with the shallow blue lines around his lips told her enough. Sweat rolled down her back as she bent to blow some more air into Bonner's lungs.

"Kid, go out front and meet the EMT's. They should be here any minute."

Lee finally moved from where he was rooted to the floor but still stood staring at Bonner's unconscious body with a look of shocked disbelief.

"Now, kid!" Annie snapped when he didn't leave right away.

She heard his feet pound down the hall at the same time she heard the first sounds of the helicopter. They couldn't get here fast enough. Cade had been doing chest compressions for almost ten minutes. He had to be exhausted, but he hadn't said a word about it. He had counted and compressed, counted and compressed and had helped her keep Bonner alive.

"Okay, we got the mask ready." Annie and Cade stepped back as the EMT's bagged Bonner. "What happened?"

"Heart attack due to an overdose of steroids," she answered.

"Have you been doing CPR the whole time?"

"Yes. He still had a slight pulse but shallow to no breathing."

The EMT's lifted Bonner onto the stretcher and hurried from the room while they issued orders into their radios. Lee had been standing by the door as the EMT's had loaded Bonner onto the stretcher and had not moved even though his friend was no longer here.

"You okay, Lee?" Cade asked as he put a hand on the shaken kid's shoulder. Lee just nodded but didn't say anything. "I'm going to follow Corey to the hospital. I'll call his parents on the way. I don't think Lee here should drive. Can you take him home?"

"No problem. Call if you need anything." She put her arm around Lee and felt the tiny shivers of shock rippling through him. "Come on, Lee. Let's get you home."

Cade lay down on his couch and closed his eyes. He was so emotionally drained that he barely heard *SportsCenter* on the television. He flung his arm over his eyes and tried to make his mind go blank. However, that was easier said than done. A red head was currently running laps up there, making it impossible to think of anything else.

There was a knocking at the door, and a part of Cade's mind irrationally hoped it was Annie. It was that small part of his mind that propelled him to his feet and sent him racing to the door.

"Don't look so disappointed to see me, brother. It makes me think you were expecting someone else." Miles Davies snapped his fingers and with a smirk said, "I know, you're expecting that cute guidance counselor you have a thing for." Miles may be the oldest of the Davies brothers, but that didn't mean he didn't deserve to have his ass whooped every now and then.

"Don't be such an ass. Where did you hear about Annie?" Cade asked as he headed back to the couch. His brother always did think he was so important. He held himself as if he were the President of the United States.

Where Marshall was always dressed in black, and Cade was usually in some form of athletic gear, Miles was never without a suit and tie. What made it worse was that when pushed, Miles was the most dangerous. He and Miles were doing a snatch and grab in the foothills of Afghanistan that turned out to be a trap. He got caught and had transmitted to Miles to get the hell out of there. Instead of leaving his brother behind, Miles took out each and every one of them in under twenty seconds. How? Cade would never know. Miles earned a little extra credit for saving his life, but that was only going to afford him so much when it came to teasing him about Annie.

"Where do you think? The biggest gossip of us all – Marshall." Miles laughed as all six feet, two inches of him sauntered in to the living room.

"Jesus. Marshall needs to learn to keep his mouth shut." Cade fell back onto his mahogany-colored, leather couch and tossed his feet onto the matching coffee table.

"When, in all of your thirty years of life has he ever been able to keep his mouth shut?" Being a rhetorical question, since the answer was clearly never, Cade didn't bother answering. "So, to hear Marshall tell it, you're ready to get married and have kids. What's the real story? Who is this woman?"

"Marriage, no way! I don't even like her. She's infuriating. She thinks I'm a helpless idiot." Cade rolled his eyes and picked up the beer he'd been drinking before Miles knocked at the door.

"Sounds promising." Cade didn't need to look at his brother to know he was trying not to laugh.

"Ha. She has stepped in front of Corey Bonner who was in a full steroid rage…twice! Supposedly it was to protect me. She told me I needed self-defense lessons. Me! Then she helped me save Bonner's life, calm as can be."

"How is he doing?"

"He's stable. His heart has taken a beating though. He's never going to be healthy again. The walls have thinned after using so much of the drug. His blood pressure was through the roof, but the doctors think he'll be able to live a normal life after he detoxes and his system basically reboots. He'll be on heart meds the rest of his life though."

"That's tough for a kid. How did Annie keep her calm? Most women would be slightly hysterical coming upon a fight and then a kid collapsing like that."

"That's just it. She's never hysterical. Instead she thinks I'm the hysterical one? I don't know what the school was like in Miami, but nothing fazes her. It just makes me crazy to prove myself to her, which is crazy in itself because she's so infuriating!" Cade leaned his head back on the couch and cursed himself for not being able to just put Annie out of his mind.

"Come on. Let's go to the Café and have dinner. We can talk it out and develop a plan of action," Miles said, standing up and buttoning up his sports coat.

"One, you can't develop a plan of action on handling Annie. She doesn't fit into any plans. Two, Summer Ridell is bound to be working tonight and she had a huge crush on you."

"I was hoping you'd run interference so I could finally eat something without being hit on. Ever since she turned eighteen and graduated, she thinks she should be getting married and having a kid or two. What's worse, she thinks she should be doing it with me!" Miles said with disgust. Miles did not cook and depended on Daisy and Violet to feed him when Mom's frozen casseroles ran out.

"You're old enough to be her father!" Cade laughed. He enjoyed goading Miles. He really did.

"I'm not that old. Damn, Cade, you can make thirty-four seem positively ancient. However, it's too old for an innocent kid like her."

"Fine, I'll go with you. I haven't eaten at the Café for a while. You can tell me what corporations you're taking apart for the better good of the little people like me."

Annie couldn't decide if she hated or loved the fact that a diner was so close. Hated the fact they didn't deliver. Shoot, no one delivered.

It was great when she wanted real food, but it was strange to have a ten minute conversation with the person taking your order when you just really wanted a chicken salad sandwich.

Over the past couple of days since her arrival in Keeneston she had been eating the most amazing home cooked meals. But tonight she thought she'd try the local cuisine. She grabbed some cash and took off down the street to the Café. It was a nice night. The stars were shining overhead, a slight breeze brought the smell of oats to her, and the full moon bathed the small downtown in a soft glow.

Bright light poured out of the large old windows of the Café onto the sidewalk, highlighting the mums that were planted in large barrels under the windows. Small bistro tables were set up outside on the nice warm night and filled with people who all smiled and said hello to her as she walked past them and into the Café.

Annie froze with one foot over the threshold when the packed restaurant fell silent. A breeze from all the heads turning at once caused her hair to flutter. Movement drew her eyes to go to a back table. Her eyes narrowed as a waitress, who was maybe just out of high school, was leaning her perky breasts in Cade's face as she picked up his plate.

A man in a gorgeous pin striped suit who was slightly taller than Cade with dark brown hair and a handsome square jaw stood and walked over to her. She noticed Cade's unhappy expression at the same time the waitress placed her hand on his shoulder and gave it a little rub.

"You must be Annie. Be easy on my brother, will you?" Tall, dark and handsome flashed a killer grin at her that almost had her forgetting about whoever this other brother was.

"Wait, who are you? Who's your brother and why should I go easy on him?" Tall, dark and handsome grinned again. "I'm Miles Davies. The brother to whom I am referring is Cade, and you should go easy on him because he's a good guy. Have a nice night, Annie."

"How many brothers are there in that family?" she mumbled as she made her way to the cash register.

"Five brothers and one sister." Annie looked down at the stranger who had clearly been eavesdropping.

"Um, thanks." Wow. No wonder she kept tripping over them. "Hey."

Annie pulled up short and checked out the man who had stepped in front of her. He was tallish, almost black hair slicked back, and did his suit sparkle? No, it must just have shine to it. "What are you doing walking into a place like this?" he asked.

"Is that a trick question?" Well, the town did have a lot of handsome men. Too bad they weren't all that bright.

"You can sit with me if you'd like." He gestured towards a small table in the back.

"I'm just here to pick up my to-go dinner."

"Well, here I am. You can take a bite out of me anytime." He raised a perfect eyebrow and gazed at her.

Annie couldn't decide whether to laugh or to kick him in the balls. He reminded her of an old man who used to live near her apartment. He yelled obscenities at her that were in a way complimentary and made her day.

"Okay. Let's get out of here. I want you...now." Annie deadpanned. She watched as his sleazy exterior cracked and he stared at her as if she had two heads. "Just kidding, hot shot, put your tongue back in your mouth." She smiled at him and when he broke out into laughter, she joined him.

"Henry Rooney at your service."

"No servicing of me tonight. I thought we covered that, Henry." Henry laughed again and she had a feeling she had made a friend. "Annie Hill. It's nice to meet you, Henry. I'm sure we'll run into each other again soon." Henry smiled and walked out the door.

Annie turned her attention to the table near the cash register where the waitress was still servicing Cade. Rolling her eyes, she walked over to them, "I hope I'm not interrupting," she tapped her foot impatiently.

"Oh! You must be Miss Hill. I'll be out here in a jiffy with your dinner ma'am." If she needed another reason to dislike the waitress, there it was.

"Ma'am?"

"Anyone over the age of twenty is a ma'am to her. Would you care to join me while you wait?" Cade stood up and walked around the table. He pulled out a chair and waited for her to take a seat.

"Won't your girlfriend get mad?"

"Sorry to disappoint you, but I like women, not girls. You really don't like me, do you?" Cade asked, his smile faltering slightly.

Feeling a little guilty about her snap judgment, she sat down and looked up at him. His eyes seemed green tonight. Sometimes they were brown.

"I'm sorry. If it makes you feel better, you're not the only one."

"Military brat tired of all the macho men?" he joked.

"No, foster care brat." Not wanting to get into it, she asked about Corey.

"He'll live, but they don't know how much damage has been done yet. We should know more tomorrow."

"Here's your dinner, Miss Hill." With a smile, the perky waitress handed her a plastic bag.

"Thanks." She pushed back her chair and froze when Cade did the same. She raised her eyebrow at him in silent question.

"I thought I could walk you home and show you the sights," Cade said in response to her silent query.

"Thanks, but Mrs. Lopez already did that."

"Well, then just allow me to walk you home to fulfill my daily gentlemanly requirement." Cade smiled at her then and her heart pounded in her chest like it did when she was going on a bust. If she thought Miles' smile was something, Cade's eclipsed it.

"Fine." She turned to go, but Cade slipped his hand onto her elbow to guide her around the table. All conversation stopped until he guided her out of the Café. Before the door closed, the noise level escalated to near deafening, and people didn't even try to hide the fact that they were staring at them leaving together.

"Is it always like this?" she asked Cade.

"No. It's usually worse." She laughed then and didn't even mind when he slipped his hand from her elbow to the small of her back. "See over there. The store with the yellow and white awning? That's my sister's store."

"That's Paige's store?"

"You know Paige?"

"I met her, along with most of the town already."

"Ah, the welcoming committee." His smile was so genuine and happy when talking about his sister and the town that Annie became lost in it.

A loud thumping started to vibrate her body and draw her out of her reverie. It drew louder and seemed so completely out of place in Keeneston. A week ago she wouldn't have even noticed it in Miami, but Keeneston wasn't a place people cruised around with their windows down and rap music pumping. It was more of a windows down and country music drifting on the breeze type place.

She looked down the street and saw a large black Escalade roaring towards them. Cade had already stopped to watch it. She wouldn't be completely surprised if some old man came running out shaking a cane at the Escalade and yelling at them to turn it down. The thought brought a smile to her face, a smile that quickly disappeared when the doors to the Escalade were thrown open as the SUV slid to a stop next to them, and three massively muscled men leapt out of the car. They were all dressed in those tear-away athletic pants and white tank tops. One man had his head shaved, one had crazy curly hair with a receding hairline and the third had black hair with bangs.

Damn, her dinner was sure to be destroyed saving Cade again. She shifted the handle, getting ready to smash it in the first person's face to reach her when Cade wrapped his arm around her waist and flung her behind him as if she weighed nothing. She stumbled backwards and fell on her bottom, landing against the old brick building. She cringed when the man with curly hair brought up a tire iron from his side. The moonlight, which had just moments ago cast a romantic glow on the street, now cast a menacing reflection off the tire iron. He raised the tire iron and swung it at Cade. She had to save him! She watched in horror as the tire iron came swinging down in an arc towards his head. He blocked it with his forearm and followed up with an uppercut that snapped the guy's head back before the man knew what hit him. She would never have guessed he had so much speed.

As the other two closed in at once on Cade, she watched the injured man stumble back to the car. She tried to get her feet under her to help, but it was already over as she stood up. With a swift kick to the knee, Cade brought the one with dark hair and girly bangs to the ground. Annie watched in awe as he crumpled to the ground, holding his injured knee. He had to drag himself to the safety of the car. With a quick strike of his hand, Cade shattered the nose of the third man. Blood flowed freely down the white shirt as the man with the shaved head scrambled into the car and tucked tail out of there.

Cade dusted off his khaki pants and turned to her. There wasn't a speck of dirt on him. The only evidence that he had just been in a fight was his hazel eyes shone bright with excitement. When he held out his hand for her, she stared at him for a moment in disbelief that he had disabled three attackers in less than twenty seconds. She looked at his large hand for a second and then placed hers in it. His hand was warm, strong, and she had to admit, she didn't want to let it go.

"Well, it's nice to see you took my advice and learned some self-defense."

Chapter Five

Cade watched Annie set the takeout bag on the small kitchen table. The way her tight jeans hugged her hips was so sexy. Her fitted Miami Dolphins jersey showed off her curves in an understated way that made it very hard for him to think of anything but what she might look like naked. Her long red hair was loosely tied back in a ponytail that swung as she walked.

Even through his lust haze, something was nagging at him. He watched as she stretched up and pulled down a plate from the cabinet for her dinner. That's when it hit him. She was just acting normally. She wasn't shaking. She wasn't crying. She wasn't scared at all. Nothing. She was acting like a mugging was no big deal. It was the same reaction he got from her after both physical altercations with Corey. He knew Miami was a tough place, but something didn't seem right.

"I am sorry about tonight. Keeneston doesn't really have much crime. Certainly muggings do not normally happen. I didn't recognize them or the car, so I'm guessing they were just punks from out of town trying to score some easy cash." He certainly didn't believe that, and by the "what, are you stupid?" look she just shot him, she didn't believe it either.

"Um, yeah. I'm pretty sure those are what are called gang members," she said to him as if he was a total bozo. She set the plate on the table and headed back to the kitchen.

"We don't have gangs in Keeneston. The Rose sisters would never allow it." He shot her a quick grin and was happy to see she momentarily returned it. He leaned his shoulder against the kitchen wall and put his hands in his front jean pockets.

"You may not have in the past, but you do now. Don't be so naive, Cade. Anywhere there are drugs there are gangs who sell those drugs. That was probably supposed to be a warning from the dealer who sells to those three kids on your team."

Annie tried not to suck in a hissing breath at her mistake. He hadn't told her there were three kids who had tested positive for S2. She knew because she got a sneak peek at the test results before he got them. She turned her back on Cade to get some silverware and hoped that he hadn't noticed her slip up.

"It sure sounds like you know a lot about drugs and gangs. But, how did you know about three of my players testing positive for S2?"

Annie set the silverware on the table and shrugged her shoulders. "Lee said something about it in the car." She turned back around and found his gaze sharp and totally focused on her face. Something wasn't right. That wasn't the scrutinizing look of a high school biology teacher. And those had certainly not been a teacher's moves against those gang members. What was up with this town? She really needed to get her computer hooked up, like now.

"Well, I'm going to have dinner now. Would you like some coffee?" she asked, hoping he would leave so she could throw the dinner in the fridge and hook up her computer. She needed to run a background check on him to see if her gut was right.

"No thank you. I need to get home and work on some lesson plans." What he needed to do was get over to Marshall's government computer and run a background check on this woman. Something was definitely off. "I have been so busy with football that I'm behind in getting my school work done."

"Well, thanks for an eventful night." Annie smiled and leaned against the front door jam. Would he hurry up already and leave?

"You're welcome. I'm just glad you weren't hurt. Make sure to lock your door." She watched him walk down the stairs and did take a moment to enjoy the view before he turned to give her a wave good-bye. She returned it with a smile and watched him as he headed back towards the Café. He really was a nice guy.

As soon as he was out of sight, she shut the door and ran into the living room. Against the far wall was a tower of unpacked boxes and somewhere in that stack was her computer. She searched for the box with her computer equipment in it, neatly at first, but when it became obvious it was hiding from her, she started tossing boxes and clothes in frustration. She finally spied the box with the word "computer" in black marker on it. Of course it was on the bottom of the pile. Wrapping her arms around the brown, cardboard box, she tugged at it until it wiggled free of the last couple of boxes surrounding it.

"Okay, let's see who you are, Cade Davies," she said as she started pulling computer equipment out of the box.

Cade slammed on the brakes and sent his SUV skidding to a stop in front of Marshall's old farmhouse. He jumped out of the car and in three long strides was on the old wood porch that surrounded Marshall's house.

"Marshall! I need your computer," he yelled as he burst through the front door without bothering to knock.

"You have a computer at home. What do you need mine for?" Marshall asked, looking up from his desk in his office next to the entranceway.

"Not that computer. The other one."

"Ah. Who are we hacking tonight?" Marshall slid his chair over to a locked armoire against the wall behind his desk. He pushed back a small panel hidden in the base of the armoire and pulled out the key.

"The lovely Miss Hill." Cade paced back and forth in front of Marshall's large oak desk. Was his brother purposefully moving slowly?

"Don't you think a date would be a better way to find out about her than running a background on her? It's more fun that way. I believe Mom calls it the honeymoon period."

"Not when she is not who she says she is."

"What do you mean?"

"I told you. She's not a guidance counselor. And I want to find out who she is. We were mugged tonight by three men, one armed with a crowbar, and she didn't even blink an eye. Went home and set out dinner all the while lecturing me on gangs and drugs."

"So you think she's a fed?" Marshall stood up and indicated the computer was ready.

"Yup. I'd also be willing to bet you my University of Kentucky basketball tickets that she's DEA." Cade flexed his fingers and went to work on the encrypted computer. "Here she is! Real name Annie Blake. Just like I thought, DEA," Cade told Marshall as he scrolled through her records. "Twenty-seven years old. Hmm."

"What?" Marshall leaned forward to try to see the screen over Cade's shoulder.

"She graduated second from the academy. That's pretty good. Let's see, after that she was stationed all around Alabama and Georgia before ending up in Miami, where she has as many commendations as she does complaints."

"Complaints for what?"

"When she arrests them, seems she likes to rough up the drug dealers who peddle to kids. It also looks like she was the reason for some very big busts. The last one was just a week ago. However, there was an issue with her beating up the drug soldier she was arresting. They patched it up by saying it was self-defense during an assault. She was transferred immediately after that."

"Why was she transferred here? We don't have any dealers here."

"Apparently we do. She's looking into an S2 drug highway that they think starts here in Keeneston or possibly in Lexington." Cade leaned back in his chair and turned off the computer.

"What are you going to do about Miss DEA?" Marshall crossed his legs and shot him a grin. He was so glad Marshall found this all so amusing.

"I think I'll help her where I can. I do have a certain skill level that could be useful. At least I can try to keep her safe."

"I don't think you have to worry about that! Isn't she the one protecting you?" Marshall laughed. "Are you going to tell her you know who she is?"

"That would take all the fun out of it." Cade smiled. He had his own idea of how to handle Miss DEA.

Annie couldn't believe it. Shock had her frozen as she stared at the computer monitor in front of her. "Son of a...," she groaned. She buried her face in her hands and muttered, "I told him to learn self-defense, and he's a freaking national hero with a higher clearance level than I could ever dream of. He must have gotten one heck of a good laugh at my expense after I told him he couldn't protect himself from a kid."

She lifted her head from her hands and sat there for a minute staring at his military photo. Wow. She might have to make that her screensaver. He was lean and muscled, his face tight and his hazel eyes serious as he stared into the camera wearing his Ranger's beret.

"Well, I might as well find out who else is in town." She tried to remember the guy's name Lily introduced her too. "Ahmed, that's it." She typed in his name and gasped at the data that came back.

No wonder the name sounded familiar. He was famous for his interrogations. No one knew how he operated, but he had led the security teams that kept the Rahman family safe and the country of Rahmi free of terrorist activity for the last ten years.

She searched Cade's brothers' names and couldn't stop the giggle that escaped. She couldn't decide whether to be angry or embarrassed at herself for thinking she was the only one who knew danger and the seriousness of law enforcement, so she just laughed. What else could she do when she was actually surrounded by military heroes?

Annie pushed back her chair on the old hardwood floor and walked over to the front window. What must he be thinking of her? More importantly, how was she going to face him again? She had insulted him and he'd never said anything. Not too many men with his resume, or without for that matter, would let a woman take a bite out of their pride like that.

"Well done, Cade Davies. Or should I say Captain Davies." He was definitely different from all the other men she knew. Maybe he wasn't as bad as she first thought.

Chapter Six

C ade placed the royal blue KHS hat on his head and took a deep breath. He hated television interviews, especially because he knew they would ask him about the dismissal of three of his players and the horrible loss they suffered last week during the scrimmage against a far inferior team. It had been a rough couple of weeks.

"Hiya, Coach."

"Hi, Steph. What's up?" he asked his fellow science teacher.

Stephanie Long taught chemistry. She was nice and loved to flirt with him, pretty even. She was petite, only about five two and had beautiful blonde hair that she kept in a French twist during school days. She always wore a pencil skirt and heels when teaching. After school, however, she wore her long hair down and switched out her tight skirts for tight jeans. She was every male student's teacher crush, and he could see why when looking at her. But, for some reason he just never felt any chemistry with her. So, he was polite but distant to make sure she didn't get the wrong idea.

"I just wanted to wish you luck for your first game. I know it's hard being the new guy, especially after losing three of your best players. What happened to them?"

"Sorry, Steph, I can't get into it. It was just a violation of team rules and was handled internally. But, thank you for wishing me luck

- I'll need it." He looked nervously over the local news crew and tried to keep his stomach calm.

"You'll do fine during your interview. You're so handsome and nice that the camera will love you. Just pretend you're talking to me." She gave him a little wink and he couldn't help but laugh a little.

"Thanks. I do feel better. I guess I'll go get this interview over with. See you on Monday." Cade smiled and walked away from the small field house to the camera crew setting up along the sidelines where his players were warming up on the field.

"Coach Davies. Could we have a few minutes?" the sports reporter asked. He looked just like any other sports reporter: middle aged, small gut, big hair and a really weird colored tie.

"Sure." Cade stopped next to him and waited until the camera was recording.

"How do you think you'll do tonight against Oakdale High School?"

"I think it will be a tough game. They are returning twelve senior starters compared to our three senior starters. They have a lot of experience."

"It has been reported that All-State linebacker Corey Bonner, offensive lineman Lee Faust, and senior wide receiver Dan Likens have all been dismissed from the team. Can you tell us why and how you will make up for their loss?"

"They violated team rules. We cannot make up for the hole left by their dismissal. They were wonderful players and have now been replaced by less experienced players. Our freshman wide receiver, Ryan Hall, has stepped up in practice and is showing a lot of promise. Running back Trey Everett is the heart and soul of this team and will provide the leadership we lost with Bonner's departure. We've taken some of the defensive players and converted them to offensive linemen. They have a lot to learn, but again, are showing great promise after only being in this position for a month."

"Thank you, Coach."

Cade nodded and headed out onto the field as the reporter wrapped up his pre-game comments.

He took in the scene and his nerves steadied. Assistant Coach Parks was warming up the offense. The defense was stretching out. The smell of the fresh cut grass mixed with the aroma of popcorn coming from the stands now filling with people. This was it, the first home game of his coaching career, and boy, did he love it! He placed the silver whistle in his mouth and gave it two short bursts. His team responded immediately and circled around him.

"Okay, men. I want to focus on execution tonight. Hit your marks, block your targets, and make your tackles. Okay, Trey. You and Ryan head out there for the coin toss. Break!" The deafening sound of clapping and cheers arose from his team as they pumped each other up.

Annie took her seat in the stands. She opted for the highest row in the bleachers so she could see everything that happened around her. Maybe, just maybe, the boss or some more of the soldiers would be here tonight. If she kept an eye on who was in the crowd, and if she could identify anyone who looked like they didn't belong, she could then also keep an eye on which people the players looked at. Then maybe she could figure out who the dealer was.

She looked around the small stadium. Apparently the first home game was a big deal in Keeneston. The place was packed. People mingled with each other, kids ran around the bleachers, and signs and pompoms waved in the air. She heard cheers as the game started and cheered when others did. She knew football. She loved football, but tonight she was not here for fun. She was here for surveillance. She glanced down at the field and saw Cade coaching one of the boys before sending him into the game. Unlike a lot of coaches she'd seen, he didn't yell at his players. He taught them. He pulled them aside and showed them what they did wrong and how to do it right. That was just the kind of person he was.

They had talked quite often since the night of the thugs. He had stopped by her office to talk, and she had politely excused herself as fast as she could. She just didn't know how to act around him. After learning who he was, she knew he would have the smarts to figure out who she was and she didn't want to risk it. He was nice, polite, and the farthest thing from the egotistical men she was used to.

Every time he saw her at the Blossom Café, he would expertly remove her from whatever grilling she was receiving from Daisy or Violet. He always would walk her home, claiming he had to protect her from errant thugs. Which, in turn, would fuel the gossip flames at the Café and cause her to listen to lectures of not buying the milk when the cow was free – or something like that from the Rose sisters.

She and Cade liked to talk about the team, and she tried to dig around to learn more information on the town. The way he would describe his childhood adventures with his brothers, or the way he helped teach Paige how to outshoot them, always had her laughing. It would only be later that she would realize they had been talking comfortably for almost an hour each time he walked her home. She would scold herself and try to remember to keep her distance. She had a job to do after all. She shouldn't be looking forward to nights on the porch with Cade.

Annie had to shake her head to focus herself on the task at hand. She was doing it again. She was here to keep a look out for drug dealers, not watch the way Cade's butt looked when he crouched down to watch a play. She didn't know why it was so hard to keep her eyes off of him. She'd worked with plenty of attractive, masculine men before. She never had this kind of physical reaction to them though. Well, maybe it was because he wasn't exactly like those men. They were macho, egotistical and always cocky.

If anyone had a reason to be cocky it was Cade. She'd seen all the medals and awards he had won while in the Army. However, he never mentioned it. He never mentioned his accomplishments and he always talked to her about the accomplishments of the kids in his class or his family. He was kind and caring and staring right at her!

She felt her cheeks redden as she realized he'd caught her staring like a doe-eyed teenager at him. Oh God! This was so embarrassing. She scanned the field and clapped when the receiver caught the ball. Maybe he would think she was just watching the game? She took a quick peek and saw he was still looking at her. Before she could look away, he smiled and gave her a wink.

She felt all eyes in the stadium turn on her. People stared at her and started whispering. They poked the people in front of them and they turned to look at her. Some smiled, some winked, and she felt her face turn an even brighter shade of red.

"You go, girl!" Miss Lily stood and waved from the front row. This couldn't be happening! Annie tried to make herself shrink as people laughed and shouted encouragements. It turned out Cade was quite the catch, but she already knew that.

She was watching him. He never thought he'd feel such pride as he did now. Cade turned back to the game just in time to see Austin throw an interception. He groaned as the safety ran into the end zone. Oakdale was now leading 21-10. The game had started off strong with a touchdown by Trey, but after the second quarter, things began to fall apart. Austin was sloppy. He wasn't seeing the field. He thought he was a running back instead of a quarterback and tried to run the ball every down.

Cade was undecided about what happened at half-time. Austin was an arrogant ass. He refused to admit he needed to hand the ball off to Trey, the actual running back, or that he was refusing to throw the ball to Ryan. Trey had stepped forward and given an emotional speech to try to charge the team. It had worked. They had run out in the third quarter and put together a great drive until Austin decided to play running back again. They had to settle for a field goal. And now here it was nearing the end of the game and Austin throws and interception.

"Austin. What were you looking at when you threw that? There wasn't a receiver around?"

"Ryan missed his route. He should have been there. He just lost the game for us, so go yell at him." Austin yanked off his helmet and threw it to the ground. It rolled over to the metal bench and came to rest at the feet of a very upset Ryan.

"Ryan didn't miss his route. He was to run a fifteen yard post, and you threw the ball right into the middle of coverage while Ryan was still five yards from his mark."

Cade saw Ryan pick up the helmet and head over towards them. Austin was a strong guy. He was around Cade's size but still needed muscle. Even though Ryan was two years younger, he was much more developed. He was already Austin's height but probably had twenty pounds on him. Cade was sure by his senior year Ryan would be All-State.

"You dropped this." Ryan shoved the helmet at Austin. "And try to show some leadership. Stop blaming others for your mistakes." Ryan turned around and headed back over to Coach Parks. He also had a maturity Austin was lacking.

"Take the bench, Austin. I'm putting your backup in if we even have another chance to score." Cade watched as Austin sulked his way to the bench and sat down, ignoring all his teammates.

Cade took a quick glance back at the crowd and saw Annie scanning the people in the bleachers. He smiled as she evaluated the threat level of every person. At least one good thing came out of this game – he knew Annie was interested in him thanks to Miss Lily! He turned his attention back to the game and watched as his defense managed to hold Oakdale to a field goal as the last seconds ticked off the clock.

Annie didn't know what she was doing. She was hanging around teenagers too much because she was starting to act like a lovesick girl. She leaned against the bleachers and sighed. Maybe he would think she was just slow to leave? Maybe she could say she was talking to the parents, who were the only ones left milling around the parking lot?

"Waiting for me?" Annie almost jumped as Cade came up behind her.

"Um. No. I was talking to some of the parents." Annie took a step away from him. She couldn't think straight when she was so close to him.

"I'm sure they appreciate you coming and supporting their sons. Some of them have talked about you, you know?"

"The parents are talking about me?" Annie stopped looking at the old cracked pavement and looked up into his eyes. They seemed browner tonight.

"No, my kids are talking about you. They really appreciate someone taking such an interest in their extracurricular activities. They said you've been trying to get to know each of them. That's real nice of you. Our last guidance counselor never sought out kids just to get to know them and to find out how they are doing in class and on the field."

Annie left her face blank. She wasn't expecting the kids to talk to Cade about her interrogations. She called them conferences. She had the boys come in and go over their classes, their goals and then tried to get them to talk about football as much as she could.

"They're great kids. I'm sorry about the loss tonight. It was a tough game." She kept her eyes on his and tried to keep her thoughts focused.

"Thanks. It was sloppy and some players need more work, but I saw promise."

Cade watched her closely. She was really good. She didn't give anything away. He had known what she was doing the past couple of weeks. She was bringing in players and questioning them. The added benefit was his players thought she really was interested in them and came out with a little more confidence. She was actually a really good guidance counselor.

"Thanks for coming to the game. It really means a lot to me." He gave her a smile and watched as she blushed again. It was really cute when she did that. It made him want to know more about what was underneath her tough DEA cover.

"To you?" she stuttered.

"Yeah. You're supporting the team and that's really great of you." Cade was enjoying himself. He liked making her feel as discombobulated as she had made him feel.

"Oh! Yes, the team. Anything for the team," she mumbled. Cade smiled. Something about this woman made him feel as if he could do anything. He looked up and saw that most of the parents had picked up their kids and headed out. The parking lot was quickly becoming empty.

"Can I walk you back to your car?"

Before she could say no, which he knew she would, he put his hand on her back and gently pushed her forward. He stopped in front of her dark green convertible. He had to focus on keeping his hand still. He desperately wanted to run it up and down her back to feel every inch of such an intriguing woman.

"Thank you, Cade."

They stopped and he watched her dig around her purse for her keys. Well, it was now or never, and if he didn't do this, Miss Lily would be mad at him and tell Miss Daisy not to feed him the next time he went to the Café.

"I was wondering if you'd like to go out to dinner with me?" Cade could swear his heart stopped beating. Was it a good sign or bad that she wasn't answering right away?

"Cade! Look out!" she screamed and tried to grab him, but it was too late.

A van skidded to a halt next to him, almost running him over. The van door was open and two men with shiny shaved heads looked out. He shoved Annie hard against her shoulder. She fell backwards against her car and out of reach of the hands grabbing him from the van. In a split second, Cade had assessed the situation. These guys were idiots.

They had fumbled when they grabbed him. They had blindfolded him, but they did such a bad job that he could still see everything. They had tied his wrists, but he could easily get out of them. It was then that he decided instead of escaping, he'd see what they wanted. He looked around and took in the guy with a broken nose and a guy in the passenger's seat with a cast on his leg. Ah, these were the same geniuses that had tried to rough him up. He had to admit, he was curious to see what they wanted.

The van was a standard utility van. There was industrial carpet on the floor. No seats except the front two. There were three men in the back of the van with him. They were all burly guys who looked like they had been using S2 themselves. So many men thought the bigger the muscles the better the fighter, but that just wasn't true. Sure they may be able to lift more weight than he could, but being a good fighter meant that you had strength, speed and precision. These guys were so bulky they'd never be able to keep up in a fight. He had a feeling though that this wasn't about fighting. This was about drugs, and he had was pretty sure he was about to meet one of the key players in the drug trade. Annie would be very happy with this news.

He watched the scenery change as they drove into Lexington. Horse farms with rolling bluegrass gave way to commercial shipping centers, subdivisions and shopping malls. They drove round and round, trying to confuse him. They thought he couldn't see, and the length of the trip would make it impossible for him to tell where they were. Well, except for the fact he had just seen that they had gone past Rupp Arena and were driving downtown. They circled around Rupp and headed back towards Keeneston. They pulled into one of the strip malls closest to the small country road that led back home and parked.

He saw the neon lights of Iron Club and Spa, one of the national chain gym franchises. There was one in Keeneston too. The lights were on, but it was after ten o'clock at night and there was no one working out. They pushed and shoved at him to get him moving. He pretended to stumble and smashed the foot of one of the goons next to him.

Even if he couldn't see, he would know it was a gym. There was a distinct smell that belonged to gyms. It was a mix of sweat, metal, rubber, and disinfectant cleaner. He was pushed through a small door camouflaged into the wall near the racquetball courts and led up a flight of stairs. At the top of the stairs was a small lobby and bathroom. To the right was an open door to a large office that overlooked the gym from behind the two-way mirrors that covered the walls of the gym.

"Take it off," a gruff voice with a slight Scottish brogue said.

Cade's blindfold was taken off, and he pretended to blink his eyes as if adjusting to the sudden light. When he brought his eyes up, he came face to face with a thug in a suit. This must be upper management.

"Good evening, Mr. Davies." The man stood from behind his desk and walked around his desk and placed a hip on the edge of it.

Unlike the goons who had a hold of him, this man earned his muscles from the streets, not the gym. That was obvious from his thickness, but lack of bulging muscles like the steroid triplets behind him. His guess would be that he was imported from Edinburgh or Glasgow to run this little drug ring. It was common to import someone with a reputation, but not well known. That way they could start a lie about how many people they had killed and the horrible acts they had committed just to gain respect. It worked because there was no way to check it out.

"By the name on your desk, I assume you are Trevor Gaylen. If there was something you needed, there is this little invention called a phone." Cade watched the red-headed Scott crack a small smile. A flash of a gold tooth caught his eye before Trevor pushed himself off the desk and came towards Cade with his arms crossed over his barreled chest.

"That I am, Mr. Davies. I'm glad you catch on so fast. I was afraid this would be a rather long, painful meeting if you were just another dumb academic." Cade stood with his arms loose, even in the face of veiled threat. "It seems that you are off to a rough start with your football team this year." Trevor stopped a couple of feet in front of him and took his measure.

"We'll turn it around. We're a young, inexperienced team."

"I thought we could enter a partnership of sorts."

"What kind of partnership? You'll let my boys use these facilities for free?" Cade watched as Trevor tossed back his head and laughed.

"Aye, you are funny, Mr. Davies. But, no. That is not the kind of partnership I was wanting. See, I have something that will help your players grow stronger, run faster, and increase their reaction time."

"And what would that miracle be? Some new vitamin supplement your gym is pushing?"

"Not exactly. It's an injectable supplement."

"Injectable, huh? As in steroid based?" Trevor grinned again, but it was calculated. He was in full sales mode.

"It's a derivative of steroids, yes, one that doesn't show up in any standard test. It will improve your players tenfold by mid-season. Guaranteed."

"And would this be called S2?"

"So, you've heard about it. Well, of course you have. You specifically tested for it during training camp. Strange that you've heard about it, considering that it has just now been submitted to the FDA for the animal testing phase. Also it's strange that you knew you had to test specifically for S2." Cade watched as Trevor transformed from the buddy-buddy salesman to the cold blooded dealer that he hid underneath a nice suit.

"I'm the kids' coach. I hear them talk in the locker room. See what they do when they think no one is around. I see and hear everything that goes on with my team. That's what being a good coach is all about."

"A good coach, yes, but not a great coach. I can make you a great coach."

"How?" Cade was interested in seeing how much he could learn for Annie. Would bringing her this information get her to say yes to a date? She hadn't, after all, been able to give him an answer to his question about a date.

"I can make you a great coach by you accepting my proposition, Mr. Davies. My very profitable proposition."

"I'm listening, but I can tell you now the mostly likely answer will be no." Cade heard the steroid triplets suck in their breath. At the sight of Trevor's eyes narrowing into cold flints of blue ice, he guessed not too many people told Trevor no, and of those, not many lived.

"No one says no to the Gaylen and lives to tell about it. What do you want me to do about it boss?" one of the steroid triplets asked.

"Isn't that a little cliché?" Cade suppressed the chuckle. It was all straight out of a bad movie.

"Nothing…for now. Let's see what Mr. Davies says after I have pitched him my proposition." Trevor took a step forward and jabbed him in the stomach.

Cade sucked in a breath from the punch he was not expecting. He had gotten caught up in laughing at the goons and didn't take Gaylen seriously, a mistake he wouldn't make again. It wasn't the strongest punch Cade had ever taken, but it was enough to make his stomach knot. Okay, time for playing games was over.

"Now, be a good boy and listen to what I have to say before you answer. As a teacher, you should know better than to make a judgment before hearing all the facts." He watched as Gaylen stepped back to lean against his desk. "This is what you are going to do. You are never going to test for S2 again. You are going to strongly recommend to all your top players that they come in for a free, six month promotional pass to the Keeneston Iron Club and Spa. They will receive free personal training from retired NFL player Devon Ross as a nice perk and enticement to join. It should also give you peace of mind to know they're being trained by one of the best."

"Didn't Ross only play for one season with the Cincinnati Bengals?"

"It's more than you played. I believe your coaching bio states you only played high school ball," Gaylen scoffed.

"You got me there. Go on. What else do you want?" Cade tried not to roll his eyes. Fighting terrorism got in his way of college ball. Apparently Trevor hadn't dug that far in his history. Not too smart on his part.

"Oh Coach, it's not what I want. It's what I can give you. I can give you the best team in the state. All I need from you is for you to coach the team."

"That's it?" Cade asked skeptically.

"That's it. You recommend the players come to the gym, you stay out of the locker room after practice, and you stop the special drug testing for S2."

"You're asking me to break the law. To supply my kids with an illegal substance."

"Not at all! S2 is only temporarily illegal. Soon enough it will be legal when we have a chance to present it to the FDA. And, I am not asking you to supply it. Simply turn a blind eye to it and in return you get a championship team."

"What about the state required drug tests?"

"Do them. By all means do everything the athletic board requires of you. Just what they require you to do. No more special testing, which, by the way, the board does not require you to do."

"And in return I get a share of any profits from the sale of your supplement or maybe from gym memberships."

Gaylen tossed his head back and laughed. "Aye, you are a funny one. But alas, no, Mr. Davies. It's much more simple. In exchange, I let that cute little girlfriend of yours live. I always did have a thing for red heads."

"N..." Cade started to say.

"And if you say no, I will take everything and everyone that you cherish from you, one by one, starting with that hairy mutt of a dog and ending with your mother, or maybe that hot little sister of yours."

Gaylen's tone had turned deadly. Cade recognized it for what it was. The truth. He would try. He may not succeed, but he believed he would, and sometimes those who overvalue their strengths are the most dangerous because they simply do not understand that they cannot win, so they keep trying. He needed to buy time to see how this would play out.

"Can I think about it?"

Gaylen relaxed and gave his salesman smile. "Of course you can. I'll give you until Monday morning. Good evening Mr. Davies."

With a flick of Gaylen's wrist to indicate the meeting was over, the steroid triplets grabbed him and pinned his arms back. The remaining man tied the blindfold over his eyes, poorly, again. He contained his sigh at these amateurs only because he knew Gaylen was trying to be intimidating. He didn't want to fracture his ego. He was a gentleman after all, and he needed to get back to Keeneston as soon as possible so he could find Annie. He had played enough games with her these last weeks, little innuendos and taunts trying to get her flustered and wondering if he really knew who she was. Well, the time for playing was over. He needed her help to protect his team.

Chapter Seven

nnie couldn't believe it. The bumbling idiots had gotten Cade into the van although he didn't put up much of a fight. Maybe his military record was forged? He always seemed to need saving. She had tried to follow them, but her damn keys had been eaten by her purse. She had to toss the whole thing on the hood of the car to find them. By that time the van was gone and she stood alone in the large parking lot.

She'd tossed all her junk back in her purse and headed home. She drove through the church parking lot which was sprinkled with cars for some sort of Bible study or singles dance, or whatever they were scheduled for tonight. There may not be many people in Keeneston, and there may not be that much of a night life, but St. Francis could throw some kicking parties.

Annie parked next to the small wood cottage house and leapt up the stairs to her front door. Unlocking the door she ran to where her computer still sat on the kitchen table – the only place she could fit it – and booted it up. She may not know where Cade was now, but she could find out where he would be when it was over.

She typed in his name and found his address. She entered it into the mapping system and stared at a dot in the middle of a field. The system said it couldn't find the location. Flipping open her phone she dialed the only number she had bothered to learn since moving to Keeneston.

"Blossom Café. What can I do for ya'?"

"Is this Miss Daisy or Miss Violet?"

"This is Miss Violet, dear. What can I do for you, hon?"

"This is Annie Hill. I need to know how to get out to Cade's house."

"Oh, bless your heart, I won! I won! I never win! Daisy Mae I won!"

Annie had to hold the phone away from her ear as Miss Violet shouted out into the Café.

"What do you mean you won? Who is it Violet Fae?" she heard Miss Daisy shout.

"It's Annie. She wants to know how to get to out to Cade's house! I won the pool! Today was my day!" There was a chorus of groans as the patrons of the Café checked their dates in the pool and even through the phone Annie bet they could see her red face. "Thank you, dear. It was about time the two of you got together. You've been circling each other ever since you got to town."

"I got twenty on a June wedding!" someone shouted.

"What?!" Annie shouted into the phone. "Miss Daisy, what was that?" Annie's stomach had flipped at hearing the word wedding. Talk about a commitment-phobe. With her history who wouldn't be?

"Oh nothing, dear. Now, you want to know how to get to Cade's. Easy. Turn right out of your house onto Main Street and keep going for about five miles. You'll see his parents' stone gate entranceway on the right. Go a half mile further and turn left into Fire Gate Nineteen there. Then make a right on the first dirt road you come to and take that for about a mile. It'll stop at his house."

"Seriously, there are still dirt roads? And what's a fire gate?"

"You'll see it. There's a break in the fence line, like a driveway, and there's a white wood marker that has the number 19 in red on it. That's the fire gate. Of course there are still dirt roads, honey. His house is almost a mile from the road. You know much that would cost to pave? Now, would you say you like the month of July or September better?"

"Neither. I'm partial to January."

"Isn't that a little soon? Oh well, why waste time is what I say. Have fun tonight!"

Annie closed her phone and stared at it for a full minute. She could just see Miss Violet putting twenty bucks on a January wedding that was never going to happen. Not that a wedding to Cade would be bad, but those were just fantasies. First she needed to make sure he was still alive.

Annie missed the fire gate twice and the dirt road once. A mailbox or a light would be helpful. She turned onto the dirt road and turned on her high beams. She drove through pastures and saw more cows than she ever had before in her life. Soon she came upon some trees and followed the dirt path through the woods.

She rounded the corner, slammed on her brakes, and sent dirt flying as she stopped before hitting a family of deer. Letting out the breath she realized she was holding, she started heading down the dirt road again. She drove around a bend and came out in an opening. A white farmhouse stood there. It was beautiful. She could tell from the architecture that it was very old, but also from the fresh paint job and what looked like a new deck, that Cade had just finished some renovations.

The house was lovely, a two-story, wood farmhouse with a large front porch that had soft-looking chairs sitting out and speakers wired for music. She pulled up to the front steps and turned off her car. The house was dark, and Cade's SUV was nowhere in sight. A tingle of worry crawled down her spine, but if half of what she read in his military file was true, then he could easily handle himself. She had to admit, she was pretty curious to find out what that joke of a kidnapping was about.

She climbed up the stairs and looked at the comfortable porch chairs, but then she looked toward the house. She wondered what it was like inside. She also knew that to do her job, and do it well, she needed proof that Cade was not supplying his team with S2 or anything illegal. Evidence like that coming to light during a trial would break any case she would make against any of the dealers. Sometimes in her job she had to do things she didn't like.

Well, if she were honest, a little B and E never hurt anyone. And think how much she could learn about Cade. She took out her pick case, but when she reached for the door, she discovered it unlocked. The knob turned easily in her hand, and she felt her heart speed up at the thought of walking around Cade's house alone.

She pushed at the door and nothing happened. Huh? It was unlocked. The door was open just a sliver. Why wasn't it opening all the way? She pushed again, but it didn't budge. Was something barricading the door? She took her pick and ran it through the sliver of open door. No, nothing was barricading the door. She took a step closer to the door and bent her knees. She put her shoulder to the door and pushed.

She heard someone grunt and the door flew open. It opened so fast she fell forward onto the old hardwood floor. It was her time to groan. The jeans had prevented her knees from being scraped up, but she had landed hard on her hands. She lay there for a second, regaining her breath, when she felt that she was not alone. She slowly raised her head and came face to face with him.

Annie stared, he stared, and neither of them moved. He had big brown eyes that seemed to look right into her soul. With his lopsided grin, he looked like he was laughing. Even his soulful eyes twinkled with some untold joke.

"Hi there. I wasn't expecting anyone at home," she said in a calm voice so as not to upset him.

Slurp! A big pink tongue lapped her across the face. She looked at the happy face in front of her and at his tongue hanging out, his white hairy jowls, and his big, black tail as it thumped against the ground, and smiled. Cade's dog looked like he had just stepped out of a Disney movie.

"What a guard dog you are. You sure know how to keep people out and then how to make them feel welcome once they can push past you." Justin's tail thumped again as he cocked his head to one side.

"Well, if you don't mind, I'm going to take a look around. Do you want to show me where things are?" Justin stood and walked beside her. His big, black nose kept nudging her hand every time she stopped rubbing his head.

"Can you show me where the drugs are?" Justin stopped walking and plopped to the ground, rolling over to expose his belly. "Hmm. I take it that your drug is belly rubs." She rubbed his belly for a second as she took in the house.

The house had just had a complete upgrade inside. Everything was new. There was an entranceway with narrow stairs leading upstairs. A half bath was tucked in under the stairs, and an office sat across the front room facing the porch. Past the stairs was a dining room that also connected with the kitchen just beyond that. Cade had obviously knocked down walls to create a large kitchen and living room area in one. The kitchen had brand new stainless steel appliances. A large island with black granite countertops and six barstools separated the kitchen from the living room. The living room held a large leather couch and two matching chairs, one of which was now occupied by Justin. A large LED television was mounted to the far right wall. The back wall had French doors that led out to a brick patio.

Annie walked into the living room and slowly looked around at the pictures and books lining the walls and sitting on tables. There were pictures of Cade with all his siblings, a picture of Cade, Miles, and another one of his siblings in military fatigues in some desert, pictures of an older couple she guessed were his parents, and then some she guessed to be of grandparents.

She opened drawers and looked behind photos but could not find anything relating to drugs or anything else illegal. She decided to run upstairs and check his bedroom before doing a search of his office. Annie hurried up the stairs and peeked into two guest rooms before finding the master suite.

A large, king-size bed with a dark green comforter sat along the far wall in the middle of the room. She walked through the door to his room and couldn't help the slightly giddy feeling she got when she sat on his bed. Against the wall opposite the bed was another LED television and a chest. She felt through his clothes and couldn't find anything. She made her way through his walk-in closet and only found a couple of old unloaded rifles. She pushed open the other door in the room and walked into a massive bathroom. A large shower with six shower heads took up most of one wall. Annie couldn't look away from the shower. She knew what she wanted to do in that shower. It was the perfect shower for it, the hot water pulsing all around, the steam rising up, the bodies… she needed to get out of here before she spontaneously combusted!

Annie lifted the small curtain next to the front door and looked out. All was dark and silent. She felt as if she were in her own world out here. Even though she was illegally breaking and entering, well, the door was unlocked she felt very peaceful out here. Knowing she was in the clear, she headed into Cade's office.

"If there is going to be any evidence of drugs, it will be in here." She sat down in his chair and surveyed his desk. He only had a bookcase and a desk with a computer on it in the room. She opened the desk drawer and found nothing. She opened one of the side drawers and found a desk full of small black cases. She picked one up and opened it: National Defense Service Medal. She picked up another box: Silver Star. There were more than ten boxes in the drawer! She picked up another one and opened it: Legion of Merit Medal. She picked up one more and opened it. Holy crap! It was the Army's Distinguished Service Cross. She put it back down in the drawer and closed it. She suddenly felt guilty for searching his house with his literally being a national hero.

She quickly went through the other drawers, and finding nothing, pushed back from his chair. She went over to the bookcase and looked at his books, finding a lot of history book such as A. J.

Langguth's *Patriots*, David McCullough's *1776*, Dan Jenkins' *Semi-Tough* and other football novels.

Annie was just about to call it quits and head back outside to wait when she noticed a heavy-duty lock on the wall hidden behind some large plants. She pushed the plants out of the way and found that it was actually attached to a door. Hmm, now this was strange. Annie pulled out her black leather lock pick case and opened it up. It took her a couple of minutes, but finally she heard the telltale click of the lock opening.

She put her tools away and put the case back in her purse before opening the narrow door. Looking around, she took a cautious step forward into the darkness. The room was pitch black, and she pulled out her small penlight. Annie aimed the light onto the wall and gasped. It was lined with weapons. She found the switch and turned on the fluorescent overhead lights and froze.

Rifles lined one whole wall. She recognized the Army's standard issue M24 Sniper along with an M40A3 and a very large M82A1 SASR. Wow, it was a beauty, a .50 caliber beauty. Along the other side of the wall were various handguns. There was an MK24, and oh, there was the new M11 also known as the SIG P228! She had always wanted to try one those. It was calling her name. She would swear to it in court if she got arrested for trespassing. She picked the M11 off of the wall where it was hanging and tested its weight and balance.

"Oh, you are one handsome guy," she cooed to it.

"Why thank you." The voice slid over her. She jumped, swinging the gun around and pointing it at her target.

"You do know it's not loaded, right Red?"

"What are you doing here?!" Annie accusingly asked him.

"I live here. What are you doing here?"

She heard the laughter in his voice and lowered the gun. Yeah, that's right. She was the one breaking and entering.

"You don't seem surprised to see me. How long have you been here?" Was he here the whole time she was drooling over his guns?

"Marshall called me from the Café and asked how I felt about getting married in April."

Annie groaned and desperately wanted to hit the light switch and hide under the large wood table in the middle of the gun room.

"I said I thought it would be lovely, but apparently my bride is in a rush and wants to get married in January."

Annie eyed the rounds for the M11 on the shelf and contemplated ending this before she died of embarrassment.

Cade only felt kind of bad for her. He was having way too much fun embarrassing her though to take pity on her. He had been halfway home when Marshall called, wanting to know all the details of their hot night together and telling him Mom was expecting him to bring Annie home for dinner on Sunday.

He had found his house still dark when he drove up and her car empty. It didn't take a genius to figure out what she was up to. He had quietly come in the house from the back door and found the faint glow from his arms room spilling out into his office. When he looked in the door, there was his dog, sound asleep at her feet. Annie was holding his favorite gun and practically worshiping it with her hands.

"If you keep touching my gun like that, I'm going to be jealous." His voice came out a little rougher than normal but her skilled fingers manipulating his gun was making him think of her using those fingers for something else. He was having a very hard time remembering he didn't want a January wedding.

Annie practically threw the gun back onto the wall and he had to laugh. She was so jumpy that he bet he wasn't the only one affected. "So, you like what you see, Agent Blake?" With a small wave of his arm he indicated his gun room.

He could see the momentary shock on her face when she realized he knew who she was, but she recovered quickly enough. He watched as she wiped her tiny hands on her jeans and then as she slowly raised her green eyes to meet his. When he looked into her eyes, he felt transported to pastures during springtime with the multiple shades of green fighting for dominance.

"I would ask you how you know who I am, but after looking around your house, I think there is a lot to you and your military record that was left out of the database." Cade smiled and rocked back on his heels. "You could say that."

Chapter Eight

Cade held the door to the gun room open for Annie. She walked into his office and leaned her hip against his old desk while he shut and locked the door. He had to look twice for the hidden panel to get the key out of in order to lock the door. Annie just looked so sexy in those tight jeans and simple white v-neck t-shirt that seemed to cling perfectly to her breasts, her hair haphazardly pulled back into a ponytail. It was driving him crazy!

Annie waited for him to finish hiding the key before asking him about his kidnapping. "So, what was amateur hour about?"

"Actually, I was getting ready to come find you to talk about just that. I think I need your help."

"Did the big bad goons scare you?" she teased.

"Ha! At first I had to go against my instinct to fight, but when I realized they were completely incompetent I had to fight from laughing. They tied loose knots and couldn't even put on a blindfold. Good news, I know exactly where the home base is. They took me into Lexington to the Iron Club and Spa where I got to meet Trevor Gaylen."

"Great. I will pass this information along to my bosses and we can get some surveillance set up. Good work, Davies. Do you think this Trevor guy is the boss?"

"No." Cade shook his head. "He's a thug in a suit brought over from Scotland."

Annie looked at him and he could see the question in her eyes, "Then what did he want?"

"He wants me to send the best boys on the team to the gym in Keeneston to train with an ex-NFL player by the name of Devon Ross. Furthermore, I'm to be in the locker room sparingly and no longer test for S2. In return, I get a championship team and you get to live."

He watched as Annie narrowed her eyes as she took in his meaning. "Well, then you have nothing to worry about. As you know, I can take care of myself." She smiled at him and his body went weak.

"It's not just you he threatened. He also threatened my mother and my dog."

"He brought your dog into it? Wow. That's low." Annie shook her head and thought about it some more. Cade was right. This wasn't the boss man. The boss usually kept to the shadows. "We think the boss, whom we call the Scientist, is the actual designer of the drug. Did he say anything that would give clues to the boss?"

"Trevor did say it was only temporarily illegal, that they were going to present it to the FDA," Cade eagerly put in.

"That way he can make two fortunes, one now, while they sell the drug illegally and then a second if it becomes approved by the FDA. That's why I'm thinking the boss is younger, maybe late twenties, early thirties. It takes around fifteen years for a drug to be approved by the FDA, and my guess is he's young enough to be able to enjoy both potential windfalls." Annie knew she was mixing her personal views with what the DEA believed, but it felt like Cade would believe in her theories where the DEA didn't want to speculate. She looked at Cade and saw him nodding his head in agreement.

"That would make sense. An older person wouldn't care about FDA approval. They'd just try to corner the street market. That would also make sense why the boss is keeping in the shadows. When they go legit, they'll need a figurehead with a clean record."

"That's right." He got it! Annie almost jumped with joy. Her bosses kept telling her it was too much of a leap to narrow the profile down to younger people. Therefore, they had too many suspects to even make a start in the investigation.

"But, S2 is not legal now, right?"

"No. S2 is currently being made with an illegal synthetic steroid that was rejected by the FDA because it caused heart failure. We've run blood and tissue tests on all the victims over the past six months, and what we're seeing is a slight change in the synthetic steroid from victim to victim." Annie was getting excited now. She was talking about her investigation, her hunches, and her own thoughts on the case.

"What does that mean?" Cade asked. She watched him cross his arms and take a seat in is black leather office chair.

Annie started to pace in front of the desk. She wanted to lay out her theory so he could understand, since it seemed like no one in the DEA seemed to. It meant a lot to her to have one person, just one, see reason in her theory.

"See, I think the Scientist has taken the illegal synthetic steroid and is making tiny alterations to it to try to correct the direct link to heart failure. Why reinvent the wheel? The synthetic was perfect, except for the fact that it caused heart failure. So, if he can fix that problem, he'd have a remarkable commodity on his hands. I'm betting that the DEA scientists will find a different chemical makeup of the drug from Corey's locker than from the drugs we took off the dealer in Miami. Somehow, I hope one of the changes will lead me to him. Maybe through a traceable chemical, something. He'll make a mistake and I will be there to take him down."

"Why go through years and years of drug trials under the FDA rules and regulations when you could make a fortune just selling it as is now?"

"I don't know. That's what I'm trying to find out."

Cade listened to Annie and felt the cold settle into the pit of his stomach. This guy was selling to kids, his kids, just to make money, and only found these heart problems to be a side effect. He didn't like it, but he'd have to delay and play ball with Trevor Gaylen for a while. He needed to find the boss and take him out before any more kids were killed, and he would bet the farm on Trevor Gaylen being the key to taking the boss down.

He pushed off the arms of the office chair and stood in front of Annie. She seemed so small next to him. He just wanted to pull her to his chest and hide her from any danger she may be in because of his deal with Trevor. He stopped himself from reaching for her though. She would kick his ass if he didn't treat her with the respect she deserved. She wasn't the only one who had gone snooping after all. His perusal through her records showed him that she was very capable of taking care of herself. It was just hard for him to accept.

"Come on. Let's go outside and talk." Cade watched her nod and walk through the office door and head straight for the back patio. He took a quick look around his living room and paused by the picture of him with his brothers and sister. It was slightly out of place.

Annie saw the second he saw the picture. She had angled it more than it originally had been. She saw that now. She also saw how he quickly scanned the rest of the area for any other signs of her search. She was so busted.

"There is still one more question I have for you," Cade said to her. His voice only hinting at the anger he was feeling.

"Yes?" Annie straightened her shoulders. She wasn't going to be intimidated by a little thing like feeling bad over an illegal search.

"What were you doing in my house? I can understand my office and the gun room, but what were you looking for?"

"I think you know what I was looking for."

"Well, are you satisfied that I am not dealing drugs to my kids, or do you need more time to search?"

"No, I don't. Thank you for offering though. I will make note of your cooperation in my reports." She was being a brat and she knew it. She should just explain it to him and then maybe he wouldn't get mad at her. It always seemed like a man was mad at her for doing her job, of course, and to be honest she never took the time to explain herself.

"Look, Cade, I know you're mad, but there is no reason to be. You know I have a job to do. You're the only one who should understand my need to make sure you are cleared before I move on to the next subject. I know you weren't selling, but I had to prove it."

She watched as Cade processed her words. "Well, I guess that clears that up. How about we go outside and have a glass of wine. I believe you owe me an answer."

"An answer?" Annie asked, relief pouring over her. He understood… he actually understood.

"I believe I asked you out on a date. Then Larry, Moe and Curly interrupted your giving me an answer. So, why don't you contemplate your answer outside?"

Annie almost jumped at the ball of fur that popped up from behind the back of a chair in the living room at the word 'outside'. She watched in stunned silence as he leapt out of the chair and ran toward the closed sliding glass door. He leapt up, his white furry paws hitting the sliding glass door at head level, his long, black coat swishing in the self-created wind as he leaned his whole body to the right. His big paws pushed the sliding door open as he fell from the air, the force of his fall pushing the door further open. Justin landed on the ground and put his black nose through the door, and with a twist of his head pushed the door the remainder of the way open.

Annie stared in amazement as Justin trotted through the door and disappeared into the darkness. "How?"

"Yeah, it's pretty wild, but he's always been able to do that. He just jumps up and slides it open."

"He doesn't look smart enough to figure that out. He kind of reminds me of a clown."

Cade handed her a glass of white wine and led her outside to the brown and green cushioned patio furniture. Annie sat down on the iron scroll chair and looked out into the night. The lawn was dotted with various trees and bushes before opening up into gently rolling pastures outlined with black fences. She closed her eyes and snuggled into the soft cushion, resting her head against the back of the chair. She opened her eyes and looked up at the star-filled sky.

Annie watched as he took a seat in the chair a few feet away from her. No wonder all the teachers in the break room swooned when he came in. His shoulders were wide, his stomach flat, and the way his jeans sat on his hips forced her to think about wild nights in bed…oh no, she was getting sidetracked and she really needed to focus on the case. It didn't matter that he was sexy as sin, nice, great with kids, and obviously secure in his sexuality. His dog did have a pink bow in his hair, after all. And it didn't matter that he seemed to be the only person who understood and supported her theories on the case. But, those things didn't matter. She was here to do a job, nothing else.

"So, what are your plans now?" Cade asked, dragging Annie back to reality.

"I want to go to the gym in Lexington. See if I can join and maybe tail Gaylen. See if I can find the drop locations and also see if I can get evidence of him dealing." Annie was also thinking about doing the same with the personal trainer. See if she could get close to him somehow. Maybe hire him to train her.

"No, I don't think that's a good idea."

"What? Why not?" Did he have a better idea? She watched as he leaned forward in his chair and set his beer on the table.

"It's too dangerous. Larry, Moe and Curly may be amateurs, but Gaylen is a pro. May I remind you, he's also a pro who has already threatened you, a pro who knows what you look like and may be instantly suspicious if you are suddenly around all the time. It's just not a good plan."

She watched as Cade ran his hand through his disheveled dirty blonde hair, his hazel eyes hidden in the shadows. Well, maybe she was wrong. Maybe he didn't get her job. No, don't jump to conclusions, she thought.

"Cade, you do know it's my job, right? I'm good at my job. I have done tons of undercover work. I can easily appear at the club and blend in as just another patron."

"No you can't. I'm telling you, Gaylen is not some street thug you trick into selling some dope to you. He'll know instantly that something is up. I won't have you placing yourself in danger."

Annie bolted up from her seat, "You won't have it?"

"That's right. I won't have it. It's a stupid move and you know it." Cade leapt to his feet and grabbed Annie's shoulders, pulling her towards him. "I don't want to see you in danger. What's so hard to understand?"

Annie leaned forward even more, "Let me set the record straight. This is my job. I'm trained for this. You don't get to tell me what I can and can't do. Do you understand? Just because I'm a woman doesn't mean I can't go into danger, Mr. War Hero, and do whatever else a man can do." Great, just when she thought he was different he goes and turns into a patronizing jerk.

"Can you write your name in the snow?" He shot her a cocky grin and she wanted to scream.

"Don't demean me! I will do whatever I damn well please and that includes running head first into danger. You don't have a say!" she yelled.

The grin fell from his face, "Then maybe I need to make myself clear," he practically growled.

Cade wrapped his arms around her and pulled her against him. He felt her breasts press into his chest as and her breathing falter as he lowered his head to hers. He captured her lips with a rough kiss. He ran his tongue along her teeth until she opened to him. His tongue surged into her mouth as he tasted her. God, nothing was sweeter than his little agent.

Annie pulled her head back and looked at his eyes flashing with desire. Damn. Her head was still spinning from that kiss. He may be a patronizing jerk, but he was a patronizing jerk who could kiss. She had to pry her hands from where they were clutching his shirt. She balled her hand into a fist and planted it right into his desire-filled face.

She spun on the ball of her foot and headed towards her car, but not before hearing him laugh, "It was a good right cross, but I can do better." Arg! She didn't know whether to go back and show him her hook or to leap on him and explore what she had felt pressing against her stomach. But sometimes a strategic retreat was necessary to win the war.

Chapter Nine

Cade glanced at the clock. He had ten minutes until he had to get to practice. His assistant coach was warming the team up so he could finish grading the tests his freshman biology class took the other day. He heard heels clicking on the floor and looked up, hoping to see Annie, but it was just Stephanie from across the hall.

"Hiya, Coach. Getting ready for practice?" She was a nice enough girl. Nice enough that they went on a date about six months ago but nothing came from it. She may be a chemistry teacher, but they had no chemistry. She also always dressed spectacularly for school, which made Cade feel like a slouch wearing his black athletic pants for practice and a royal blue t-shirt with KHS across the front in white.

"Trying to."

"Bless your heart! That eye looks horrible." She placed her finger on his chin and raised his face to get a better look at his black eye. "What happened to your eye? There's a teacher's pool on trying to guess what happened," she giggled.

"Well, I wouldn't want to give you an unfair advantage. All will be revealed when enough time for speculation to run rampant has passed and when everyone has placed their bets," he laughed.

"Oh! I'm sorry. I didn't mean to interrupt. I'll come back later." Cade snapped his head from Stephanie's grasp and right into the clearly pissed off face of the woman he couldn't stop thinking of.

"You're not interrupting. I'll let you all talk. Cade, we'll talk more later. Have a good practice." Annie watched as Stephanie straightened up from leaning over the desk and thrusting her cleavage into Cade's dazed face. "Bye now!"

Cade watched as Stephanie strutted out of the room. When he turned to look at Annie, he knew he was in trouble. She stood with her arms crossed, which resulted in her breasts being presented to him. He heard her clear her throat. Uh-oh. She'd caught him staring at her chest. He just couldn't stop digging himself deeper into the hole he was in.

"It's not what it looks like." Dig. "I mean, nothing was happening." Dig. "I mean, she doesn't mean anything to me. She was just looking at the nice shiner you gave me."

"Yeah, sure. Look, I just wanted you to give me a list of the players who were the closest to the three players who were using S2. I want to call them in first for a counseling thing I'm going to do with the players on peer pressure and drug use."

Cade glanced at the clock and saw he was already late for practice. "Can you walk with me to practice and we can talk more about it? Please." Annie gave a quick nod of her head and headed out the door without him.

Annie was so pissed off she would swear her red hair had turned into flames. She was all ready to come forgive him when she spotted his face in the chemistry teacher's breasts and her hands all over him. If only he had not spoken a word to her last night and kissed her, then she'd finally get laid. She didn't even want to think about how long it had been. But she couldn't fool herself. She wouldn't have gone through with it. It just wasn't her style.

They walked down the empty hallways winding toward the football field. Blue lockers lined the walls heading toward the double doors at the end of the hall. They pushed through the doors and into the hot summer heat. Humidity engulfed her and held her tight as they made their way across the parking lot to the practice field.

"What the hell?" Annie didn't quite know what to think of the picture in front of her. The players were in a circle, and inside the circle were two people dressed in large padded sumo wrestler outfits.

"The guys were really down after our last loss so we thought it would be a good idea to have a fun practice. We're still teaching tackling and blocking, just as sumo wrestlers." Cade grinned and watched his assistant coach belly bounce Ryan Hall across the circle.

"Who is that?" Annie asked, pointing to the giant bouncing kids around with his sumo belly.

"That's Coach Parks. He's the offensive coordinator." They stood and watched as Trey Everett tried to block the belly but got flattened. Coach Parks held up his hands in victory. Austin Colby nodded to the group, and on a yell the whole team leapt onto Coach Parks. Parks fell dramatically to the ground with the kids as he tried to throw them off of him.

"Okay then. You might need to rescue him. I'll write down the names of the kids you recommended I start with and call my boss. I will let him know about the deadline you have tonight with Gaylen and see what he wants you to do and also run my plan by him. I'll give you a call later to let you know what to do,"

"Okay. Look, Annie, we need to talk. About last night."

"You got practice, Coach. We can talk later." She cut him off and turned back to the building. She didn't want to hear that last night was a mistake, and she'd bet her job that what he was going to say.

Annie closed the door to her office and took a few minutes to stand in front of the desk fan she had bought to cool off. Her office was small and windowless. Her gray metal desk was covered with papers and student files. She had no pictures on the walls, only generic college and university posters that were sent to her in the mail. She had no plants, not even fake ones, and no personal items except for a pair of sneakers in case she needed to run after a kid someday.

She sat down on her cheap desk chair and picked up the phone to call Special Agent Romero. As she was patched through, she picked up the files of the students Cade had told her about. First up was the quarterback, Austin Colby. He was best friends with Bonner and the most likely to give her information.

"Romero," she heard her boss snap as he picked up.

"It's Blake."

"What do you have for me?"

"Last night the head football coach was snatched from the parking lot by a team of idiots." A little laugh escaped as she remembered Cade retelling the story.

"You're laughing? Is he hurt?"

"No, far from it. He went along with it to get us information."

"He knows about the investigation? How in the hell does he know about an undercover investigation?"

"Ah. About that. You have your database up?"

"Yes. But I don't see how that has anything to do with how a high school football coach could discover our investigation. Are you sure he isn't the boss?"

"Yes. I have searched his desk at school and his whole house. Type in the name Cade Davies. You have a higher clearance level than I do. Maybe you can learn more than I could." She heard Romero type in the name and waited while he was silent.

"Jesus Christ. A Distinguished Service Cross? Is he for real?"

"Sure is. He also hacked the DEA database and discovered my identity and more within the first week I was here."

"Then I guess I don't need to be worried about him being involved. He'll make one hell of a witness if it ever goes to trial. So, what did he find out?"

"He was taken to see Trevor Gaylen at the Lexington Iron Club and Spa. He thinks Trevor is hired upper management from Scotland. Trevor gave him a choice. No more S2 testing, turn a blind eye to any locker room dealing, and get his top players into the Keeneston Iron Club and Spa for personal training with Devon Ross. If he chooses to do this, he gets a championship team. If not, then his dog and the women in his life, including his mother and sister, are killed."

"Okay. What else is there?" Romero asked.

"I have a plan. Cade gave me a list of kids who were close to the guys that tested positive for S2. I want to call them in for counseling on handling the pressure of sports and classes and bring in drugs and peer pressure."

"Tell Coach to accept the deal this Gaylen guy is offering. Tell him to pretend to turn a blind eye but document everything. I want intel that will lead us to the boss. Also, have him keep an eye out, and if anything gets too serious, and it looks like the kids are in danger, we'll put a stop to it. We don't want anything to happen to these kids. I want you all to watch, listen, learn. Talk to the kids, but don't talk to them about S2 specifically. Get to be their friend or at least not the teacher everyone hates. I want to learn the major players in the drug trade. I want to know the dealers, the supplier, middle management, upper management, and the boss. I want all that information and all that evidence before we take down the ring. Because when we take it down, I want everyone in jail. I don't want anyone left to try to take over the business and continue to endanger these kids."

"Yes, sir."

"How is the boy doing with the heart problem?"

"Better. He still isn't back at school yet and may not be able to for a while."

"Okay. I will send someone from the office to the rehabilitation center to talk to him. I will let you know what we get from him. You're doing well Blake. Call in next week at the scheduled time."

"Yes, sir. Good-bye."

Annie hung up the phone and put her feet up on the desk. Crap. She had really wanted to act more aggressively, and she had a feeling

Cade would not be happy with doing nothing to protect his kids. She picked up the files on her desk and started reading them. She wanted to know all about these boys before she began calling them in to talk to them.

Annie put the file she was reading down and looked at her silver watch. It was past six o'clock. She had probably missed football practice, and there was a good chance Cade was already gone for the day. She stuffed some more files into her bag and ran out the door. She raced across the parking lot and breathed a sigh of relief when she saw that Cade's SUV was still parked by the field house. She pushed open the door to the locker room and wrinkled her nose. It smelled like sweat, dirt and grass. The smell was overpowering.

"Cade?" She peeked around one of the lockers but didn't see anyone. She went off in search for him, passing rows of lockers and benches. There was a large meeting room with plastic chairs and a chalkboard covered with X's and O's that took up most of the wall.

It looked like she turned the wrong way so she headed back for the door and then kept going past it. She looked down more rows of lockers until she saw a light coming out of a door at the end of one of the rows. She headed toward the light and noise reached her ears. As she neared the light, she heard singing, very bad singing. Was that Taylor Swift? No, couldn't be.

Annie paused to smile to herself as he continued to sing. She walked through the door and froze in her tracks. Cade was singing alright, singing butt naked in the middle of a huge room with shower heads lining the three walls.

"Oh my God!" She felt her cheeks go bright red at the sight of him. He was even better without his clothes on. His muscled arms, his chest sprinkled with dark blonde hair that came together in a tiny trail that led past his well-defined abs straight to his...

"Annie, can I help you?" he laughed. He turned to her fully so she got an eyeful and then some. She covered her eyes with her hands, more to hide the fierce blush than to prevent her from looking. It had been a long time after all, and this was, well, this was art and it deserved to be appreciated.

"I'm sorry. I was just going to tell you about the conversation with my boss." She shifted her ring fingers slightly so she could peek out and study the artwork.

"Okay, so what did he say?" She heard him chuckle, but she was really busy appreciating the artwork to look up and see his face.

"Oh, um, he wants you to take the deal with Trevor. He wants us to gather intel and evidence so we can bring the whole ring down at once. I know you won't like it, but he does have a good point."

"If there's one thing I know how to do, it's keeping my head down and gathering intel, even though all my instincts tell me to do something to protect the people." Damn. He grabbed a towel and wrapped it around his waist. She dropped her hands and realized why it was so hard for some guys to keep their eyes on her face, 'cause his muscled chest was not allowing her eyes to go any further upward.

"What did you do for the Rangers? Both my boss and I tried to access your whole file and we couldn't. Everything is sealed."

"It's not sealed. It's just not written down. The things I did were off the books. Surveillance, rescue, and well, things that may make the paper, but you'd never be able to connect it to the United States." Cade shrugged and pulled on a t-shirt.

"Well, I guess this isn't as important as what you did, but you are saving an untold amount of children's lives."

"I know. That's the only reason I'm going along with it." Annie watched as he walked out of the showers and felt an odd sort of panic as she realized she didn't ever want him to walk out on her. And she certainly didn't want Miss Perky, the chemistry teacher, seeing what she just saw.

Chapter Ten

Annie pulled on her KHS sweatshirt and clapped her hands together as Trey Everett ran for eight yards. The crisp mid-October air mixed with the scent of leaves covering the ground, the noise of the band playing, and the crowd cheering was warming. It filled her with the feeling of being a part of something and she loved it.

She wasn't so much in love with the fact that over the past six weeks she hadn't gotten any closer to learning who the boss of the drug organization was. It had been quiet. No other contact with Trevor, no thugs stopping by, nothing. She had tried poking around at the Café for the local gossip. She did hear an interesting story of some drunken horse groomers riding a horse down Main Street, and teenagers tipping cows, but there was no talk of any drug use.

The big talk recently had been about the Homecoming Parade and game. And, what a parade it had been! Each class built a float that carried its Homecoming Court, and the football team had three floats. A lot of the area businesses built floats as well. Ashton Farm had a float pulled by horses. Henry Rooney shined in one of his suits on top a gavel-shaped float. Paige Davies put together a Derby hat float for her store, Southern Charms, and Pam Gilbert was dressed up as a referee on a soccer field float for the Parks and Recreation Department.

People lined Main Street decked out in blue and white. They cheered the floats, waved to the people on them, and talked to all their neighbors. The Rose sisters had set up an outdoor food booth and showed the Homecoming Court what it really meant to hold court. Everyone in town made sure to stop by to pay their respects before heading home.

The town was excited for Homecoming. The team had gotten off to a rocky start but had won the last five in a row. They had squeaked by in a couple of them, and it still looked like they were trying to find their groove, but a win was a win. Cade had told her that he didn't know whether to be thrilled or horrified, thrilled they were winning, horrified that they still didn't seem like a team after all this time.

She enjoyed their talks at night when he walked her home from their standing Wednesday night dinner at the Café. They would have dinner, and he would walk her home. They'd sit on the porch and talk about the team and her guidance counselor job. It seemed like that was the only time they could talk. It seemed like every time she tried to talk to him at school, Stephanie would come and sit down and start chatting with them. Every now and then she'd see that flash of desire shoot across his face, but then it was gone before she could decide what to do about it. It really was better this way, though. She had a job to do and romantic entanglements would just hinder her.

Annie had been interviewing the team over the past months and had found a few kids that had more information than they were sharing. Teenagers. They always thought they were so smart. In reality, they were so easy to read. She knew they were lying to her the second they started spinning their tales. They were so cocky that they hadn't even noticed when she tricked them up on their story. No reason to lie about what you did over the weekend or what you do at the gym, but they did.

Right now it looked like Cade was going to kill one of those kids. Cade had his hand in Austin Colby's facemask and was forcibly trying to get him to pay attention while he explained something. But even from the stands she could tell Austin was having none of it. His body language shouted defiance.

"Hey. What did I miss?" Paige Davies slid into the seat next to her.

"Well, Cade seems to be struggling to get Austin to do what he wants. We were down by ten, but Trey just ran it thirty yards for a touchdown. The fourth quarter is about to start. What were you doing? You hardly ever miss a game."

"Cole and I were in Tennessee visiting his mother. I made him turn on the siren so I could catch the end of the game." She grinned and Annie instantly saw the family connection. She had gotten to know Paige over the past couple of months. They sat together every game and sometimes McKenna joined them. It was strange to have girlfriends. She had never had any before.

"Colby! Jesus, are you trying to kill me? I called a running play! Are you blind?" Cade screamed. He could feel his blood pressure rising more than it did when he was under enemy fire in Afghanistan when he rescued an ally prime minister who should have known better than to enter a war zone without having the area secured.

"I thought I was open for the run, so, it was still a running play." Austin refused to look at him. Instead he kept his eyes on the cheerleaders. He had refused to take any criticism and instead blamed every other player on the team.

Cade looked at the clock. There were two minutes left in this game and they were down by three. "Okay, now listen. I want you to call a slant rout to Hall. Got it?" Austin didn't bother to acknowledge him as he ran onto the field after practically tripping over his ego. Cade took a deep breath. They hadn't been covering Hall very closely, and if Colby would actually pass the ball, Hall would make good yardage.

The ball was snapped. Austin stepped back to throw to a wide open Hall and tucked the ball and ran instead. He barely made it back to the line of scrimmage before he was taken down.

"Time!" Cade yelled to the referee. The whistle was blown and the team made their way toward the sideline. Cade took a deep breath and counted to ten. He would not kill Austin... he would not kill Austin, he chanted in his mind.

"You're busting my rhythm, Coach. Let me do my own damn thing." Austin yanked off his helmet and glared.

"I'm going to say this once Austin. Once. So help me, if you do not do what I tell you, I will run you to the ground at practice and then make you run more."

"Yeah, right. I am the best player on this team. I don't have to do nuttin'."

"Try me," Cade barely whispered as he hardened his gaze. Austin rolled his eyes and put his helmet back on. "Slant route to Hall. Got it?"

The team lined up and the ball was placed on the line. Cade heard no noise but the whistle of the referee starting the clock. The ball was snapped. Hall took off. With a quick stutter step he lost his guard and was headed for the end zone. Austin raised his arm back and threw the ball. It spiraled through the air and bounced off the ground on the opposite end of the end zone from a wide open Ryan Hall.

The crowd groaned as the band picked up. A loss that should have been a win. Cade was livid. The team gathered around him for the post game prayer, all except Austin who headed straight for the tall Devon Ross in his Cincinnati Bengals warm-ups and gold chains. Cade looked into the emptying stands and immediately focused in on Annie. She saw it too.

"Amen," Parks said. The team broke and headed for the locker room.

Cade watched as Trey Everett headed straight for Austin. Devon nodded at him, and Trey sent him a look that could freeze Hell. Austin turned to Trey, and Trey grabbed his jersey at the neck and dragged him by his pads away from Devon. Cade watched as Trey yelled at Austin until something hit home, and Austin reached out and shoved Trey. Trey took a step back and then shoved Austin hard. Austin went flying and landed on his butt on the field.

A couple of people in the stands clapped, and Austin hurried to stand up and stormed off the field in a huff. Devon came over to Trey and Cade figured it was time he got involved. He headed over toward them, but before he got there, Trey shot Devon the finger and walked to the locker room.

Cade looked back to Annie and their eyes locked. They both understood what had happened. Austin was on S2 and Trey knew about it and didn't like it. She had found her weak link, and he would bet Trey would be in her office first thing Monday morning.

"Tough loss Coach." Stephanie saddled up next to him and slipped her hand through his arm. "It'll be okay though."

"No, no it won't. I'm watching my team implode."

"But they were great! It was just one bad play."

"I wish. They're aggressive and not listening to us. Instead they are fighting with each other and not using their heads. They have talent, but they just need to get out of their own way."

Forty-five minutes later Cade hurried out of the locker room. Tonight settled it. He needed to see Annie and tell her they needed to work on this together. He was hopeful they could work together *closely*. They had been talking and getting to know each other more over the last couple of months, and what he discovered was that he liked her. They worked well together and he knew it. He looked out over the parking lot to where kids were getting in their cars, parents were chatting and tires were squealing. Squealing? Cade watched as a black Escalade turned down a row of cars and headed straight for him.

They slammed on the brakes, and the steroidasaurus triplets from his last visit to the gym jumped out with bats. Great, just what he needed. At least it wasn't Larry, Moe and Curly. "Our boss said you were wavering on the deal we have. You better get out of the way of your boys. Boss is turning them into champs," one of them said.

Honestly, with their tight white t-shirts and shaved heads they all looked the same.

"No, your boss is turning them into aggressive, egotistical teenagers who think they know everything. Look what it got us. A loss. Tell your boss he's making the team implode." Cade was so angry he had to talk himself out of beating them up then and there, staring parents be damned.

"This is just to remind you to keep your mouth shut." Bats were swung, headlights were smashed, windows were shattered, and the hood was dented as they busted the SUV up. Cade rocked back on his heels and tried not to laugh. They had done it again.

"Hey! What are you doing to my car?!" Coach Parks yelled as he sprinted towards them from the field house. The triples froze and looked from Parks to the car they were currently destroying. One of the men, the one with the tattoo of himself on his forearm, at least Cade hoped it was of himself and not one of his buddies, pulled out a piece of paper.

"Says he drives a year old Black SUV. Toyota." One the three men leaned forward to look at the front of the car.

"Ford. Oops."

"Dammit, Steve. Boss is going to be pissed." He shoved the guy he called Steve and then noticed Parks was closing in on them. They began to push each other and trip over one another as they leapt back into the Escalade and tore out of the parking lot.

Cade shook his head and tried not to laugh at the mess-ups the lackeys Gaylen had sent continued to make. He looked at the damaged vehicle. Poor Parks, he wasn't going to take this very well. He loved his SUV. He fell to his knees in front of his broken headlights, his hands stretched up to the heavens and cried, "My Baby!" before collapsing into tears.

Chapter Eleven

A nnie sat on the old floral couch and looked at the wall. She put the glass of Sangiovese down on the small, wood side table and leaned forward. She had lit candles in the living room and poured a glass of wine in an effort to relax. She hoped it would trigger something as she looked at the wall where she posted all the notes on the case. There were pictures of the players with different color yarns attaching them to other players and pieces of evidence, but so far nothing was connecting them. There was no common thread.

Just this afternoon she had received the information that S2 had spread from Kentucky to Florida and now to Texas. She had looked through the file before the game but couldn't figure out how it had gone from Miami to Houston. Hence the wine and candles. She took another sip of wine and looked at the cases. The only common factor was that the buyers were all high school athletes. With a sigh, she slouched back against the couch. This was what her Friday nights had consisted of for years now, and boy it was almost as depressing as the fact she couldn't figure out the connection in these cases.

The knock at the door surprised her. Maybe the Rose sisters had taken pity on her again and brought her some food. They had surprised her once a week with some home cooked goodies that made her excited every time the door rang. She did kind of feel like Pavlov's dog, but if it was any more of the pumpkin spice cake that

Miss Violet had dropped off last week, she'd happily drool. Suddenly giddy to see what goodie awaited her, she got up and hung the picture of some saint over her notes before bounding to the door and quickly opening it.

"Hi." Oh crap. That was not who she thought it was going to be.

"Hello, Cade. What brings you by tonight?"

She tried to hide herself behind the door. She was wearing a pair of baggy flannel bottoms from Victoria's Secret and an old Florida State t-shirt that was a size too small. She had kind of filled out some since college. She was definitely not in any kind of outfit to see Cade in, especially when she desperately wanted to apologize for the punch. It was a good punch, though, but he didn't deserve it. She knew that now.

She just didn't really know how to deal with men who might care for her, and she believed that he did care for her. She was used to men putting her down, always thinking that because she was a woman she could not do what they did. They didn't want to be her partner in the field because they didn't trust a woman to have their back. They didn't want to go undercover with her because they never thought she'd be able to pull it off. And they never wanted to hang with her after a case because she wasn't one of the guys.

"Something happened after you left that I thought you should know about. Can I come in?"

Oh double crap. He looked so good in his jeans and black pullover. Of course, not as good as he looked out of them. She took a quick look down at her black flannel pants with pink polka dots and shrugged. It wasn't like he was interested in kissing her again.

"Sure." She opened the door and waited for him step inside. "I'm guessing what happened wasn't too bad since you are smiling. Come into the living room. I was just having some wine and trying to find the common connection to all the cases that have appeared in Kentucky, Florida and now Texas." She walked into the living room and took the saint picture down, leaving him to follow.

He stopped in front of the wall and took a quick glance at it. He stood with his hands on his hips, the same hips that she had dreamt about straddling. She downed the rest of her wine and coughed when it went down wrong.

"You okay?" Cade turned and asked.

"Yes," she croaked. She took a seat on the couch and watched as Cade grinned. Oh, no, don't do that. She needed more wine to handle sexy smiles.

"Wine?" she asked and bolted straight up.

"Sure." He followed her to the kitchen and took the glass of wine she poured for him.

Cade took a sip of wine to hide the smile on his face. She was so flustered and it was such a good look on her. So was that shirt she was wearing. It fitted her like a glove and outlined those breasts he desperately wanted to feel. It was a shame he would never get that chance. She had made it clear he was to keep his hands to himself. It was strange for him. Most women flung themselves at him and his brothers. As a result he actually hadn't wanted to date anyone, anyone until the redhead sitting on the couch next to him punched him, that is.

Now he couldn't stop kicking himself for kissing her. It was a great kiss, but it had scared her off, and for that he'd always be mad at himself. So, he was stuck longing for her from afar. He was nice when he passed her in the hall but didn't impose himself on her. He looked for her every game but made sure she didn't see him looking at her. God, he was a mess.

"So, what happened after the game?" she asked.

"Ah, the triplets came back for a visit on command from Gaylen."

"The Three Stooges?"

"No, the steroid triplets."

"The bald ones with no necks?" she asked.

"Yup. They somehow found out I was unhappy with the team's performance and came to remind me to keep our deal."

"How did they know you weren't happy?"

"Anyone at the game could tell I was not pleased."

"Yes, but the triplets weren't at the game. Someone must have told them. And that someone is who we need to find." He watched as Annie jumped up and took a yellow index card from the small side table and wrote out 'Mystery Game Watcher' on it and stuck it on her board with a link to Gaylen. Annie stared at the wall for a couple more minutes, then sat back down on the couch. She turned to him, "What happened next?"

"Well, this is where it gets funny. I walk out of the field house and start heading for my car. When I'm about twenty feet from the car, I hear tires squealing. The triplets jump out with bats and start destroying the car." At her shocked expression he smothered a laugh. "But they destroyed the *wrong* car."

Her hand covered her mouth and he heard a muffled, "No!" Her green eyes were wide in both horror and laughter as he watched the emotion play over them. "Whose car was it?" she asked through her fingers still covering her mouth.

"Coach Parks,"

"Oh! Poor Parks! He's such a nice man." She lowered her hand from her mouth and Cade couldn't tear his eyes from her lush lips. Just one kiss. That was all he wanted. "What did Coach Parks do?"

"He yelled at them and then they started arguing over what car they were looking for. Apparently the guy named Steve gave the others the wrong description. Then Coach Parks started yelling and running at them so they high-tailed it back to their car and took off. Parks started to cry then."

He watched as Annie's face turned red. Her shoulders were shaking, but she wasn't laughing. Then as if erupting, she laughed. Tears started to roll down her cheeks as she grabbed his upper arm as she laughed.

"I shouldn't," she gasped out, "be laughing. Poor Parks! But it's too funny thinking of the guys messing up over and over."

Cade felt the rumbles in his belly as the laughter came. Annie's face was bright red, and he placed his hand on her arm, just as she was doing to him. Suddenly he wasn't laughing anymore. They were close and touching, and her eyes were looking into his. Suddenly he didn't know what to do.

"Um, more wine?" she asked as she broke eye contact and jumped up.

"Sure." He stood and handed her his glass, but she didn't move. She was standing right in front of him, and this time she met his eyes and held his gaze.

Cade watched as she leaned forward. Was she going to kiss him? No, she wouldn't do that. She made it clear, no kissing. But, she took another step forward. He felt the soft outline of her breast as it brushed against his fleece pullover. He watched as she tilted her chin up, offering him her lips.

Cade didn't know what to do, so he just stood still, debating. Kiss. Punch. Kiss. Punch. He was debating when the choice was taken away from him. Her lips met his. He felt her hesitatingly kiss him. He had to admit it wasn't his finest kiss. He was just too shocked to do anything. Finally his baser instincts won out, and he felt all restraint leave his body. It was definitely worth another black eye.

He opened to her then and felt her tongue tentatively seek entrance. That was his undoing. He was tired of being still. He wrapped her in his arms and pulled her against him. Her body was so damn sexy. She was all lush curves and felt as a woman should. He applied more pressure to her lips and slipped his tongue around hers. God, he wanted her, and wanted her now. The couch was somewhere nearby, and all he cared about was getting her naked and exploring the fullness of those breasts and the gentle curve of her hip.

He took a step back and bumped into the small side table on the far end of the couch. Thinking it was the couch, he moved to sit down, bumping onto the table top instead. He put his hand out behind him to steady himself when his foot got tangled in the phone cord. He tried to kick it off, but instead lost his balance and fell back onto the table.

Annie couldn't believe she had done that. It was so obvious he didn't want to kiss her. But, she'd been thinking of kissing him before he came, and it just sort of happened. She had never chased a guy in her life, but it seemed to work. He had wrapped his arms around her and the kiss had turned hot!

And then it ended. What the heck? Annie opened her eyes and found Cade falling backward onto the table, the table covered with lit candles! He landed in the middle of the table, the action causing some of the candles to fall to the ground. Annie immediately stomped them out with her fuzzy socks.

"Wow. That was smooth," Cade murmured as he righted himself.

Annie was about to throw him a smile when she saw it. "Cade! Your arm. It's on fire!" she said slowly, not wanting him to panic and start running around making it worse.

He looked down at his arm, and she was pretty impressed that his eyes didn't even go wide. He slipped his arm out of the sleeve and pulled the fleece and the t-shirt stuck to it off. He folded it carefully, wrapping the shirt over the fire and extinguishing it.

"Well, that was convenient. I wanted your shirt off anyways." She shrugged and stepped forward to grab the smoldering shirt and toss it in the sink. "Now. Where were we?"

"I'm pretty sure I was about to do something like this." She felt herself be scooped up into arms. She thought for a moment to fight it, but when had she ever let herself be treated like a woman? No, she was going to enjoy it.

He carried her through the door to her bedroom. She felt right in his arms. He looked over her head and into the room and froze for a moment. A twin bed? That was seriously going to limit his smoothness in bed.

"Is everything all right?" He heard the nervousness in her voice. He would do whatever it took to banish any signs of nervousness.

"It's perfect. Now, I think it's unfair you have seen me naked, but I haven't seen you naked yet."

"I had my eyes covered, remember."

"Liar." He set her down and brought his lips to hers. Softly, slowly he tasted her. He reached for her shirt and stripped it off before looking down at her. She was gorgeous, and he was going to show her just how amazing he thought she was.

He ran his hands down her sides and over the curve of her hips. Her skin was so soft. It was ivory and there was a sprinkling of freckles covering her shoulders. He leaned down to kiss them. He worked his way up the column of her neck and grew bolder when he heard her moan in satisfaction.

His hands slid under the elastic band of her sports bra and cupped her breast. His hand got stuck, though, as he tried to remove it to help take off the blasted thing. Smooth, Davies, real smooth. He was so nervous. He knew it already. He just wasn't going to admit why it was so different this time. Cade slid his hands down her hips, under those cute pajamas, and down her legs while he pushed them to the ground.

It was going to be hard to make himself take his time. He felt himself losing control, something he prided himself in never doing. But getting a glimpse of her lush body was enough to snap any control he had left. His mouth came down on hers as he felt her fumble with his button as she tried to push his pants down. Screw control. It was overrated. There was something to be said for uncontrollable sex. He led her backwards a couple of steps and lowered her to the bed. New goal: to make sure she enjoyed it so much she'd forget to punch him.

Trevor Gaylen looked out over his domain. The gym was full, and the profits were up in both the legal and illegal incomes. All those thirty-something men down there getting wind of a new drug and thinking it would turn them into teenagers again had turned into a very profitable secondary market. Denial. It was a profit maker, that's for sure.

Before getting into S2, he had sold leftover biochemical weapons materials to middle-aged women, promoting the promise of youthful appearance. It was a great way to dispose of all the outdated weapons materials no longer selling on the black market. S2's new secondary market worked the same way. Men hit their mid to late thirties, their wives started to have babies, and they were faced with the fact they were no longer eighteen. Or, what he was seeing more of, was the thirty-seven year old bachelors trying to get laid at the college bars and being turned down because they were too old. S2 made them feel young again. They could lift more. They could run faster. They could trim up and get those six packs they always wanted.

It all boiled down to denial. Denial you were too old to nail sorority girls. Denial you were too old to keep up with the high school players on the rec room basketball courts. Denial you were now a mature woman and had wrinkles. And what did all that denial equal? Money.

At the knock on his door he turned to the video monitor that sat on his desk. His men were here. He pressed the buzzer that unlocked the door and waited for them to file in. The three men he had sent to remind Coach Davies to stay on track were staring at their feet. The three imbeciles who had previously failed looked like they were gloating, for their failures were now being replaced with newer failures. They were all screw-ups. It was hard to find good drug soldiers these days.

"I got a call from Boss. Said the wrong car was destroyed. Also said it drew a lot of unwanted attention from parents when the owner of the car started screaming and Coach Davies started laughing. Do you have anything to say?"

"I read the note with the information wrong. I don't know why I thought it was a Ford. They both looked the same and were parked near each other. It was my mistake, sir."

"Well, Steve, I respect someone who takes responsibility for his mistakes. But, because you made that mistake you will now be the carrier of the new shipments coming in. If you get caught, your punishment will be the jail time you get. If you don't get caught, there will be no punishment." Gaylen took a seat in his black leather desk chair and pulled out the most recent sales information.

"The latest orders are in. This is a big order, Steve, so don't mess it up. Remember, this is your chance. Pick it up tomorrow and deliver it to our contacts at the Convention Center. The Personal Trainers of America are having their annual conference in Lexington this year. They'll be arriving Friday, and their product must be delivered to them soon after.

"Ross has really expanded our market with his NFL and trainer contacts. We will have new markets in Georgia, California and New York by the conclusion of the conference. Texas is booming while Florida is holding strong. All in all, business is going well. If Steve manages the pickup and drop, we'll all be looking at some bonuses."

He paused and let it soak into their dimwitted minds. They certainly had more in common with dumbbells than lifting. However, they were loyal and you could never beat that.

"Now, back to our main problem. Boss says Coach Davies is wavering on his end of the deal. I'm afraid we need to send him a reminder of what will happen if he decides to no longer participate in our deal. Doug, you take your crew and make a little visit to remind the Coach of the repercussions of getting cold feet."

★　　　★　　　★

Annie hung up the phone with her boss after updating him on the case and begging for a rookie to be sent to the school for an assembly on drug abuse. He wasn't too happy about it, but that was what rookies were for. She had done thirteen assemblies when she was a rookie in Miami. Much to her surprise she had really liked it. She liked interacting with kids and being there for them, especially the ones she knew she could help. This undercover gig wasn't so bad. She actually liked going to work although it was strange to not be armed. She was getting used to it though.

A knock at her closed door had her looking up through the glass window to see who it was this late after school. "Come in," she said when she saw Trey's face.

"Am I interrupting you, Miss Hill?" he asked with a slightly nervous look on his still maturing face.

"Not at all, Trey. What can I do for you?"

"I need help." He sat down in one of her visitor's chairs as if the weight of the world were on his young shoulders.

"Are you in trouble?" She'd be shocked if he was. He seemed the perfect young man.

"No, ma'am, but some people I know are doing something that makes me uncomfortable. I'm pretty sure it's illegal and it's affecting the team. I just don't know what to do because I know they'll be in trouble." Trey pushed back a long lock of blonde hair that had fallen forward and into his eye.

"Who will they get in trouble with, Trey?"

"Their parents, Coach, and shoot, ma'am, I don't know who else, but I'm guessing the police wouldn't look too kindly on it."

"What are they doing that could get them in trouble? Are they in danger?"

Annie held her breath. This was it. It was her break. If Trey would just un-shoulder some of the load, she could make her case.

"I don't think they are in danger. At least they don't act like it." He paused and looked up at the ceiling before looking her in the eyes again. "I just don't know if I should turn them in and risk ruining the rest of their lives."

"Do they know what they are doing is wrong or that it could ruin the rest of their lives? It seems if you tell me what it is, I can help you

make that decision. You don't have to do this all on your own."
Annie kept her gaze steady but gentle.

"That's it!" Trey bolted from his seat. "I'm going to talk to them first. Straight up. I'm going to make sure they understand what they are doing to the team and what the consequences are if they get caught. I am the captain of this team, and I need to act like it. Thanks, Miss H!" And with that her best lead walked out the door.

Chapter Twelve

Annie pulled the baked spaghetti out of the oven and almost cried for the first time in her life. Things had changed, and she wasn't entirely sure what to think about it. Almost a week ago she and Cade had made love for the first time, and since then they had been together every night.

Usually Cade would pick up dinner after practice, and they would talk about their day and about the case. They would watch some television, which would inevitably end up with their clothes tossed around the room and them naked on the couch some time later.

She would then kick him out when it started to get late. There was just something about spending the night sleeping with someone that was just too intimate and serious for her brain to handle. Cade seemed to take it well though and never complained when she started glancing at the clock.

One thing she had made clear was that there was to be no affection at school. She didn't particularly like the fact that people knew about her personal life and wanted to keep it separate as much as possible. First off, she wasn't one of those touchy feely people who liked public displays of affection, and she would never even think of doing that at school. Second, she knew it didn't make sense, but in her mind if you were in a relationship, it made you vulnerable. She was vulnerable to speculation from her peers and friends and vulnerable to her enemies because they now knew her weakness. It also had the bad side effect of people judging her on her relationship as opposed to the job she was doing.

Annie stared at the burnt meal and began to try to scrape off the blackened top as she thought about when she was younger. When she was fifteen, her foster mother had been a serial dater. She had depended on man after man to give her an identity. She would be so and so's girlfriend, never herself. She would depend on the boyfriend of the month to provide for her and in return she was his doormat.

Annie had been mortified by it and had taken pains to always be the one in control and to never lose her identity in a relationship. As a result, she was more inclined to go on a couple of dates and then the relationship just drifted away into nothingness. The men usually were intimidated by her anyway and because of that tried to exert control over her. She would not let them make her fit their concept of a "normal" woman who would sit eagerly by the phone waiting for them to call or who would do whatever she could to make him happy. She always got a kick out of that.

Being the simpering trophy girlfriend just wasn't her style. She was too busy to worry if he called her or not. Most of the time she forgot about calling him at all, and most of his calls went to her voicemail. But, as she scraped another burnt layer off her failed attempt at cooking, she realized that this time was different. Cade didn't complain about her job. He didn't complain about the fact she didn't call him. He didn't complain about the fact that when at school she wanted to keep it professional. He didn't even complain when her fears surfaced, and she hurried him from the house when it got late. Fears of those nights at the foster home always surfaced. It was why she couldn't spend the night with anyone. Not realizing it, she stabbed the casserole dish with her knife as the flashback assaulted her.

Annie pulled on the old, ratty white undershirt that served as her nightgown and jumped onto the cot that served as her bed. The thin mattress sagged under her slight form as she pulled the musky covers over her head. She had turned twelve years old today, but no one knew it. It was just another night in Hell. She'd been at this foster home for four weeks, and her only escape was school that started last week.

She shared a room with two other girls, Stacy and Sarah. They were both eight years old. She was the big sister, and the girls looked to her to protect them, but she couldn't. She had tried, oh, how she had tried. She had received a broken rib for the effort along with a black eye and probably a concussion, but she had never seen a doctor.

The floor board creaked, and a shadow blocked the light coming under the door from the hall. Hell had arrived. Stacy and Sarah stifled a cry and pulled the covers tight to their little chins. Annie heard the door open and closed her eyes. She started working over the science problems from class that day and tried to block out the screams coming from the girls. The first night she was there she had jumped on his back and tried to stop him from hurting them. She had saved them that night, but she had been so badly beaten that she couldn't stop him again.

As she huddled under her blanket that hadn't been washed the whole time she'd been there, she thought about her science teacher Miss Whitebuckler. School hadn't started yet when she had arrived, and after the scars from her beating faded, she had been enrolled in school. Miss Whitebuckler would help. She was a tough but fair older woman who had taken a liking to her. She knew no one else would listen to her. Social services thought she was a liar and stopped investigating the claims of neglect and abuse she had told them about.

The sobs reached her ears along with the crack of the belt. She knew she couldn't stand it anymore. She peeked out from the covers to peer at the broken floor lamp near her bed. She slowly slid out from the side of the bed and onto the floor. Her knees scraped along the rough hardwood floor as she crawled to the lamp. The long rusted pole was solid enough to be of some assistance. She hadn't been labeled a troublemaker for nothing, and this time she knew what she was up against.

Her fingers wrapped around the cold, iron rod as she crept quietly to the large figure facing the bed. The girls' cries masked the sound of her approach. She lifted the pole high and with all her strength brought it down on his head. The sudden silence was deafening. The pounding of her blood running through her body was all she could hear. Stacy and Sarah stared at her with their eyes wide as they watched his body fall to the floor.

"Grab your thing. We're getting out of here," Annie told them. The girls scrambled to grab what little they had. She pushed hard as she lifted the window and boosted the girls through it before he could wake up.

Miss Whitebuckler had found them the next morning huddled under her desk in their night shirts when she had arrived at school. True to Annie's belief, she had helped and had made sure charges were filed again her foster parents. Annie had been moved to a group home and had never seen Stacy and Sarah again, but she saw them every night in her dreams.

Annie looked down at the casserole dish and saw that she had scraped the whole dinner into the trash can while she had been dragged back in time. It was her first attempt at making dinner for Cade, and it had failed miserably. She had never even tried to make dinner for a man before. Maybe this was a sign that she wasn't ready for such intimacy yet.

She picked up her phone and hit speed dial. "Blossom Café, what can I do for ya'?"

"Hi, Miss Violet. I need help."

"Oh, bless your heart, you tried to cook, didn't you?"

"Yes. It's burnt to a crisp and Cade is due here any minute. What do I do?"

"We'll take care of everything, dearie!" As Miss Violet hung up the phone she heard her yell, "Henry, don't you move from that seat! I need your help."

Annie hung up the phone and smiled. This town sure did know how to cheer her up. She set the small table with two mismatched plates she had bought at a St. Francis fundraiser and poured some wine. She wasn't surprised by the knock on the door. It was either the Roses to the rescue or Cade.

"Hey there, sexy." Annie rolled her eyes, but smiled when she saw the takeout bag hanging from his finger. "Prince Charming here to save the day. Now, don't I deserve a kiss for rescuing the damsel in distress?"

"Just try it, Rooney," came the cold voice.

"Dammit, Cade, you're ruining a moment here." Henry winked at her and she laughed.

"Thank you, Henry, for the rescue." She leaned up and placed a kiss on his cheek. "Now, go before you get into any more trouble." With a wink of his ice blue eyes, Henry gallantly lifted her hand and placed a kiss right above her knuckle. Something sounding rather similar to a growl reached her ears, and Henry gave her a smile that told her he knew he was tempting fate and enjoying it.

"Good-night, my dear. If I can ever be of assistance, you have my number." Henry shot Cade a cocky grin and then slowly walked down the stairs whistling.

"What was he doing here?" Cade asked a little sharply. Annie felt her eyebrows rise at his tone and turned to head into the kitchen.

"Oh you know. He brought dinner by, so we had a quickie on the kitchen table. Nothing out of the norm."

Cade felt his blood pressure shoot through the roof. He knew she was joking, but some primal instinct in him wouldn't let him laugh it off. He wanted her so happy and pleased that she'd never think of another man again. "Well, I can't be said to be outdone by Henry."

Cade swept her into his arms and silenced her protests with a searing kiss. He lowered her to the counter and shoved the bag containing their dinner away from them. He planted his hands beside her and leaned over her, possessing her mouth. He pushed her plum-colored business skirt up her hips and stripped off her panties. If it was the last thing he ever did, he would make sure the only thoughts she had about this kitchen were of him.

Annie stood on the porch and leaned into Cade's goodnight kiss. Tonight had been as close to perfect as she could ever dream of. Dinner had been great. They had laughed, swapped stories and, well, she couldn't forget about the kitchen sex that had started on the counter, continued against the refrigerator before ending up with her laid out on the kitchen table and him over her. All in all, it was a spectacular night.

"It's getting kind of late, isn't it, Mr. Davies!" Annie jumped away from Cade at the sound of the authoritative voice.

"I was just saying good-bye, Father James," Cade chuckled.

"Good-bye's involve words, not tongues, Mr. Davies." Annie heard the amusement in Father James' voice as he walked across the parking lot towards them after locking the church doors. She still had the urge to cross herself as she tried to smooth down her rather mussed hair.

"I'll see you at school tomorrow," Cade said as he grinned down at her. "Sleep tight, and if you get cold, just go to the kitchen to warm up." He winked, turned and bounded down the steps after giving Father James a quick wave.

"Now, my dear child, how do you feel about September weddings?"

"Father! I thought priests weren't supposed to gamble." Annie couldn't believe it. That stupid pool the Rose sisters had going was growing by the minute.

"Gambling on the holy sacrament of marriage is, I'm sure, exempt. Plus, we really need a new roof for the church and winning the pot could help. Now, about September."

"Good night, Father." Annie shook her head and walked back into her house, leaving the little man standing at the base of the stairs by the statue of the Virgin Mary.

Annie had the files of the boys she thought were using S2 pulled out and was looking over them for common connections. The files contained the school's file plus the ones she could pull off the federal database. It seemed that everyone in Keeneston had common connections. They all went to school with each other or attended the same church, were in the same Boy Scout troop, and often playing the same sports.

She was having a very hard time finding the type of illegal connections she was used to finding in Miami. There they shared a jail cell, same probation officer, etc. This was infinitely more difficult to connect. She was also getting frustrated. She felt as if she were missing something. She knew the soldiers, Larry, Moe and Curly and then the steroidasaurus triplets. She knew Devon Ross, the personal trainer, had to be the dealer, and Trevor Gaylen was upper management. So, who was the real boss? And why were they targeting high school boys? With Ross's connection to the NFL, it just didn't make sense. The pro's had money and lots of it. High school boys didn't have money, and they didn't win Super Bowls, endorsements or anything else drug lords could use as blackmail for extra income.

She leaned back in her chair to take a break and saw the clock on the far wall. It was already six o'clock! She gathered her files and slipped them into her black leather satchel before turning off the lights and locking her door.

Annie looked down the long, dark hallway and decided something was wrong. The lights were normally not turned off until seven when the janitorial service got done with the cleaning. She stopped and listened and heard the faint sound of voices making their way to her. She couldn't tell if they were male or female. She slipped her hand into her bag and grabbed her mace. She slowly made her way down the hall to the main intersection. The voices had stopped, and she was having trouble deciding which hallway they were coming from.

She slowed her breathing to quiet her body so she could listen better. The hair on her arms stood on edge as the sound of high heels clicked down the hall to the right of her. They were coming towards her. Annie pressed herself against the small space on the wall with the intersection on her right and against the beginning of a row of lockers on her left.

The *click click click* of the heels echoed around her. They grew louder with each step as the person neared her. Was this the boss? Was this a dealer? It just seemed too strange for the lights to be out and the school deserted for anything good to come from this meeting.

Annie relaxed her body and listened in order to time her attack. There was only one person who fit that sound, and she knew she would be able to take her easily. The woman neared and Annie shifted her body slightly toward the hallway. She took in a deep steadying breath and on the exhale made her move.

She rounded the corner, keeping her right shoulder against the wall for protection in case shots were fired and wished she had her gun instead of just the mace.

"Freeze!" Annie was startled when the woman let out a high-pitched scream and flapped her arms up and down as if she were trying to fly away. "Jesus, Stephanie! It's me, Annie."

"Oh my God! You scared me half to death. I heard someone down here and thought it might be kids getting into trouble. Then you jumped out, and I was sure I was going to die." Stephanie had her perfectly manicured hand over her heart and managed to still look beautiful even though she was scared out of her mind.

"I thought the same thing. I'm sorry I scared you." Annie had slipped the mace up her sleeve as soon as she assessed that there was no threat and reached for her bag. "Are you leaving for the day? You sure are here late."

"I just finished grading papers. If I take them home, I get caught up watching television and end up not grading at all. So, I stayed late and finished. Now I can get home and watch *The Bachelor* without worrying about grading."

Stephanie picked up a very cute Coach bag that matched her dark pink sweater set and slung the strap over her shoulder.

"Well, I'm just heading home, too. How about we walk out together?" Annie waited for her to agree, and then they headed down the back hallway towards the teachers' parking near the football field.

"I would have thought you would be getting ready for a big date or something. There is talk that you are all hot and heavy with Coach Davies."

Annie wasn't sure, but it sounded slightly snappish. "No. No plans for tonight. I just thought I would curl up and watch some television too."

She didn't address the rumors of her and Cade. If it were up to her, no one would know about her personal life. Not that she was embarrassed about Cade. Really it was quite the opposite. But then it made her have talks like this with people she didn't really know.

"So you two aren't serious?" Stephanie nudged her and gave her a wink.

"I don't know. We haven't talked about it, so I guess not." Thanks, Father James. For a priest he sure had a big mouth, and she was pretty sure these rumors originated with both him and the Rose sisters.

" 'Cause, if you were serious, I could give you all kinds of advice."

"That's nice, but not necessary."

Oh, this was getting bad. She did not do girl talk. She opened her bag and started scrounging around for her keys so she could get out of this conversation as soon as possible.

"You know, from when Cade and I dated. So, if you ever want to have some girl time and compare notes just let me know. It would be so much fun!"

Annie paused mid-reach to her car door. She had a feeling this was some sort of power struggle but not one she wanted to be in. She'd ask Cade and see what really happened.

"Thanks, Steph. That's real nice of you. But, like I said before, we're not serious. Have a good night and thanks for walking out to the car with me." Annie opened the car door and tossed her bag inside.

"Okay, well, the offer is open any time! Bye!" Annie jumped into her car and took off before Stephanie could do more girl talk.

Chapter Thirteen

"Austin, what the heck are you doing?" Paige screamed from the stands. "Oh, this is not good, not good at all," Paige said to her as she sat down.

Annie agreed. It wasn't good. They were playing T.H. Morgan, who happened to be one of their biggest rivals, and were falling apart. Austin wasn't listening to a thing anyone said and was pointing fingers at his teammates. In return, his teammates were ignoring him.

"What is going on with them? It's as if two separate teams are out there. Team Austin and Team Everyone Else." Paige sat down in frustration and glared at Austin's back as he threw yet another incomplete pass.

Annie watched as Austin began to yell at Ryan for missing the catch, when in reality the pass was nowhere near Ryan to begin with. Ryan had made some impressive moves just to manage to get in reach of the horribly thrown ball. The team did have athleticism, but they were just not working together.

"Annie, you may want to go home right after the game and hide."

"Why would I do that?" Annie asked, alarmed at what Paige said. Did Cade tell her who she was?

" 'Cause my brother is going to be madder than a bear with a thorn in his paw after this game."

"Oh, well, I'm used to men being pissed off. No big deal."

"You deal with pissed-off men as a guidance counselor?"

"Sure. Cade may be able to throw a tantrum, but not nearly as well as a seventeen year old. Then I get the pissed-off parents. So, yeah, I think I can handle Cade in a snit." Annie turned to look at Paige as she started to laugh.

"A *snit*?" Paige laughed. "I have never heard the word snit associated with my brother before. That's priceless."

Annie zipped her fleece coat up and let Paige have her laughs. She knew the real reason Cade was pissed. It was obvious the team had talent, but S2 was inflating egos and creating tension among teammates.

She cringed when T.H. Morgan scored a touchdown, pushing the lead to seventeen. Cade threw his playbook to the ground and grabbed Austin by the horse collar when he tried to go out onto the field. She couldn't hear him from where she and Paige sat, but she could read his lips and was pretty sure he just told his quarterback to sit his ass down on the bench for the remaining two minutes of the game.

Austin tore off his helmet and threw it into the table full of water. Cups went flying and water shot through the air as he stormed off towards the locker room. Cade signaled his sophomore quarterback to get out onto the field. The poor boy couldn't weigh more than a hundred and fifty pounds. But, there was no fear in his eyes as he took his orders and headed out into the huddle.

Annie had always thought of herself as tough, but those last two minutes had aged her ten years. Maternal instincts she never knew she had came out in full force for little Bobby Rudd. She had met with him to go over his grades at mid-term and was astounded by how smart he was. He had a 4.0 and was signing up to take advanced placement classes on the recommendation of his teachers. He was skinnier than a rail and carried a book with him everywhere. He was a nerd and was putting himself in danger out on that field.

Annie watched in horror as the huge, beastly linebackers shoved at the offensive linemen while trying to get to little Bobby. Bobby back pedaled with the ball and looked downfield. Ryan was sprinting down the sideline. Bobby raised the ball and threw it seconds before a linebacker crashed into him, ramming him to the ground.

Annie shot to her feet and gasped. He had to be broken in half. Paige lunged to her feet, unconcerned for little Bobby who was surely dying on the field. "Come on, Ryan!" she screamed, forcing Annie to look downfield.

The ball was spiraling downfield right for the outstretched hands of Ryan Hall. Ryan managed to find another gear and leapt into the air, snagging the ball. He landed, twisted to avoid a defender, and kicked it into high gear again, running for the end zone.

Annie turned back to see little Bobby standing whole and apparently uninjured as Ryan ran in for the touchdown. Bobby smiled and casually headed to the bench as if throwing a forty-yard pass resulting in a touchdown was no big deal. She didn't think she could like the kid any more than after their meeting, but there were obvious sides to Bobby that she hadn't even begun to know.

The last seconds of the clock clicked off, but even with Bobby's heroics, they had lost by ten. "Come on. Let's go check on Cade. He looks ready to explode." Paige grabbed her hand and tugged her down the metal stairs of the bleachers to the field. She went straight to her brother and gave him a hug.

"Bobby!" Annie yelled as the boy started past her towards the locker room. "Are you okay after that hit?"

"Miss H? Sure I am. That's what the pads are for. Thanks for coming out to watch the game," Bobby said in a voice that was still high.

"You're welcome, Bobby. That throw was amazing."

"Just physics Miss H. Hey, can I stop by Monday to go over that forensic book that you gave me? I finished it already. It was fascinating. I was hoping we could talk about it some more, and if you had any more criminal forensic books, I would love to borrow them."

"Sure. I'll bring a couple of my old textbooks from college, and we can go over some old cases. Do you think it's a field you would be interested in going into?"

"It sure is. I love science, but I can't see myself in a lab. Maybe in the FBI or something where I'm out in the field. That would be cool."

"I'll place a call to Paige's husband to see if Special Agent Parker can join us. Maybe he would give you some tips. With your smarts you could go into a specialized branch such as behavioral analysis or biochemical terrorism."

"Thanks, Miss H! That would be awesome. See you Monday!" She watched as Bobby ran off the field and gave his dad a high five and his mom a hug before heading into the locker room.

Cade said good-night to his sister and walked over to where Annie stood staring after Bobby Rudd. "Do I need to be jealous?" Cade whispered into her ear as he came up behind her.

"Maybe after he hits puberty. That's one kid who is going to make a difference in this world. Sorry about the game. And sorry for the frustration."

"It's getting worse. I don't know how much longer I can turn a blind eye."

"I'm hoping it will be over soon. I'm talking to Bobby again on Monday. He's too smart to not know about what's going on. Maybe I can find out some more."

"I better get going so I can give my post-game breakdown. Justin is spending the night with Marshall and his dog Bob, so I can spend a little time with you tonight if you don't have other plans."

She turned to him and smiled. Those emerald eyes sparkled and Cade couldn't help himself. He leaned down and kissed her right in front of all the players, parents, and staff who had come out to see the game. He tightened his arms around her. He loved the feel of her in his arms, but he also knew she'd be mad. She was not in favor of any touching in public, and he had gone and claimed her as his in front of the whole town. So, he held her close in hope that she couldn't get off a good punch.

"Okay, I'll see you tonight," he heard her muffled voice say from where he had pressed her head to his chest.

He released her slowly, surprised by the lack of reprimand, and smiled. Oh, yea, she liked him!

"Be safe going home," she rolled her eyes as he watched her head for her car.

"So, that's what you've been busy doing after practice," Coach Parks chuckled. "What do you think of December? It's a romantic month, isn't it?"

"Ha-ha. Come on, let's go see if we can salvage this team." Cade didn't know if he could or not, but he was going to try.

Cade pulled open the cold steel door to the locker room and walked down the hall to the meeting area where the team met after games. The usual noise of fifty-seven boys talking about the game, girls, and the start to the weekend was absent. Instead only one voice rang out.

Cade stood at the open door and stared into the meeting room where Trey Everett was up by the chalkboard addressing his teammates who were sitting in the blue chairs waiting for the post-game breakdown.

"I don't care what your excuse is Austin. You know that you are not playing as part of the team. You want to go to college on a football scholarship – we all do! But you won't get there by yourself. I know what you are up to. Hell, this whole team knows what you and the others are up to and we're saying we're not putting up with it anymore. Everything we do has consequences and if you all continue down this path, I will turn you in myself. Further, if things don't change right now we will refuse to go on the field with you."

Austin shot up, his long hair wet from sweat sticking to his head, "You can't do that to me. I can't afford to go to college without a scholarship!"

"We know. So, what's it going to be? Quit S2 and rejoin the team, or have Bobby here start for you? He sure did a good job tonight, didn't he?" Trey leveled Austin with a stare and held it. Trey may be one of the nicest guys Cade knew, but he was also one of the toughest when pushed, and it looked like Austin had pushed him to his limit tonight.

Austin sat on the chair deflated. "I thought I was helping the team."

"You're tearing it apart," Ryan said as he stood. "I may only be a freshman, but you all know what I want? I want a championship. I want to see the town plastered with posters announcing the new state champions and our name on the water tower. I know we were given no chance at winning this year, but if we play as a team, we can do it."

Cade waited, not wanting his presence to be known as the boys murmured their approval. "So, Austin, what do you say? Are you with us?" Trey asked. The room quieted down and all eyes turned to his quarterback.

"All the way to State," Austin smiled. The room erupted in a chant of "State! State! State!"

Cade walked into the room after a moment of celebration and waited for the boys to quiet down as they saw him head to the front of the room. "I guess I missed something?"

"Nothing much Coach. We just made a pledge to work together all the way to State," Trey said from his seat.

"Sounds like a good pledge. Before we can make it to State we need to look at what has been working for us and what hasn't. How about a late night tonight gentlemen, and then some hard practices next week so we can show our opponents we're not letting anything get in our way. 'Cause, if we win next weekend, we can finish second in the division and be in a good position to make a play for the championship."

Cade watched as the same players who last week couldn't wait to leave, leaned forward in their chairs to get a better view of the breakdown. Not a single person complained at staying late, and not a single person looked at the clock as they went over the game.

Chapter Fourteen

A nnie changed out of her jeans and into her black, winter running pants. They were soft, comfortable, and perfect for a crisp night like this. She pulled on her Keeneston High sweatshirt and headed for the kitchen. She opened the small microwave and took a sip of the hot chocolate she had made.

It normally took Cade about an hour to finish up after a game, so she expected him any minute. She grabbed her Florida State fleece blanket and headed for the porch. She would just snuggle up in one of the chairs outside and wait for him.

She took a seat on one of the two chairs and took a deep breath of the clean air. The smell of turning leaves and lit fireplaces was so different from that of the sea air, pollution, and fruit that was Miami. The stars were bright in the dark sky and for once she felt at peace.

Headlights turning into the parking lot drew her gaze from the stars to the speeding black Escalade that squealed to a stop in front of her cottage. Seriously? She was finally feeling peace, dammit!

The doors opened and the three men who had attacked Cade on the sidewalk a couple of months ago jumped out.

"Can I help you boys?" She was so not in the mood for this. That just went to show how the slower country lifestyle was affecting her. She had always been in the mood for a fight in Miami.

"You pissed off the wrong person, lady," the one with the receding curly hair and the Playboy Bunny tattoo on his forearm said. Of course they weren't wearing coats. They had two hundred and fifty pounds of muscle to keep them warm.

"Me? I don't remember pissing anyone off. Hmm, I did cut off old Mr. Lyons the other day, but he was going twenty-five in a fifty-five, and I really didn't want to drive all the way to Lexington behind him. Are you boys his great-grandsons?"

Clearly not knowing what to say, they paused in their approach and looked at each other. "Um, we got a message for your boyfriend." Larry tried again. It was hard to take him seriously. He really needed to cut his hair.

"Oh, should I get you a piece of paper to leave a note on?" she asked sweetly. She took a sip of hot chocolate to hide her smile. She watched over the edge of her mug as the one she called Moe tripped over the Virgin Mary statue and fell face first into the bald one she called Curly.

Annie stood and shifted toward the railing and the small garden gnome dressed as a priest that stood in front of a large fern. Larry had turned and glared at Moe and Curly who were stumbling their way up the stairs towards her.

"Oh dear. I would take that as a sign."

"A sign?" Moe asked.

"Sure. I mean, you were tripped by the Virgin Mary. You may want to go to church or something." Annie went ahead and crossed herself for good measure. The action caused the men to pause and stare at the statue. She pulled her cell phone out and hit the record function. She set it on the rail and reached out to grab the gnome priest. She had him hiding behind her back before the men turned around.

"As I was saying, we got a message for your boyfriend that we need to give him." Larry tried again. This time he was doing a pretty good job at his intimidating scowl, but the clear lack of intelligence in his eyes just made her think of a bad off-off-Broadway actor.

"And that message would be?" she asked politely.

"That he needs to remember the agreement he made and keep his mouth shut. Now, this will only hurt a minute. Sorry about this. You seem like a nice enough lady," Larry told her as he advanced toward her.

"It's okay. I guess you're just doing your job for...." She arched her eyebrow questionably at Larry.

"Mr. Gaylen."

"Shut up!" Moe hissed as he hit Larry.

"What? How is she supposed to know who the message is from if we don't tell her?" That caused Moe to pause, and he looked to Curly who nodded as if it made all the sense in the world.

"Is Cade going to remember this agreement? I mean, he does all this work at school and then with the team and on his farm. He makes agreements all time. Maybe you should tell me what the agreement is so I can remind him. I'm sure he didn't mean to forget it, but he just has so much going on." She watched the guys look at each other again and shrugged. This was going to be easier than she thought.

"Tell him to keep his mouth shut about the drugs or his mother's next. Now, come here and don't scream. We'll just make it worse if you scream." Larry took another step toward her.

"I'm afraid I am rather frozen in place by fear. You are very scary men, and I fear I can't come to you."

"Thank you, we'll come to you then." Larry gave Moe and Curly a nod and waited for them all to get on the small porch. They had to walk single file to where she was standing at the railing.

She tightened her hand around the priest gnome's head and waited for Larry to reach her. One more step. Now! She tossed her hot chocolate mug at Larry's face.

"Ow!" The mug hit him square in his large nose. Using her left hand, she swung the priest gnome in a large arc and connected with Larry's receding hairline.

Larry dropped instantly to the ground. Using the momentum of her swing, she brought the little gnome back up with an arcing backhand, hitting Curly under the chin and dropping him unconscious to the ground on top of Larry.

"Amen," she said to the little priest. "I told you. You should have taken the fact that you tripped over the Virgin Mary as a sign."

Moe looked a little hesitant, but was tougher than she gave him credit for. He launched himself over his downed comrades and hit her square in the stomach. The impact sent her flying backwards onto the wood porch floor as the priest gnome sailed through the air and into the bushes.

"Umph." The wind was knocked out of her as all two hundred and fifty pounds of dumbass landed on her. She opened her mouth to suck in some air as Moe got to his feet. With one booted foot, he pulled back and struck out at her midsection.

She curled into a ball and the hit reverberated up to her arms. He brought his leg up, intending to stomp on her side. She waiting until his leg was high in the air, making him the most unstable. She kicked out with her upper leg and made contact with his knee. Not having both feet on the ground, he teetered and fell backwards.

Annie didn't waste any time. She scrambled to her feet and leapt over the pile of dumbass, trying to grab the chair to swing at him. Before she could reach it, he dove and caught one ankle, sending her crashing to the ground just short of the chair. She kicked out, making contact with his face, but he didn't let go. He got to his knees as she continued to kick as hard as she could at the arm holding her in place.

He may be stupid, but he was strong. She couldn't pull free. He leaned over her, and she made contact with his gut only to have him punch her. She had been able to throw up a block that deflected the punch from shattering her nose, but she'd have one heck of a bruise on her cheek. Her teeth even hurt after that punch.

Thinking he had brought her into submission, Moe stood and reached down to pick her up. She brought her knees to her chest and quickly kicked out with them. She hit him hard, square in the chest. The force sent him stumbling backwards and into the railing. Arms pinwheeling, Moe lost the fight with his balance and fell backwards off the porch.

She went to stand, but everything swam in front of her. She prepared for another attack from Moe, but it never came. She grabbed the chair to steady herself as she slowly stood. When the swimming stopped, she made it to the rail and looked over.

The Virgin Mary stood resolute over the immobile Moe. A smudge of red blood on top of her head was the only evidence of what had happened. She had told him it was a sign. Annie found herself crossing herself again. Living in a priest's home was starting to affect her, she decided, as she reached for her phone. She narrated what she had seen and then stopped the recording.

She punched in the number to Romero's cell and waited for her boss to pick up. "This better be important," was his gruff answer.

"I just had a visit from three of Gaylen's men."

"And?"

"And they are unconscious on my porch. What do you want me to do with them?"

"Depends. Did you get anything good out of them?"

"Yeah. I recorded it all. Even their saying what the deal was between Davies and Gaylen."

"Good. Email it to me then call local authorities. Have them arrested for trespassing only. They'll get bailed out with little fuss. I doubt they'll tell what really happened and that will help keep Gaylen in the dark. If the police say anything about assault, tell them you found them like this and just assumed they were drunk. Assaulting a lady will make too much noise, and Gaylen will most likely lie low for a while."

Annie paused for a second and listened to the background noise. It sounded like he was watching a British film. "Hurry up Vin. this is the best part," she heard a woman shout.

"Sir, are you watching *Pride and Prejudice*?"

"No!"

"Really? 'Cause it sounds like Lady Catherin de Bourgh just arrived at the Bennett house and that really is the best part, well, besides the whole Colin Firth in the pond scene."

"Shut up, Blake. It's date night. Call the police, email me the recording, and don't mention this again." Before she could tease him more the line went dead.

Just three minutes later a Keeneston County Sheriff's cruiser pulled to a stop in front of the cottage where she sat on the steps waiting. Two men emerged from the cruiser. One was tall and lanky, probably early forties. The other was younger but much shorter and had the beginnings of a mustache.

"Hiya, ma'am. What happened here?"

"Hi, I don't really know. I think the men were drunk and came here for some reason. Maybe they expected Father James and wanted to confess. Well, two are passed out up there, and this one looks like he tripped, and when he fell, hit the Virgin Mary."

They looked at her strangely, and she was worried for a minute they were going to question her further or ask why her cheek was swollen and starting to turn color.

"You're Annie Hill aren't you? Cade's girlfriend?" the short one asked. "Well, we're right pleased to finally meet you! I'm Dinky, and this is my partner Noodle. We've heard so much about you."

"You have?" They wanted to talk to her about Cade and not about the three unconscious men? Maybe she had gotten hit harder than she thought and was hallucinating.

"Can I ask you a serious question, ma'am?" Noodle asked in a slow voice full of twang.

"Um, sure." Okay, here was the interrogation she was expecting.

"What do you think of March? It's such a beautiful month to get married. Just the start of spring, new beginnings and all that stuff." Annie stared at Noodle and could hardly blink. Apparently wedding pools were big business in Keeneston.

"Um. What about these guys?" She gestured to the men who were starting to stir, their moans reaching their ears.

"Oh, don't worry about them, ma'am. Dinky, can you take care of them?"

"Sure, just talk loud so I can hear ya'." She watched Dinky head off to the men and start to cuff them as he read them their Miranda warning.

"So, March is a nice month, isn't it?"

"Seriously? Why does anyone care who Cade's dating?" This really was very puzzling to her.

"Well, geez ma'am...."

"For the love of God, stop calling me ma'am. It makes me feel old."

"Yes, ma'am. I mean, yes Miss Hill. Anyway, Cade has been chased after by ever girl in the county from the ages of sixteen to eighty. Probably half the ladies over in Lexington too."

"He's what they call a catch," Dinky yelled over. Annie rolled her eyes and sat back down on the step as Dinky started to load the barely conscious men into the cruiser.

"See, he never dates seriously. In fact, he and his brothers usually run in the opposite direction of any single lady." Noodle became serious, or at least she thought he did. He leaned closer to her and in a hushed tone asked, "So, how did you do it? How did you catch him?"

"I don't know. But, maybe it had to do with the fact that I was never chasing him to begin with."

"What she say?" Dinky yelled from placing a slightly bloody Moe into the cruiser.

"She said it was because she wasn't chasing him," Noodle shouted.

"That's deep," Dinky mumbled as he closed the fully loaded cruiser.

"You know, that makes sense, ma'am. I mean Miss Hill. It's just like noodling a catfish. You wiggle your finger, but it's the fish that has to come to you."

"Dang, Noodle. That's very philosophical." Dinky came to stand next to Noodle, his hands resting on the big, black utility belt around his waist.

"Excuse me? Noodle, fish, finger?" What the hell were these guys talking about? Whatever it was, they apparently thought it made perfect sense.

"You know, noodling." Noodle looked at her as if she were speaking a foreign language.

"Yeah, noodling," Dinky chimed in ever so helpfully.

"I'm sorry, boys. It's been a long night. Maybe you could tell me what noodling is."

"She is from Miami. It's not like it's really the South," Dinky told Noodle, who readily agreed.

"It's when you catch a catfish with your bare hands. You find their hole and stick your hand into it, wiggle your finger so the fish bites it, and then you pull the catfish out." If he had been a teenager, he would have added, 'like duh'.

Annie didn't know how to respond, so she didn't. She just found herself looking back and forth between the two of them. They reminded her of golden retriever puppies, and she had the odd sense to pet and cuddle them.

"Do you think that's why I have trouble dating, Dink? Maybe I just need to let them chase me."

"It's worth a shot."

"Thanks, Miss Hill. I'll give it a try. If it worked on Cade, it's good enough for us to try, huh Dinky?"

"Sure 'nuf."

"Have a good night, ma'am. Shoot, Miss Hill, don't forget, March is the perfect month for a wedding. Just make sure it's after the NCAA tournament. I think we'll go far this year. Go Big Blue!"

Annie waved good-bye as they got into their cruiser and took the Three Stooges off to jail. She needed a drink. What was Big Blue? She had been afraid to ask after stupidly asking what noodling was. All she knew was she wanted to get inside, get warm, and put an ice pack on her swollen cheek.

Chapter Fifteen

Cade ran the film again for the players. They had been there for two hours and it was close to midnight. Coach Parks had gone outside and told all the parents that the team wanted to stay and work on preparing for the playoffs. Between upperclassmen and the coaches, all the kids without cars would be driven home.

"Coach? Your phone is buzzing again."

"Thank you, Hall. Just ignore it."

"But, Coach, it's the third time it's gone off in under a minute. It's probably important."

Cade snatched up the phone and looked at the caller ID. He didn't know who was calling, but it was a local number. "Yes," he snapped as he pressed the answer button.

"Cade? Noodle."

"Kinda busy here. Can I call you back tomorrow?"

"Oh, sure, sure. I didn't really need to talk to you. I just thought I should let you know I just came from haulin' three big fellers off Miss Hill's property. She was fine, but there was one heck of a bruise forming on her face. Looks like something real nasty went down there although she's only claiming trespassing. I figured it was best not to push."

Cade froze. Bruise, three men, this was serious. "Is she okay? Are you sure?"

"No. That's why I'm calling you. Miss Hill is real nice, but I take it that she is a real independent type. She tried to feed us a line that three guys were just passed out drunk as she sat there with a swollen cheek, and the way she moved showed a tender midsection also. For all she wants to appear innocent, she beat the crap out of these guys and I'm beyond impressed. However, she is choosing to keep us in the dark. Since she's your girlfriend, I'll respect that. Just call us if you need us. But, if I were you, I would be heading over there right quick to check on her."

Cade's heart had stopped beating as soon as Noodle had told him about Annie being injured. "Thanks, Noodle. I'll go over there now." Cade ended the call and turned to his team. "I'm sorry I have kept you guys so late. It's about time for you all to head home. Upperclassmen please give at least one of the lowerclassmen a ride home. I'll see you for practice on Monday. Expect to stay late. We have a championship to win!"

The boys cheered and headed out to the parking lot as Cade grabbed his things and sprinted to his car. If only he had been there. He should have been there. This was all his fault. He was nauseous at the thought of the fear she must have gone through with three men attacking her.

He knew she was trained, but still, three men! How did she take down three men? It didn't matter that she had. He should have been there. His phone rang, and he opened it immediately as he tore out of the high school parking lot.

"Annie?"

"No, it's Daisy Mae. Where in all of Jupiter are you? Why aren't you with Annie? How is she?"

"I don't know. I just got the call from Noodle. On my way there now. Call waiting, it may be her."

"Give her a hug for me."

"Annie?" He was desperate to hear her voice.

"No, but speaking of Annie, why weren't you there to help her? Three men, Cade! Three! Is she okay?" his sister's chiding voice asked.

"I don't know, Paige. I'm speeding there now."

"Well, give her a hug for me."

"How is every one finding out about this anyway?" It wasn't like Noodle to spread gossip…much.

"Father James saw the lights and went to check it out. He called John Wolfe, who called all the Rose sisters. Miss Lily called Kenna, who called Dani who called me. You know, the norm." He should have known. That was the normal grapevine chain. "Cade. Don't smother. She won't appreciate it if you do."

"I never smother." He heard his sister give a little snort and hang up. Okay, maybe sometimes he smothered.

His tires skidded as he took the turn into the church parking lot too quickly. The little cottage was lit up, but nothing appeared out of sorts. He tried to pay attention to Paige's advice and slowly walked up the steps.

"Oh! It's you. Post-game breakdown run late?"

Cade almost jumped at the sound of Annie's voice coming from somewhere nearby. "Annie?" He looked around on the porch but didn't see her.

"Down here." He leaned over the railing and saw the bushes move.

"What are you doing down there? You should be in the house, with the doors locked, and a medic looking after you!" Whoops. Well, he had tried to take Paige's advice at any rate. From the way her hands went to her hips, he guessed she didn't care that he had made an effort to remain calm.

"I'm looking for something." She turned her back to him and disappeared back into the bushes.

"Shoot, Annie, I'm sorry. I was just so upset when I heard that you had a visit from Gaylen's people. I should have been here to protect you."

"Ah-ha!" She popped back up, holding up a gnome that looked suspiciously like a priest. "Hate to burst your bubble, but I didn't need you. I had him. He took out Larry and Curly."

Cade watched as she came up the stairs and turned to him. His fists clenched in anger as he saw the massive, swollen bruise on the side of her face. "I could have protected you from that."

Annie felt her temper rising as she put the little gnome back in place. Her face throbbed, her side ached, and he was spouting macho bull when all she really wanted was a hug. She didn't know which made her more upset: that he was pulling his protection act or that she needed him to hug her.

Tonight had taught her one thing. She was tired of being alone. She was tired of working so hard and then coming home to an empty house with no one to share her day with. It frustrated her. She had never felt these desires before, and she wasn't quite prepared to handle them.

She loved the sex with Cade, but she found herself wanting more of the moments they snuggled on the couch watching a game, laughing and talking. She turned around from where she had place Lil' Jim, her new name for the priest gnome, and looked at Cade.

"I'm sorry, Sparky." Cade's shoulders slumped as he took a seat in the chair by the door. "I just can't seem to stop myself from being an overprotective ass."

"What?" Did she hear him right? An apology and an endearment. She was pretty sure she had never received either of those before. It felt nice. Comfortable.

"Damn, I'm out of my element here. I care for you. You have to know that. When I heard you were hurt, I just blamed myself for not protecting you." He held up his hand to stop her from speaking. "I know. Trust me, I know you are more than capable of taking care of yourself. I have seen you in action and I have read your file. None of it matters to me. I trust you to have my back in a fight, but it still doesn't mean that I want to see you in a fight. It goes against every instinct I have to think of you being hurt and not wanting to prevent it. Please tell me you understand."

Annie looked at him. His speech had been firm, unyielding, but his eyes seemed to implore her to understand. Surprisingly, she did. The trouble was she had those same feelings for him. She wanted to protect him. The meaning of that protective feeling and the warm feeling that came over her when he said he cared about her was just too much for her to contemplate. What she did know is that she understood and couldn't be angry at him for acting the way he did.

"Yes, I understand. You're a good man, Cade, even if you do call me Sparky." She winked at him and opened the front door. "Want to come in?"

"Sure. But, it's pretty late and you need your sleep."

"Would you stay the night?" Annie bit down on the right corner of her lower lip. She knew it was a big step, but it was a step she was ready to take. Cade would chase away any nightmares she might have.

"I would love to. Come on, let's go inside. Let me take care of you tonight." Annie walked inside, her cheek throbbing, her side aching, but she had never felt better.

Chapter Sixteen

Annie tried to roll out of bed, but the sharp pain froze her in mid movement. The pain was from the bruised rib. When she moved a certain way, it felt as if someone was hitting her rib with a chisel.

She closed her eyes and took a deep breath to force her muscles to relax. She swung her feet off the side of the bed and quickly stood, a hiss of breath escaping from between her teeth.

Cade had made her see a doctor on Saturday after they woke up. The doc said that by Wednesday the pain would decrease and in a couple of weeks would be gone altogether. It couldn't happen soon enough—she hated not being one hundred percent.

All weekend Cade had stayed with her. She had fallen asleep in his arms every night, and he had chased away all the bad memories that used to visit her in her sleep. But, it was time for her to do her own job. She had a meeting with Austin Colby that she didn't want to be late for.

Cade walked down the hall and couldn't stop the grin from appearing on his face. He'd never been so excited to get to school before, but this weekend had been nothing short of amazing.

"Hey, Coach."

"Hi, Austin. You're here early. Don't you normally run in while the bell is sounding?"

"I had a meeting with Miss Hill."

"You did? How did it go?" Annie had failed to mention this meeting when he had left her after dinner last night.

"Good. We went over my classes and talked about football. I'm really excited for Senior Night. I'm ready to show them what we can do."

"The team needs a leader, Austin. Trey can only do so much. If you help him, you all could go really far."

"We already thought of that. I talked to Trey on Saturday, and we're having lunch together today to come up with a game plan to keep everyone motivated." Who was this kid? Cade wasn't going to complain though. "I better get to homeroom. See ya' at practice, Coach."

Cade nodded and headed to Annie's office. Maybe she'd have found something out. Her door was open and he rapped his knuckles lightly on the window in the center of the door. Annie was at the filing cabinet with her back to him, and he watched as she slowly straightened. She was still in a lot of pain.

"Hey, Sparky. How are you feeling this morning?"

"Still hurts, but the more I move around the better it gets."

"Make sure you take it easy. I'll bring over some stuff the trainer uses on the players tonight and maybe that will help some." He hated seeing her slowed down in any way. She was always so sure of herself and her movements that it seemed strange to see her hesitate in any way.

"Thanks. I'm willing to try anything." She slowly made her way to the door and stopped next to him to watch the kids hanging out by their lockers talking before the bell rang.

"How did your meeting go this morning?"

"Good. I tried to get some info out of him but got nothing. He's clean though. I could tell. He wasn't sweating, his pulse wasn't jumping, his eyes were clear. It will take another week or so to get it all out of his system, but at least he's stopped taking it. I'm hoping that when he's fully clean he'll change his mind and talk to you or me about it."

Cade heard the bell ring and watched as the kids started to slam their lockers and head for homeroom. He glanced down at Annie and knew if she looked up she'd see the wicked glint in his eye.

"Well, I better get to class." He leaned down and kissed her lips. For a moment he forgot where he was as he deepened the kiss. It would be impossible for him not to. Her lips were made for him to kiss.

Whistles brought him back to reality, and he reluctantly broke off the kiss. He heard Annie groan and turn back into her office. Looking over his shoulder, he saw the students who had been so frantically getting to homeroom all staring at him instead.

"Have a good day, Sparky." He gave Annie a wink and then turned to his audience, "Aren't you all late?" With the spell broken, the kids scattered and he was left in silence as he made his way to his classroom.

Gaylen wiped the sweat from his face. It was a good thing they were on the phone and Boss couldn't see Gaylen reacting to the threats. He was rather partial to his balls and would like to keep them if at all possible.

"You're failing, Gaylen. You know what happens to people who fail me, don't you?

"Yes, Boss. They disappear."

"But not before they beg for death," the voice whispered over the phone. Gaylen felt his Adam's apple lodge in his throat. From the orders he'd carried out on behalf of his boss, he knew that was the truth. "I want to know why Austin has stopped coming to the gym, and I want that reason taken care of. Do you understand?"

"Yes, Boss." Gaylen sighed in relief when he heard the phone disconnect. He took out the handkerchief in his black suit's front pocket and dabbed at his forehead.

He needed to appear under control before he paged Devon. A man didn't rise to his position by showing weakness or fear – no matter how well deserved. He moved away from his desk and over to the bank of windows looking out over his empire.

It was the middle of the day, yet his gym was full. He had millions of dollars of product arriving tomorrow and a team of soldiers to do his bidding for him. His suits each cost over a thousand dollars. Not too bad for a kid who grew up on the streets of Glasgow, one of the most dangerous cities in the world. He had fought for every penny he stole and every trinket he had gotten by mugging tourists.

He was never scared those dark, cold nights spent trying to keep warm, not like he was now. Now he knew what wealth and reputation were, and he didn't want to lose them. He was betting with his life that he wouldn't. He turned back to his desk and hit the intercom.

"Hen, be a dearie and send Devon up when he gets done with his client." Gaylen released the intercom and sat back down in his leather chair. He needed to move some money around and develop an exit strategy, just in case he couldn't pull this one off. He didn't want to stick around to see what the boss had in store for him.

Cade listened to the band play the fight song and took one last look around the jammed packed parking lot before heading into the locker room. He had been in his office studying the playbook until he had made his way through the whole thing. They had a chance to do the impossible tonight. If they won, they would come in second in the division and make the playoffs. They had an inexperienced team, a leader who for most of the season was on drugs and so out of control the team almost imploded, and a brand new coach. It seemed impossible to him, especially with only three starting seniors.

However, here they were on the cusp of the playoffs. It was the last game of the season, and the team's seven seniors were being honored. He hung out by the door, taking one last look around as the cheerleaders got in place with the paper banner for the boys to run through, and then headed inside.

"Our season doesn't end tonight. It starts tonight!" Cheers erupted from the group of players surrounding Trey and Austin as they stood on the wooden bench in between the lockers.

"We may be the underdog, but we've been the underdog all year," Trey continued. "And you know the thing about underdogs? No one sees 'em coming!"

"We're going to be firing on all cylinders tonight, boys. We're a clean, new engine, and we're going to work as a team tonight. I know it was my fault that we weren't a team before, but we will be tonight and we will be when we win State!" Austin yelled as the team broke out in chants of 'State'. They turned to each other, hitting their shoulder pads before jumping up and down in a circle around Trey and Austin.

"I guess I don't need to do a pre-game speech," Cade said to Coach Parks. He turned to his boys and raised his voice, "Your time is now, gentlemen. Go out onto that field and take it!" Sometimes less was more, he thought, as the boys ran past him onto the field.

Annie clasped her hands nervously and then rubbed them on her thighs as she waited for the start of the fourth quarter. So far it had been back and forth with neither team holding the lead for long.

"Here you go. I thought you might like some." Paige handed her a hot chocolate and took the seat next to hers.

"I was afraid you weren't going to make it back in time. I don't know how much more I can take," Annie laughed.

She had never gone to a high school sporting event before coming to Keeneston and was drawn in by how hard the boys tried.

It was killing her that they were fighting for every yard. They were currently tied and she couldn't imagine what their parents were feeling.

"I wouldn't abandon you. You're the only person who will sit with me during a game." Paige turned around and looked up the stadium. "See the large group sitting about fifteen rows up. Couple in their fifties with three strapping men next to them?"

Annie turned around and looked up into the stands. They were easy enough to spot. All the women and some of the girls in the stands were trying to get closer to them. It was easy to see why. They all looked like slightly varying versions of Cade. "Yes, I see them. Your family?"

"That's right. My own family won't sit next to me. Oh! Here we go! Come on, Austin! Watch the coverage!" Paige screamed.

Annie tried not to crush the little white Styrofoam cup she held as a massive linebacker broke through the line, causing Austin to scramble out of the pocket and make a run for the first down.

"Look at that." Paige hit her arm, causing her to spill some of the hot chocolate. "That cocky safety is all over Ryan. He's holding him up so he can't run his route. Come on, Ref! Defensive interference!"

Annie watched the next play, and sure enough, that kid was jawing at Ryan. This was accompanied by gestures that mimicked the trash talking. Even she wanted to go on the field and give him a talking to.

"Ref! You watch number 35. He's holdin' our boys 'til the cows come home!" Annie turned at that familiar slow, elegant voice coming from Miss Lily. A KHS blanket was lying over her standard flower print dress, her white hair covered with a beautiful, light pink knit hat with a big white flower sitting jauntily off to the side.

Looking around, she saw that the entire town was here. She had walked down to the Blossom Café the other night to get dinner, and the town was covered in the school colors. Signs were posted on the doors of businesses announcing they would be closed for Senior Night.

Her attention was turned back to the field as the cocky safety shoved Ryan, sending him flying to the ground. Cade was on the field yelling at the referees, and she was pretty sure one of the Rose sisters called the ref a horse's ass. The bench was yelling at the offense on the field as they huddled on third down.

The boys clapped and lined up for the play. The ball was snapped and Ryan ran along the sidelines as number 35 covered him. Ryan stopped, turned, lowered his shoulder and hit number 35 square in the chest. The benches emptied as Ryan's teammates jumped up to cheer. Annie looked around and saw that the people in the bleachers had done the same.

Cade watched as his team went nuts. They were waving towels in the air and screaming encouragements to the offense. It was a wasted down. The pass to Ryan had overshot him when he decided to pull his little stunt. But, it seemed the boost in the morale of the team made it worthwhile.

"Time out!" Cade yelled as he signaled the referee. He waited for the boys to run over to the sidelines before he said a word. "Okay, gentleman. We have two options. One, we punt the ball away. Two, we go for it on fourth down and ram the ball down their throats. What say you?" He made eye contact with his team and knew their choice by the smiles on their faces. "Austin, blue slant thirty. You think you can do that?"

"Only if it's to Hall, Coach." Cade looked between Austin and Ryan and knew by the determined look in their eyes that they would move Heaven and Earth to make this play.

Paige reached over and grabbed Annie's hand. "Oh my God, they're going for it!" There was a collective gasp from the crowd and then all at once they erupted in cheers to encourage the boys.

The ball was snapped. Paige squeezed her hand tighter, and Annie held her breath as she watched the play take shape. Austin dropped back as Ryan burst from the line and blew by the safety who had been pushing him around all night. Ryan never looked back. He sprinted straight down the sideline for ten yards before slanting towards the middle of the field.

Austin pulled his arm back and released the ball with everything he had, his back leg raised off the ground with the effort. The football sailed through the air in a tight spiral. The cheers stopped as everyone waited to see where the ball would land. Ryan leapt into the air, arms outstretched, and plucked the ball from the night sky. Cheers burst forth from the crowd as feet pounded the metal bleachers. Annie and Paige involuntarily stood up as Ryan landed on the ground and stumbled forward into the end zone.

Cade smiled and shook hands with the opposing coach. Hall's touchdown had sparked the team. The defense prevented any more touchdowns, and Austin threw for two more. It had been a huge victory going into the playoffs and a wonderful Senior Night for the guys.

Students poured onto the field to celebrate the victory with their friends. Parents hugged their children, and several mothers cried knowing their sons were soon graduating. Cade searched the crowd for Annie. He found her immediately. Her red hair danced in the wind as she and Paige made their way onto the field.

He shook the hands of the parents who approached him while fighting through the growing number of people on the field to get to Annie. All he wanted was to wrap his arms around her and celebrate – just the two of them.

"Annie!" He waved his arm in the air and drew her attention. He smiled when he saw her face alight with a smile of her own. Paige waved back as he moved around some cheerleaders hugging their boyfriends.

"Well done, Coach!" His sister clapped excitedly. "The playoffs! I can't believe it."

"Thank you, Paige. But now, there is something I have to do." He turned to Annie and saw her wrinkle her brow in confusion before he wrapped his arms around her. The feel of her body against his was all the celebration he needed. He lowered his head and brought his lips to hers.

"Hey, Bro, I think you're embarrassing our mother." Miles' serious, yet sarcastic voice cut through the crowd noise.

Cade sadly pulled away from Annie's warmth to glare at his older brother. "As always, you have impeccable timing, Miles."

Miles just smirked and rocked back on his heels. He was still in his suit from work and looked ridiculously out of place in the sea of denim. Cade wrapped his arm about Annie's waist and tucked her against the side of his chest. "Mom, Dad, I would like you to meet Annie Hill. Annie, these are my parents, Marcy and Jake Davies."

Annie stood frozen against Cade's side. She had never met a man's parents. Actually, she had never met many parents at all and was wholly unfamiliar with the situation. Did she say something? Did she shake hands? Luckily the decision was taken from her when Mrs. Davies pushed Cade aside and grabbed her up in a matronly hug.

"It's so nice to meet you. I have heard so many wonderful things about you. This is my oldest son Miles." Annie smiled and shook hands with the very serious looking man with an eerie similarity to Cade. "And this is my second son Marshall, and my youngest son Pierce."

My, if she were seven years younger, Cade would have some competition. Pierce was handsome in a sexy, laid back, country boy way that made her know she'd like him instantly. Marshall just looked tough. She could easily see him as a soldier. "It's nice to meet all of you."

"Well, I know you young people will want to celebrate tonight's victory so we won't keep you. It's was very nice to meet you, Annie. I hope to see you at our Sunday dinners soon. Good job, son. I knew you would be a wonderful coach." Marcy patted Cade's cheek.

"Thanks, Mom." The group watched as Jake Davies led his wife through the crowd towards the car.

"We hate to tear our dear brother from such a lovely lady, but we had thought to have a guy's night out to celebrate the victory. Will, Mo, Ahmed, and Cole are going to join us," Marshall said.

"That's alright. Annie's going to hang out with us girls tonight. We don't need any of you men to have a good time." Paige grabbed Annie's hand and pulled her over to her side. "That is, if you would like to join us. Dani, Kenna and I are going over to Miss Lily's for a spa night with lots of chocolate, which any woman would tell you is way more satisfying than a man."

"I would love to join you. We will see you gentleman later." Annie grinned, linked her arm with Paige's, and followed her off the field.

She had never had a girls' night before. While she was terrified about the prospects, the mention of chocolate focused her mind so that all she could think about was getting there as fast as possible to sample the treats. She glanced over her shoulder and shot Cade a grin, conveying that he would need to prove himself against the chocolate. Paige was right, chocolate could be very satisfying.

Chapter Seventeen

Annie hoisted herself into Paige's old pick-up truck and grinned. There were two rifles mounted on the back window and an adopt-a-pet bumper sticker on the tailgate. Paige was her kind of girl.

"So, what is this thing we're going to?" She hoped she didn't sound as naïve as she felt.

"We're just going to put on a movie, eat some chocolate, paint our nails, give each other facials and talk about guys. You know, a typical girls' night."

Paige drove down Main Street and turned at the second and last stoplight in Keeneston. She drove up a slight hill lined with old houses with even older trees. The houses and lots were large and square. No cookie cutter neighborhoods squeezed onto postage stamp sized lots here, no condos reaching for the sky and no apartments stretching out over the land. Instead there were tons of green grass, bagged leaves sitting neatly on the curbs and landscaped yards surrounding picture-perfect colonial and Victorian houses.

They turned right into the driveway leading to a pretty, white Victorian with a large wraparound porch. A porch swing swayed gently in the cool fall breeze as lights blazed from inside.

Paige parked next to a sexy, red BMW M6, a brown piece of crap Lumina, and two Buicks the size of a small country. Interesting. The

M6 was her dream car. But, with a sticker price around a hundred grand it would always only be a dream.

"Wow. It must be nice to marry a prince. That's my dream car." Annie pointed to the red BMW.

"Oh, that's not Dani's car. That's Kenna's. She used to be a real hot shot attorney in New York City. She bought it as a gift to herself when she made junior partner. Dani drives that brown and rust Lumina."

She saw Paige smile when she choked and then coughed. A princess drove a Lumina?

"I can see what you are thinking. Yes, Her Almost Royal Highness drives a clunker. She's very attached to it and insists on keeping it. I think she just really likes to rile the king.

"See, Dani refused to touch her sizable trust fund when she was younger and earned every penny she had. The first thing she bought was this car. It breaks down all the time, has no heat, and can be heard from two counties over. But, it's hers. The king thought she was a gold digger out to snare his son and was rather mean to her. Then he had to eat crow when he found out she was the daughter of one of the richest winery owners in Italy. She found it all very amusing and even went to pick up the king at the airport in her Chevy. He drove all the way to Keeneston in that car, and Dani had never been happier."

Paige opened the door and hopped out of the truck. Annie slowly lowered herself to the ground and looked at the house. This was the stuff of nightmares: giggling, gossiping, and girlie bonding. She squared her shoulders and took a deep, steadying breath. Hey, she had taken down drug lords, how hard could a girls' night be?

The front door opened before Paige and Annie had made it up the steps. Annie felt her eyes widen at the sight before her. One of the Rose sisters, probably Miss Lily, was at the door with her white hair pinned tightly away from her green face.

"Well, bless the Saints and color me happy! Daisy Mae! Violet Fae! Paige brought Annie!" Miss Lily hollered into the house. "Come in, come in." She opened the door wide as Annie climbed the steps to the porch where two more green colored faces came into view.

"Annie we are so glad you could join us! Hurry up and take off your coats you two. Ya'll gotta catch up. We've already started the facials," Miss Violet said as she started helping her off with her coat.

Annie gulped. You can do this. Just stay quiet and listen to the conversations. Maybe she could even learn something. Paige grabbed her hand and led her down the hall and into a cozy living room.

"Hi, Paige. Welcome, Annie! I'm so glad you could join us. You two have a seat right here and we'll get started." With her burgeoning pregnant belly and her auburn hair tied up in a topknot to keep the green gook out of it, Kenna pointed to the loveseat. Annie cringed at the sight of a bowl with green mush in it and the paintbrush in Kenna's hand.

"It's great that we get this chance to talk more. I know we've hung out some at the games every now and then, but this really gives us a chance to get to know each other. I mean, you're dating Paige's brother – that practically makes you family," Dani said as she came at her with some gauzy type thing. Oh God, what were they going to do to her?

Paige flopped down on the couch and picked up a piece of fudge from a pretty plate sitting on the side table. "I'm glad we're doing this too. I needed some time away from Cole and his wedding planning. I swear, if he and my mother come at me with another invitation design, I'm going to scream. I thought guys weren't supposed to be involved in the wedding planning process."

Annie looked around as the girls all laughed.

"And I thought they weren't supposed to be involved in the pregnancy either, but I too had to escape Will. He's following me around and practically clucking. We've been here thirty minutes, and he's already texted me three times, making sure I'm okay. I just had to call Ahmed and bribe him with a little known law to get him out of testifying in a committee hearing if he'd lift Will's cell phone from him tonight."

Kenna put the paintbrush into the goop and stirred it. Oh God, was she coming at her with that stuff? Annie jumped when she suddenly felt her hair being pulled away from her face.

"Sorry! I didn't mean to startle you. I was just going to put this wrap on so you don't get that stuff in your pretty hair," Dani said, holding up a strip of the gauzy stuff.

"Um, okay." Annie tentatively sat down and let Dani wrap the gauze around her face. She sat in terror as Kenna came towards her, paintbrush in hand.

"So, what about you?" Kenna asked as the first glob of green gunk was smeared on her face.

"What about me?"

"What does Cade do to bug you?" Kenna smeared some more gunk on her face and waited for her answer. What should she say?

"Come on, dearie. Don't be shy. We've all been there. Men are simple creatures, and sometimes it helps to talk to your friends about it so you don't one day smash a freshly made apple pie in his face," Miss Lily said as she sat in the floral embossed chair across from her.

Annie looked around and saw everyone looking at her. Her mind suddenly went blank. She couldn't think of anything. Wait, what did he do that ticked her off?

"Well, he has a tendency to think he has to protect me from, well, from everything." Annie saw heads nodding and felt some of the tension in her shoulders ease.

"I once took out a man twice my size with a crepe pan. Men, so clueless sometimes." Annie whipped her head around to look at Miss Violet, who was sitting so primly on another floral chair, the green gunk on her face having dried into a light lime color. She couldn't be more than five feet tall and looked pretty much like Merriweather, the short, round fairy godmother in *Sleeping Beauty*.

"Miss Violet!" Paige exclaimed.

"Don't look so shocked, Paige. You, after all, shot an assassin."

"Yes, but that doesn't have the flair of taking him out with a crepe pan." Paige leaned back against the couch and folded her arms over her chest. Annie would swear she was pouting.

"Back to Annie. It's a good sign he's being protective. It means he cares," Miss Violet said.

"Definitely. So, is it true you're getting married?" Dani asked as she grabbed some more fudge.

"No! We haven't discussed the future at all. I'm sure he doesn't think it's serious. You never know when I'll be transferred again." Did Miss Lily just roll her eyes?

"Well, then you better hurry up and tell him you love him," Kenna said as she swiped the goo across her forehead.

"What?"

"Oh don't look so shocked. We all know it already. So, spill." Miss Daisy gave her a stern look. Annie looked around the room and saw that everyone there, including Paige, all thought that they were in love.

"It's too soon. We've only known each other a couple of months."

"Oh nonsense. You don't have a man practically living with you when you don't love him," Miss Lily told her.

"He's not living with me!"

"That's not what Father James says." Miss Violet gave her sister a wink.

"Yea, and Cade has missed three Sunday dinners at my parents' house. He's never done that before." Paige leaned her head back as Kenna attacked her with the green gunk.

"Would you care to revise your previous statement?" Kenna asked as she dipped the paintbrush in the bowl. If her tone had been cold instead of joking, Annie could see why she was rumored to be such a good attorney.

"Okay, so maybe it's not casual." That was the closest she was going to get to telling them the truth, the truth that she was starting to feel way more than she had ever felt before. She snapped out of her thoughts when she heard laughter. "What?"

"Just tell him you love him. It's so obvious that you both are crazy about each other, but if you want to keep being delusional, I guess that's your business." Kenna put the paintbrush back into the bowl. "I have to go to the bathroom again. I swear, this kid is doing jumping jacks on my bladder."

Paige and Dani started talking about weddings as the Rose sisters started in about a pie contest they were sponsoring. Annie rested her head against the back of the couch and closed her eyes. She didn't want to show the women the fear in her eyes. They were sharp enough to see it. It was fear that her face was going to be ripped off by whatever this goop was. It felt like her face was pulled so tightly you could bounce a quarter off of it. Who was she really kidding? It was fear they would see the confusion in her eyes. The more she thought about it, the more she thought they were right, all those feelings she was having that couldn't be defined or explained. Oh no, she was totally in love.

Her eyes popped open and she found the three wise faces of the Rose sisters looking at her. "Told you, you loved him," Miss Lily said as the other sisters nodded their heads.

Cade accepted the beer Will handed him and took a long slug of it. He was under attack. It didn't look like an enemy ambush but it was. Instead of the mountains of Afghanistan, it was a bonfire and cornhole boards. Instead of insurgents, it was his brothers and his best friends, which only made it more dangerous.

"Come on, Cade. Just admit you are in love with her." Will sat down on the bench next to him.

"Just because you are whipped by your wife doesn't mean I'm in the same situation."

"I'm sorry, my friend, but I agree with Will. You're very much in love with her," Mo said as he tossed a cornhole bag.

"Yea, Bro, you've missed three Sunday dinners. Ma is already picking out places to hold the wedding." Marshall laughed as his bag knocked Mo's from the board, and Mo murmured something he guessed was a curse word in his native language.

"A real man is one who can admit his true feelings."

"Give me a break, Ahmed. You have never expressed any kind of feelings."

"That is because you are not my true love." Ahmed turned away from the group and walked away.

"Deep, but true." Cade rolled his eyes at Miles. He looked at his watch and hoped it was late enough for him to get home and away from these busy bodies.

"I'm about to head home. Want me to give you a ride?" Cole asked.

"That would be great. Thanks for the victory party guys. Good night."

Cade followed Cole to his Explorer and climbed in. They were at Marshall's farm, and it was only a matter of minutes to his place, but he couldn't get there fast enough. The truth was catching up with him and he didn't want to face it in front of anyone else.

"You know, I fought like crazy to not love Paige."

"You really think this conversation is appropriate with her being my sister and all?" Crap. Now he was trapped in the car. He should have walked.

"Love happens. It's what you do with it that matters. If you embrace it, it will give you a joy you have never known was possible. If you ignore it, it has the power to haunt you."

Thank goodness. There was his house. "Thanks for the lift."

"Any time. Think about what I said."

Cade nodded and practically leapt out of the Explorer. He didn't want to hear any more about love. He just wanted to have a beer, watch *SportsCenter*, and pet his dog.

Cade set down another empty beer bottle and was still no closer to where he wanted to be. He wanted to be comfortably single again like he had been before Annie. Then he didn't have to worry about if she felt the same. So, he had set out to drink himself stupid in hopes to forget about his fear, his fear that his love wouldn't be returned.

He groaned when he heard the knock on the door. If it was Marshall here to give him hell again, he wouldn't be held accountable for his actions. He gave Justin a pat and got up after he hopped off his lap. His brother just didn't know when to stop. Cade couldn't wait until Marshall fell for some woman and then he would have his payback.

Cade yanked opened the door and froze. He wondered if he had drunk too much and was hallucinating his desires. Annie stood in his doorway looking like a vision. He heard himself whisper her name as he reached for her. She came eagerly to his arms as his lips met hers in unspoken desire. He scooped her up, kicked the door shut and carried her upstairs.

He placed her before his bed and gently removed her clothes before shedding his. She reached up and with her finger slowly traced his jaw line.

"I love you," he heard himself whisper before he lowered her to the bed.

Annie gasped for breath. She was sure she was being tortured. She couldn't breathe and her face was wet. But then something tickled her. She struggled to open her eyes against the attack. When she managed to open them, she came face to face with Justin lying on her chest. His big hairy paws were planted beside her head, and his face was inches from hers. Slurp! She was drowned again in another doggie kiss.

She gave him a pat and encouraged him to get off the bed. Cade was still asleep next to her, but Justin obviously wanted to go out. He jumped off the bed and danced around, waiting for her to get dressed.

"Okay, come on, big boy." She headed down the stairs and into the living room. Justin ran behind her, his feet slipping on the hardwood floor as he took a corner. He regained his footing, sped past her and ran headfirst into the sliding glass door.

"Oh my God, are you okay?" Justin just ducked his head embarrassingly and wagged his tail. She opened the door and he bounded out onto the patio.

She headed into the kitchen in search of coffee. She needed stimulation to be able to contemplate what Cade had said last night. He couldn't possibly mean it, could he? She had never been loved before. The vulnerability of it and his potential to hurt her was downright scary.

"Good morning." Annie looked up from pouring her coffee to see Cade leaning against the doorjamb. His bare feet poked out from his jeans, and his arms were folded across his chest as he smiled at her.

"Good morning, I hope I didn't wake you up." She suddenly felt a little shy. Should she bring up what he had said last night? Or, what if he didn't mean it? Or, if he didn't even say it, and she had imagined the whole thing?

"No, you didn't. It was the mighty ram there." He nodded his chin to where Justin was staring into the room, pink tongue hanging out of the corner of his mouth and matching pink bow falling out.

"I had been meaning to tell you that Trey came by my office. He seemed close to telling me more details on S2 but wanted to confront the users himself. I assume he did so. He hasn't been back to see me since."

"That's right. He took the team over and got them to come together better than I ever could. I know one of the boys was Austin, but as you have probably noticed, he's clean now. I haven't figured out who the others were, but maybe Trey will tell you now that they're clean?"

"I'll try on Monday. Well, I better get dressed and get home. I have some paperwork I need to get to my boss."

Cade stared after Annie's quickly retreating form as she scuttled out the door and to her car. Maybe it was the wrong move to break out the L word last night, although, it wasn't as if he could have prevented it. Those words had come tumbling out of their own volition as soon as he had seen her.

He had also seen disbelief and a little fear streak across her beautiful face before he kissed it away. Maybe he should have talked about it with her before she left, but she had seemed so skittish that he didn't think it would be a good idea. He was hopeful his plan of giving it time to sink in wouldn't result in her running for the hills, or else he'd be left chasing after her.

Cade pulled the curtain away from the window in his office and looked out. He smiled at the cloud of dust her vehicle was leaving behind. It would be a fun chase though.

Chapter Eighteen

Cade felt the smile spread across his face as his last student left the room. He had a free period until his senior anatomy class started. He needed to go see Annie and invite her for dinner at his parents for tomorrow night.

He had gone to his parents' house for the weekly family dinner and been cornered by both his mother and Paige. He was ordered to bring Annie to dinner or else all homemade food would be cut off. Not that he couldn't cook, but his mother made a peanut butter fudge pie that was to die for. On top of that, the only person she had shared the recipe with was Paige, and they were sticking together on this.

"Hiya. How is our winning coach doing today?"

"Hi, Steph. How are you?" Cade looked up and saw Stephanie in her usual black pencil skirt and matching sweater set. Her hair was pulled back into a little bun at the base of her neck. She was holding a covered plate and Cade wanted to groan.

One of the reasons he had asked her out was because she had been so kind. She had brought him homemade treats and had talked with him about his students. But, after that first date, it became weird. She was sweet, but she was always there. Now she was standing in front of him with a plate of home cooked food and a smile on her face.

"Really good. I made brownies yesterday and had these left over. I thought you would like some." She placed the plate on his desk and he tried to smile sincerely.

"These smell great. Thanks, Stephanie. I'm just getting ready to go see Annie. My mother has pronounced that it was time she meet the whole family properly in the form of a dinner."

"Really? It's that serious?" she said, just a little too seriously. "I mean, that's great. I just didn't think you'd ever get serious about someone."

"Kinda took me by surprise, too. Well, thanks for the brownies. I'm sure they're as delicious as always. I better give Annie the bad news!" Cade stood and walked out into the hallway with Stephanie.

"Good luck at the dinner. I better get back to making up the pop quiz my junior chemistry class is going to get this afternoon." Stephanie walked back into the classroom and shut her door. God, he hoped he had misread those signals. He liked Stephanie. She was sweet but not right for him.

Annie smiled at Samantha and reached out for her hand as she led her toward her office door. "Sam, I promise, you'll do great on your SAT's. You have been studying for a year with a tutor. You're a 4.0 student. Just relax and have confidence in yourself."

"Thanks, Miss H. I'll let you know how I do on my next practice test. Oh, hello, Coach Davies. Do you have the test scores back from our genetics test?"

"Yes, you'll get them in class today. But, Sam, Miss Hill is right. You need to have some faith in yourself. You put in the time to do your homework and study and as a result you did very well."

"How…."

"You'll see in class."

"Oh, okay. Bye, Miss H, Coach Davies." Annie watched as the young girl hefted her backpack on her small frame and headed off towards her next class.

"Good afternoon. How was your weekend?" Cade asked her.

"It was good. Got my reports done and even was able to meet with Romero on Sunday. How about you?" Annie went back to her desk. She needed some distance from him or she might just beg him to love her.

"Well, that's why I'm here. I am here to deliver a royal proclamation from my mother. You are invited to family dinner at the farm tomorrow at six."

"Me?"

"Who else but the woman I have been spending all my time with?"

She watched as Cade walked around the desk. She dug her nails into the arms of her chair. She just didn't know what to do with all these emotions. Emotions were something fairly new to her. "Tomorrow?"

"Yes, and if you know my mother, she won't take no for an answer. We'll talk about it more tonight when I come over with dinner. Sound good to you?" He smiled and she felt herself melting. Little devil, he knew what he was doing.

"Okay, tell your mom I will be there. How about some meatloaf from the Blossom Café? I had never had meatloaf before, but I find myself quite addicted." She smiled up at him. No woman could say no to him when he looked at her like that.

"Looking forward to it. I missed you this weekend."

Annie's mind was whirling at that proclamation. She wanted to ask him more about it, but he turned around, winked and sauntered out of the office. Oh that man was waging war on her. Surely that meant he loved her!

That knowledge put an extra bounce in her step for the rest of the day. Nothing, not even a faculty conference this afternoon, would ruin her mood!

Annie shook her head and tried to focus on the papers in front of her. She was trying to figure out which players had used S2 and which she could flip. Austin was at the top of her list, but he wasn't talking. She had called him into the office today just to talk. He was polite and talked about the stress of leading the team and about the worry of college scouts, but nothing about S2 and bad influences.

Annie would get there though. She'd build a good relationship with him and then slowly extract the truth. She glanced at the clock and gasped. She was due at Cade's parents in less than an hour. Annie scooped up her files and tossed them into her shoulder bag. She had to hurry if she wanted to have time to get home and change for the meeting of the parents.

It terrified her more than any meth user waving a gun around. Parents. She had never had any and was scared of the unknown. She reached for the doorknob and turned it. Nothing. It didn't turn. She must have been so nervous that she had accidentally locked it. Annie looked at the lock and grew confused. The door appeared to be unlocked. She tried again to pull the door open but nothing. The blinds rattled against the small glass window as she yanked on the door.

"Hello? Is anyone there?" Silence met her. She pulled up the blinds and looked out the window but saw nothing except an empty hall. What was going on?

Annie was reaching for the desk phone when she was plunged into darkness. She tripped over one of the chairs and landed against her desk. Now what? With no outdoor window, her office was pitch-black. She reached out with her hands and felt around her desk for the phone. She grasped it and brought it to her ear. Silence. The electricity outage must have disconnected the phones as well.

Something nagged her though. The power outage could explain the phone but nothing could explain the locked door. She lifted the leather flap of her bag and rummaged around for her cell phone. Finding it, she activated the screen and the brightness lit up the room enough for her to see. She looked down at her phone and cursed. No signal. Impossible.

Someone in the S2 ring must have figured out who she was. But, if they figured out who she was, why were they just locking her in? Shouldn't they be trying to kill her? None of this made any sense. What did make sense though was that she was going to have to break her door's window to unlock the door.

She touched her cell phone screen again to light up the room. She looked around and grabbed the blue plastic chair resting against the well with its metal legs. Annie hated breaking glass. It was always such a mess. She gripped the chair on each side and rammed it into the window. The impact reverberated up her arms and into her chest as she watched the window splinter and crack. With a couple pokes of the chair's legs, the glass shattered and fell to the floor in the hallway.

Now, if she could just unlock the door. She carefully slid her head through the window and looked down to a sight she was not prepared to see. There, in the door lock was a thin piece of metal broken off. There was no way she'd be able to unlock the door. She was going to have to climb through the window. What took her back more however, was the small black rectangular object that sat a couple of feet from the door: a cell phone jammer. What the Hell was going on and who was responsible for it?

Annie took off her jacket and laid it over the broken glass. She tossed her bag through the window and placed the chair against the door. She stepped up onto it and looked at the broken window. Oh, this was going to hurt. She hiked her dark green skirt up around her waist and stuck her left leg through the window. She had to grip the side of the window to keep balance, the broken glass puncturing the palm of her hands, as she grasped the sides. She hissed but kept a tight hold until she was precariously perched half in and half out of the window.

The glass poked at her bottom as she sat on her jacket but didn't cut her through her jacket. Blood started to trickle down her forearm as she ducked her head and bent far enough over to squeeze her upper body through the window. Shards of glass tore into the back of her neck, ripping out her hair as she popped free. She slowly started to adjust her weight to her bottom half as she inched herself further out the window. She moved her right leg through the window as well and twisted towards her left until she was perched on the window facing the hall. She pushed off the window and leapt to the ground, rubbing her bottom as she stood up. That had hurt.

Annie shoved her skirt into place as she listened for her assailant. Nothing. Not a sound. She slowly walked down the hall to where the switches were. She flipped them but nothing happened. The circuit breaker must have been thrown. She went rigid when the slightest noise reached her ears.

Someone was here. She placed her right hand on the wall and started to turn when she heard a footfall directly behind her. Before she could turn around, something was brought down on the back of her head. She staggered forward and fell head first into the lockers before everything went dark.

Annie heard the muffled sound of someone running away and forced herself to open her eyes. The hall appeared blurry, but she could make out a dark figure running for the exit. She pushed herself up and tried to chase after the figure, but the world spun. She focused on the end of the hallway until it came into focus. Annie ran down the hall, each pounding footfall like a hammer against her head.

She slowed when she reached the door to the parking lot. Her hand closed around the metal rod as she carefully opened the door. Annie peered out into the parking lot. Not seeing anything, she stepped out and looked around. No footsteps, no dark figure, just her car in an otherwise empty parking lot.

"Dammit!" She pulled out her phone to call her boss and then swore again. She was due at dinner in less than five minutes. She ran for her car as she dialed Romero's direct line.

"Romero."

"Something is going on, and I don't know what. I was just imprisoned in my office with a lock pick broken off in the lock, electricity cut, and a cell phone jammer sitting outside my door."

"What happened?"

"I broke the window, crawled out and was hit from behind and into the lockers as the perp fled. I didn't get a good look at all. But, I wasn't seriously hurt, and it was certainly not an attempt on my life. It doesn't make sense at all."

"Okay. Where are you now?"

"On my way to meet Cade's family for dinner."

"It's a good thing you disclosed this relationship or I'd be pissed. Hell, I still am pissed, but it works with your cover. From your file, I know you never have done this before which means this is serious for you. I remember the first time I met my in-laws. My father-in-law met me at the door with a large carving knife. So, I guess I'm saying good luck. I'll send a forensic team over to the school to see if we can lift any prints and to figure out who is behind this. Do you think your cover is blown?"

"No. If they knew who I was, wouldn't they have killed me or threatened me in some way? That's what isn't making sense to me." Annie skidded her tires as she turned onto the dirt road leading to the farmhouse.

"I agree. Keep your cover for now. I'll let you know what we learn."

"Oh my God!" Annie screeched.

"What is it? Are you okay?" Romero asked, practically jumping through the phone.

"I just looked in the rear view mirror. I have a huge bruise on my forehead, a lump on the back of my head, blood running down both arms where my palms were cut on glass, and I think I left a chunk of

hair on my window. Plus, I just pulled up to the Davies' house."
Annie didn't notice the muffled laughter as she attempted to clean up.

"I'll be in touch with the results from the crime lab. Have fun, Blake."

"Yeah, right," she mumbled, but Romero had already hung up and her time had run out.

"She's here!" Paige screamed over the NFL pregame show. Cade blew out a breath as Pierce jumped over him.

"Oh, this is going to be so much fun," Pierce said with a devilish glint to his eyes.

"I hate to sound like the voice of reason here, but maybe you all should not interrogate her like you all did with me. I am FBI after all and can handle it. She's just a counselor," Cole told the group as he moved to the door with the rest of the family.

"As much as I would relish grilling her as much as Cade grilled and tormented my dates, I really like her. So, boys, behave." Paige gave her brothers a stern look before opening the door.

Cade had to push his brothers away so he could walk down the steps and meet Annie at the car. This must be her worst nightmare, and having everyone staring at her probably didn't help.

He hurried down the stairs to her car and smiled as he watched her frantically brushing her hair. Her nervousness was so cute. Cade walked around to open her door and froze when she looked up at him. Cade yanked open the car door to get a better look at what he thought he saw.

Yup, he was right. She had a huge bruise on her forehead. Her hands and arms were covered in blood and she was missing her jacket. And something was wrong with her hair.

"Are you all right?" He gently placed his fingers on her face to move it so he could get a better look at the bump on her head. He then ran his hands over her arms and found the source of the blood.

"I'm fine now. Sorry I'm late."

"Screw being late. I'm taking you to the hospital."

"No! Really, I'm fine. The blood is dried and I don't want to cause a scene."

"Sparky, no matter what, you are going to cause a scene. Now tell me what happened, and quickly, before they get impatient." He directed his eyes to his family who were all staring at them intently.

"I got locked in my office. The electricity was cut and a cell phone jammer was placed outside the door. I broke the window and crawled out, hence the blood and missing hair. I went down the hall to try the light switch when I heard a noise behind me. Before I could turn around, I got smashed over the head and fell headfirst into the lockers. I saw a figure in the distance but not enough to have any kind of description. I gave chase and found an empty parking lot, and that is why I was late to dinner."

Cade's heart didn't slow down after her explanation. Who would do this to her? "Do you think your cover is blown?"

"No. I don't know what this was about, but it didn't feel like it had to do with the case. The agency is checking it out for clues now."

"Are you all coming in?" he heard his mother ask.

"Sorry, Ma, but Annie had a little accident." That excused everything, and the family rushed down the steps, his mother leading the way.

"Oh, bless your heart! Are you hurt? What happened?" his mother questioned as she hurried toward a wide-eyed Annie.

"I was carrying too much stuff and tripped on some loose gravel in the parking lot. I'm afraid I went head first into my car."

Cade tried to hide his smile at her explanation. It was a good one, and it had his mother and Paige ushering her inside to get fixed up. All awkward greeting was now pushed aside. His mother was in her zone. Having six kids, she became something of an unflappable nurse.

Annie's head was spinning, and not because of the whole being bashed over the head thing. It was spinning at the conversation going around the table. She had learned the whole family history and even some about the black sheep of the family, Cy, who apparently only showed up every now and then.

She had been fussed over, bandaged up, and then plied with homemade food by Mrs. Davies, who insisted on being called Marcy, or in a not so subtle hint, Mom. Pierce was trying his hardest to interrogate her but was failing miserably. Cole was trying to run interference. Marshall and Miles were trying to intimidate, and Mr. Davies sat by quietly eating his food, watching everything.

Every now and then she would swear Cade was cursing and planning the downfall of his brothers. She found it all very strange, very chaotic, and very comfortable. So, this was what it was like to have a family. She liked it very much and was quite envious.

"So, dear, are you going to be spending Thanksgiving with your family?" Marcy asked from the head of the table.

"Thanksgiving?" Annie repeated. She never celebrated Thanksgiving. She couldn't cook and was always alone, so it never seemed important.

"You know, the holiday that's on Thursday where you traditionally eat turkey and stuffing and lots of dessert and watch football," Pierce joked.

"Pierce," his mother whispered harshly. "Ignore him. Now tell us about your family. Are they are in Florida?"

"Um, I really don't have much of a family. My mother died when I was ten, and I was raised in a series of foster homes," Annie stated matter-of-factly. People often got upset when she told her story, but to her it was the only thing she knew.

"No family! Oh, bless your heart! Everyone should have a family. No father, or grandparents?" Marcy exclaimed as she placed her delicate hand over her heart.

"I don't know who my father was. I don't think my mother knew either. My grandparents are dead. I have, or had, an aunt in Louisville, but haven't heard from her since she refused to take me after my mother died. I heard from a cousin, Chrystal Sharp, but I'm not too keen on family who only want me to fill out a family tree." She took a deep breath and plastered on her 'I'm okay with it' smile. "That's why I didn't realize Thanksgiving was this week."

"Well then, you will simply join us for Thanksgiving. Cade, you pick her up at noon. We'll be your family and that's that."

"Marcy, you don't...." Annie started to say she didn't have to do that. It hardly bothered her anymore to be alone on holidays.

"Enough. You're coming. You're family. Now, Marshall, what's this business about your wanting to run for sheriff?"

Annie hid her smile behind her napkin. The table had shifted all of its attention away from her and to Marshall. Marshall in return stared at his mother in disbelief.

"How did you know that? I didn't tell anyone."

"Mothers always know these things. Just like I knew every time one of you snuck out of the house. So, tell us about your decision to leave the private security practice and going into public service."

"I haven't decided yet. I just found myself wanting something different. I am getting tired of doing the same thing day after day — installing security systems, providing protection for celebrities coming to town, and so on."

"Well, you sure don't have my vote."

"Miles!" Marcy gasped.

"I was just kidding, Ma. I think it would be a wonderful thing. The sheriff is getting rather old and has been pretty sick recently. Some new blood never hurts. And think of all the potential women he could get when wearing his uniform."

"That's it, Miles Jackson Davies. No dessert!" Marcy reached over and grabbed the slice of pumpkin pie sitting in front of him. Annie watched in disbelief that this big, serious, tough guy hung his head and pouted when his mother took his dessert away. Marcy might not look like it, but she was a force to be reckoned with.

Annie loved when she stayed at Cade's house. His king-size bed was so much better than her little twin one. She pulled the sheets up to cover herself as she curled up against Cade's warm body.

"About Thanksgiving," Cade started.

"Yes?"

"Well, my parents eat pretty early, and Dani and Mo are having an open house party that evening. I know it would be a long day, but I would love it if you came with me to their house after dinner with my family."

"Sure, that sounds like fun," she agreed as he turned off the light and wrapped her up in his arms. After a couple of minutes she heard his breathing slow and she knew he was asleep.

The bed on her side dipped and Justin crawled over to her. He rested his head near her pillow, gave her a wet kiss, and wagged his tail. Her two boys. Her family. The thought rocked her to her core. She had lived most of her life thinking she never wanted a family, never needed a family, but not after tonight. Tonight showed her what she could have: a loving husband, interfering in-laws, brothers, sisters, children and even a dog.

She could see herself in this house filled with noise and love. She had lived in silence too long. She finally knew what she wanted in life. She wanted the dream, and she wanted it with Cade Davies. Damn, what was she going to do now?

Chapter Nineteen

Annie looked in wonder at the mansion in front of them. There were BMW's parked alongside pick-up trucks and Buicks that were older than she was. All the wings of the mansion were lit up and it looked like something out of a fairytale.

"Wow!" Annie couldn't think of any other word to describe it.

"I know. But, after you meet Mo it won't look nearly so ostentatious. He's really laid back unless he needs to cut some red tape."

"I only met him for a second, but he seemed really nice." Annie thought back to her first week in Keeneston and snickered. "Actually, the Roses wanted to set me up with Ahmed when I first moved here."

"Really? Well, I know who we're avoiding tonight," Cade said as he parked the car next to a large, blue tank of a car from the seventies. Annie shook her head. "Oh, you think I'm joking. No, ma'am. If Ahmed decides he wants you, he would just kill me and take you."

Annie laughed as they walked up the steps toward the party. They entered through the open doors into a huge foyer. Marble floors, antiques, crystal chandeliers, and priceless artwork hung on the walls. When she looked closer, she saw family snapshots on table tops and other little homey touches throughout the area.

"Oh, there you are! We were hoping you'd come." The Rose sisters bustled over to them, dressed in their finest floral dresses and matching hats.

"Why, I have never seen such beautiful women. How are you ladies doing tonight?" Cade kissed their cheeks and grinned down at them before Miss Daisy smacked him on the arm.

"Don't you be sweet talkin' me in front of your girlfriend. She might decide you're a rascal and not marry you."

"Howdy, ma'am, Cade," a tall, wiry man with slicked back light brown hair said. He was handsome in his black suit and tanned skin.

"Happy Thanksgiving, Noodle. How are your parents?" Cade asked. Holy cow! She didn't even recognize him!

"They're doing well. They are walking around here somewhere. Have you had any more problems, Miss Hill?"

"No, thank you, deputy." She smiled at him before Cade started talking fishing with him. She decided to go walk around some and see more of the house while they were discussing baits and lures.

The sitting room was packed with people. She recognized most of them, even if she couldn't remember their names. They all waved or stopped her to say a couple of words to her as she made her way to the bar set up on the far side of the room.

"Annie," a smooth voice encompassed her.

"Your highness?"

His eyes gleamed as he silently laughed at her. His manners were way too good for him to actually laugh out loud. "Just call me Mo. Everyone else does."

"Oh, well, thank you, Mo, for inviting me."

"You're part of the town too. Danielle talks very highly of you. I hoped you and Cade would join us for dinner soon."

"I'd like that. Thank you." He was so different from Cade, but they both had the same kindness. Cade exuded power through his quiet strength. Mo exuded power through his bearing.

Annie talked with Mo until he was cornered by Pam Gilbert to discuss fundraising for new school computers. Annie quietly excused herself and continued through the room. She was enjoying her time on the outskirts of the room as she watched the people of this small community talking and laughing.

Just the sight of the whole town dressed up and happily chatting away made her want to belong. She had a man she loved, in a town that welcomed her. She even kind of had Justin and the Davies family.

An older, portly fellow with black pants, dark orange dress shirt and suspenders came towards her, sporting a big, bushy gray beard. He smiled, and his large belly jiggled as he waved to some people across the room.

"I just wanted to tell you that I'm so glad you have come to join us." He shook her hand and smiled jovially.

"Thank you, Mr...?"

"Wolfe, John Wolfe. It's about time the law did something about those drugs. Keeneston is such a perfect town, but we just aren't prepared for such things. And, that Devon Ross is as sleazy as they come. I really hope you can bust him soon." Only through years of training did she hide her shock. She put on a gentle smile and gave a little laugh.

"I'm sorry, Mr. Wolfe, but I'm just a guidance counselor, not a cop."

"A cop? Of course you're not a cop, missy, you're DEA," he said matter-of-factly. "Now, you just let me know if you need any information, and if I don't already know the answer, I can find out for you. It was a real pleasure meeting you. All the kids at the high school just love you. I hope you decide to stay around after this case." He gave her a wink as he waded back into the crowd.

Annie stood still, feeling a bit silly as she stared after him. How was that possible? Had she just been punked? She smiled again and started to mingle. Lesson one, never show a reaction. So she talked to Dani, Kenna and Paige and allowed herself to be dragged around the room and introduced to practically everyone in the town by the Rose sisters before Cade caught up with them.

He came up beside her and lightly ran his hand down her back before resting it on the curve of her hip. "Are you about ready to go home?" he whispered into her ear. His warm breath danced over her skin, resulting in goose bumps and shivers that were definitely not caused from being cold.

Home. The word meant something now. She gave him a full smile and nodded. She really wanted to get home and be with him. He expertly extricated her from the conversation and steered her out of the room. She slipped on her coat when she noticed John Wolfe again.

"Hey, he knew I was DEA. Did you tell him?" She casually nodded in his direction.

"Who, John?"

"Yes, he came up to me and told me he was glad I was here to clean up the drug mess and offered any information I needed."

"He's a local legend. He knows everything, but no one knows how. I'm not surprised he knows about the drugs, and I'm not surprised he knows you are DEA. I would be surprised if we ever found out how he knows all this. If he offered to help, take him up on it. He and the Roses are the heart and soul of this town. He'll find out anything you need and will move heaven and earth to protect Keeneston." Cade leaned over and gave her a gentle kiss on the lips before saying good-bye to some of his friends gathering their coats.

They approached his home, and she saw the curtain in the front window move aside and a big black nose press against the widow. A purple bow was tied in his hair today. Justin barked his greeting as he bounded toward the door with his hair flying and bow bouncing.

A sense of peacefulness settled over her as she watched Justin land two big paws on Cade's chest and cover his face with his kisses. She may not have experienced the feeling often, but she knew what it was. She was happy, and she was in love with a man and his goofy dog.

Cade laughed as Justin bounded around. Annie slipped out of her coat and leaned against Cade. He slipped his arm around her shoulders and tucked her head against his chest.

"Cade?"

"Yes."

"I love you, too." She felt the hitch in his breathing as he heard her soft words. He spun her around and kissed her fast and hard. His hands were everywhere, and she was suddenly standing there in nothing but her black bra, panties and heels.

"God, I have been dying to tell you how much I love you, but I was afraid I would scare you away." His tie went flying and landed out of sight. "I was afraid before. I'm glad you didn't push it. But, I know it now with certainty. I know what I want, and it's you." She didn't speak anymore after that. He didn't give her time. He decided to show her a kind of love that didn't need words.

☆   ☆   ☆

The playoffs. Jesus, the playoffs. Cade took a couple deep breaths and wrung his hands. He was stalling going into the locker room. He knew it, but he couldn't let the boys see his nerves. He had never made it to the playoffs. Heck, he'd never coached before either. How was he going to do this?

"Coach?"

"Austin, what can I do for you?" Cade watched as his quarterback squared his shoulders and looked him right in the eye.

"Over Thanksgiving, I realized something. We both know I was supplementing with S2. I told myself it was for the team. To help win State and to help me win a scholarship. I thought it made me better, but it made me worse. I had dinner with Bonner, and he's still in physical therapy and has to take all these medications. I don't want that to happen to anyone else. I realized what happened to Bonner could happen to me or any of my teammates who are taking S2. I have talked to the team. We're all clean now, but I know what I need to do. I need to turn myself in to you as a drug user. I know you'll want me off the team. Maybe I could get some counseling from Miss Hill and come back next year?" Austin stood his ground and was prepared to take his punishment. Cade couldn't help but respect him. He had grown up.

"After the game, let's meet in my office in the field house with your parents and Miss Hill and discuss the situation. I am very proud of you for talking to me. It shows great leadership, Austin. Real quarterbacks need to lead on and off the field."

"Yes, sir." Austin went back into the locker room and Cade felt his adrenalin surge. He had a plan and it would work if he got some help from John Wolfe.

Cade ran the length of the sidelines, cheering Trey on as he made his way to the end zone. There was one minute left in the rematch game against their rival T.H. Morgan and they were tied. Austin had passed the ball to Trey who had leveled one defender and twisted out of another tackle forty yards back. He had broken free and was heading for the end zone to give Keeneston the lead.

Trey tucked the ball against his chest as he lunged past the last defensive player to reach the end zone. The whistle blew and the referee's arms went up causing the stadium to erupt.

"Come on, men! Huddle up! The game is not over. They still have time to score." Cade called his defense around him as the extra point was kicked. "Stick to your man. Don't give them an inch. You win this, and you play at Commonwealth Stadium from now on."

The defense took the field with determination. The quarterback from T.H. Morgan pulled his arm back and released a canon of a ball that shot downfield. Cade almost closed his eyes, but he couldn't look away. If the receiver caught this ball, there would only be Aiden, the freshman safety, there to prevent the touchdown.

He watched as Aiden stuck with the receiver as they bolted downfield. Aiden turned his head to locate the ball coming right to the outstretched hands of the receiver. The five feet nine inch Aiden leapt into the air at the same time as the receiver. Hands battled, bodies clashed, the ball was caught, and the crowd gasped as the two players landed in a heap on the field.

Cade stopped running, his eyes never looking away from the two forms on the ground. The referee pulled the receiver off of Aiden, looked down, and blew his whistle. Cade couldn't blink. He didn't want to miss the signal. The referee pointed back downfield. His shrimp of a freshman had intercepted the pass. They had won!

"Austin! Knee the ball until time has expired. We're going to Commonwealth Stadium, boys." He was surprised Austin could even hear him between the team cheering and the screams coming from the crowd.

Cade took a moment to hear the cheers, to see his players celebrating. Parents were jumping up and down in the stands along with the rest of the town. He had just brought a team of inexperienced underclassmen to the state semi-finals. On top of that, he may have just cracked the case for Annie. His happiness drained out of him. What would happen when she solved the case?

"Annie!" He found her hugging his players, along with Paige, as they made their way into the locker room.

"Cade! Oh, congratulations! This is just so unbelievably wonderful! She wrapped her arms around him and squeezed tightly.

"Bro, you're amazing! I'm afraid I may have broken Annie's hand though," Paige rasped out, her voice raw from cheering.

"Thanks, Paige. I'm sorry to abandon you, but Annie is needed for a parent meeting. I'll talk to you soon, though, okay?" He gave her a kiss on the cheek and escorted Annie to the field house as Paige continued to high five the players.

"What's going on? Is everything all right?" Annie asked as she hurried to keep up with him.

"Austin has seen the light. He wants to confess all. We're meeting with him and his parents right now. And, I have a plan," he smirked.

Chapter Twenty

A nnie and Special Agent Romero stood looking at the Keeneston County Utilities box truck that was parked in front of John Wolfe's house. She didn't know if it would hold the three agents and equipment without the bottom falling out. The truck was mostly rusted and was missing a muffler and a side mirror.

"Where did you get this, um, truck?" Vincent Romero asked. He stood with his hands on his hips and wearing the DEA traditional uniform of a gray suit and black tie. His dark hair was sprinkled with gray around his temples and slicked back with some gel.

"This is ol' Bessie. She's the county's one and only utility repair truck. I borrowed her from my cousin's, brother-in-law's, son's best friend," John told him as if that was common. What wasn't common was the way he was adjusting his sweatpants and pulling at the t-shirt he was wearing. "Do I really have to wear this getup?"

"Yes, John. You don't wear suspenders to work out in. Come on. You know what to do. Give us forty-five minutes until you head to the gym. Let these guys finish wiring you up." Cade stepped back as one of the agents explained to John the hidden video in the sweatband he positioned on John's head.

"Are you ready, Austin? Do you have any questions?" Romero asked Austin, who looked more comfortable in his baggy athletic shorts and KHS football shirt.

"So, Miss Hill isn't a guidance counselor at all? She's actually a DEA agent?" Austin scratched his head and stared disbelievingly at Annie.

"That's right," Annie answered.

"That's cool. Do you have a gun?"

"Yes, but I've found most everyone in Keeneston has a gun."

"True. My mom has a .38. I guess it's not so cool then."

"Do you know what you're supposed to do?" Annie asked again. She feared working with kids. They tended to think they were on television instead of in real life. As a result, they could get hurt.

"Yup." The tech gave him a KHS sweatband and waited for him to put it on.

"There are two cameras in yours: one in the H and one hidden in the logo on the back. You don't have to watch him to get video, so just do everything naturally and forget the cameras are even there," the tech explained.

"Austin, you need to give John about ten minutes to get used to the area before you go in. We'll be right outside."

"No problem. I owe my team this." Austin climbed into his mom's minivan and flipped open his cell phone to waste time while he waited.

"Okay, let's do this," Romero called out. Techs gathered equipment and hopped into black government-issued cars as John pulled at his sweatpants again.

Annie, Cade, Romero and an agent introduced as Jones, hesitantly climbed into the back of the utility truck and took off for the gym. Annie tried to appear confident, but it was hard when her whole case was resting on a senior citizen and a teenager.

The truck was silent. Everyone was holding their breath as they watched John walk into the Keeneston Iron Club and Spa. The video was up, and they looked at the television monitor as they listened to the audio through headphones.

John walked into the club and asked for a tour and the free week's pass that was promoted for potential members. He was shown around by a perky blonde in tight black spandex pants and an equally tight, white tank top. By the end of the tour, Annie hadn't seen much but the ass of the perky blonde, but at least John remembered to stop at the machines that faced the free weight area.

John thanked the girl and settled down on one of the machines. On cue, Austin sauntered in, shot the same perky blonde a thumbs up, and headed to the locker room. He dumped his things in a locker and headed for the free weights. It only took a minute for Devon Ross to appear. They picked him up first on John's feed as he not so casually made a beeline for Austin, who was doing bicep curls in front of a mirror.

"Long time, no see. How are you?" Devon asked as he shot a glance to the large two-way mirror on the second floor to where Cade said Trevor Gaylen had an office.

"I was grounded, dude. Totally sucked." Austin changed arms and continued to work out.

"Did your parents find your stash?"

"Hell no. I didn't come home on time. I was too busy with this hot blonde if you know what I mean. The 'rents totally freaked. But, since I couldn't get to the gym, I couldn't replenish. I'm running on empty, and I have the semi-finals next week. I need to catch up on my supplements." Annie was relieved when Austin heaved the weight back on the rack and grabbed another one.

Austin didn't look at Devon, but he didn't avoid him either. They were just two guys talking in the weight room. She had to give him credit, he was doing really well. Even John was doing his part. He moved to another machine slightly closer to the guys and attempted to work it while he casually kept his eyes straight ahead. When he moved machines, he turned his sweatband just enough to the side where Devon and Austin were in frame, but he was looking to the left of them so he wouldn't draw attention.

"Dude, this is harsh. I can't believe this is burning. I've gotten spoiled with the supplements. Here, spot me." Austin tossed some weights on the bar and lay down on the bench. Devon stood over him and spotted him as he cranked out a set on the bench press.

"How many supplements do you need?" Devon asked as he helped put the bar back in place.

"Two weeks. I need enough to get me through the championship game."

"Damn right. State champs all the way. It'll be seven hundred."

"No prob. Grandma sent some money for my college fund last week."

"Okay. Meet me in the locker room in fifteen minutes."

"Sure, dude. I got one more set here. Can you still spot?"

Annie wanted to cheer. He pulled it off so far, even asking him to stay around while he did another set. John got up and moved to another machine as Devon moved to talk to some other people working out. Romero gave a chuckle as the sounds of heavy breathing came across the audio. John was not enjoying himself. They all broke out into grins when John murmured something about needing some pie before he died.

Fifteen minutes later Austin made his way to the locker room. Devon was already there with a brown paper bag. Without talking, Austin unlocked his locker, got out a bag with money in it and tossed it to Devon.

"You got any needles in there? I'm running low on them too." Austin opened the bag and looked in, giving the camera a good shot of the needles and two vials of S2.

"Move in," Romero said into a walkie-talkie. Moments later the locker room was full of agents with Dinky and Noodle representing the local law enforcement.

Devon and Austin were put in cuffs and arrested. Devon was placed in one of the DEA vehicles with Agent Jones and taken to Lexington. Austin was put in the Keeneston Sheriff's Department cruiser and taken home by Dinky and Noodle.

"Good job, Blake. We didn't get enough to take down Trevor, but Devon strikes me as a talker. I'll let you know how the interrogation goes." He hopped out of the truck and signaled for the driver to take them back to John's house. Her cover was intact, an arrest had been made, and her kids were now safe. It was a good day.

Trevor felt the sweat break out on his forehead. The digitized voice coming over the phone was beyond angry and wanted blood. He had watched from his office when Austin came in and started working out. He hadn't been in for weeks. Stupidly, he had been relieved to see him. The prodigal son returning and all of that. Devon had raced upstairs and explained that he had been grounded for staying out all night with some girl and needed enough S2 to make it through the championship game.

Trevor had foolishly given the drugs to Devon, thinking that the boss would be happy to have the star player back on board. He had stood there, watching through his window as Devon made his way to the locker room. He watched as Austin finished up a set of squats and followed after him. And then his world crashed down on him as he watched men in bad suits and a couple sheriff's deputies race through the gym and straight into the locker room.

Devon and Austin had been led out of the room in handcuffs, and his heart had stopped beating. Austin didn't have enough evidence to convict anyone but Devon. On the other hand, Devon had enough knowledge to make things very hot for him.

Trevor had known right then that the next forty-eight hours would determine one of three things: he'd be dead, in jail, or on the run. He had a contingency plan, of course. Any smart criminal did. He had a fake passport declaring him as one Travis Golden, a Bahamas resident. Further, he had a nice little bank account already established there under that name. Then the phone had rung and the Bahamas were looking better and better.

"How the hell did you let this happen? Who told the cops? Was it that little brat?"

"I don't think so. He was arrested as well." Trevor wiped his forehead and sat down in his chair. Acid was building in his stomach as more and more curse words spewed forth from Boss.

"It must be Davies then. Rough him up a little and kill that stupid slut of a girlfriend. That should teach him to keep his mouth shut. And for God's sake, get someone into that holding cell with Devon and take care of him before he talks."

"Blood or no blood?" Trevor asked.

"Normally I would have you rip his damn tongue out and slash his throat, but that would garner too much attention. He's diabetic. Have someone shoot him up with insulin. Go to his house first and plant enough evidence that the cops will be forced to stop their investigation. Let Devon take the fall for everything. He was stupid enough to get arrested."

"What about our next shipment of S2? Won't the cops be surprised to see it again if we have any more health issues?"

"Not if you take care of this tonight. If not, I'll order your death. Got it?"

"Yes, Boss."

"Now, the new shipment has been altered slightly, so it won't be the same as what Devon just got caught with. Leave the rest of your supply at Devon's place. Hopefully this strain won't result in so many deaths because of heart issues. Thank goodness for all these brats. Better than rats, and they actually pay me to be my test subjects. Profits were way up this quarter. At least you're not failing me financially. But, Trevor, you go with them tonight to make sure the job is done right. Davies is not to be seriously injured, got that?"

"Yes, Boss."

"The girl on the other hand... feel free to make a statement." The phone disconnected and Trevor relaxed some. If tonight went well, he wouldn't need to leave town. If it didn't go well, then he needed to get gone.

He pulled out an eight inch hunting knife he kept in his drawer and slid it into his holster against his back, hidden by his black sports coat. He sent a text to the boys and headed downstairs. Tonight he would get back in the boss's good graces. Boss wanted a statement kill and what Boss wants, Boss gets.

Chapter Twenty-One

"Humph. I can't get the door to open." Steve had his shoulder against the door and was trying to quietly push it open.

"It's probably locked." Trevor tried not to roll his eyes. His boys were good for violence, but that was about it. They were definitely not hired for their intelligence.

"It's not locked, Mr. Gaylen."

"Move over idiot, I'll get it." Doug pushed Steve out of the way, and with his curly hair sticking out in different directions he put his shoulder to the door and shoved. The door flew open, and Doug face-planted in the entranceway coming nose to nose with Justin. "Shit! It's a big hairy dog."

"Slit its throat." Trevor shoved Steve forward before the dog could alert Davies and his girl that they were there.

"No need. It's a nice dog," Doug whispered. Justin thumped his tail, turned and trotted upstairs.

Cade awoke in the middle of the night with the feeling someone was watching him. He felt the warm breath on his face and slowly opened his eyes. Justin's face was no more than an inch from his. Justin's brown eyes were looking right at his, and he brought his big paw up and slapped him in the face with it.

"Go back to bed, Justin. It's the middle of the night," Cade whispered to his dog. But, Justin didn't go lie down, and he didn't jump on the bed. Instead he pawed at him again and looked at the door.

Cade was about to roll over to ignore him when he heard a noise that wasn't right. It was a creak that didn't fit in the normal noises his house made when it settled. He quickly got out of bed and slipped on a pair of Bearded Collie boxer shorts that were lying on the floor. They certainly weren't the most intimidating, but his Ranger boxers weren't at hand.

He crawled onto the bed to wake Annie up, just to find her already awake. "I count at least five, possibly more," she said as she slipped on her panties and a t-shirt.

"Those aren't good odds."

"They're learning, but they're still not too smart. Got any weapons up here?"

"Bat or knife?"

"The priest gnome worked pretty well, so I'll go with the bat." He tossed a Louisville Slugger across the bed and watched her take position on one side of the door. If Cade wasn't worried sick about her, he would have appreciated her fighting knowledge. They would bottleneck them so they could have a fighting chance.

Cade picked up the portable phone, dialed 9-1-1 and tossed it back down on the bed while it rang. He could hear them easily now and didn't have time to talk to the operator. They would trace the call, but he knew they were too far away to make a difference now.

Annie pressed herself against the wall and closed her eyes. She counted the footsteps. Seven against two. Those odds were definitely not good. She knew she could take two, but that would leave five to Cade, and there was no way he could handle that. She would just have to take more on because there wasn't a chance in Hell she'd let anything happen to him.

She tightened her grip on the bat and tried to control her breathing. Her plan was to bottleneck them in the doorway. Two could probably get through at once, but then it would be one on one. If they went down, the thugs behind them would have an even harder time getting through the door.

Annie heard the men stop. One tried to creep quietly forward but was about as quiet as a buffalo. She watched the doorknob turn and knew it was time to protect Cade once again. It always seemed like he was getting in trouble.

The door swung open and Larry and Curly came busting through. Annie heard the sound of Cade's knife tearing through Larry's jacket. Curly looked to his injured friend and Annie swung away. The contact with the back of Curly's head reverberated up her arms. Annie didn't have time to smile as Curly crumpled to the ground, landing on top a moaning and bleeding Larry. Two down, five to go.

Moe and one of the roid triplets tried to fight their way in, but they both couldn't get over their two downed comrades. As the hairless ball of muscle made his way through, she decided Cade could have him. He was really big. A girl does need to recognize her limitations after all. Anyway, she wanted a reunion for her and her Three Stooge partner who was having trouble trying to climb over his friends.

"Long time no see." When he looked up from trying to untangle himself, she smacked him with the bat. His nose wasn't straight anyway. Maybe they could finally fix that in jail.

Moe went tumbling backwards as the blood gushed from his nose. He stepped backwards and into, well really more like onto, the unconscious Curly. Moe's arms pinwheeled as he lost his footing. Annie watched as he lost his fight with gravity. He collapsed against the door, his head smashing into the frame. Annie watched him for a second, but he didn't move. He had been knocked out when he had fallen.

"Jesus Christ. Do I have to do everything? Just kill her for crying out loud. How hard can it be?" a Scottish accented voice said.

"Gaylen, is that you? You know, if you wanted to come for a visit, you could have just called." Cade walked to one side of the pile of downed thugs, wiping the bloody blade of his knife on his Beardie boxers. Too bad, blood was hard to get out and those were really cute boxers.

"You know why I came, Davies. You leaked our operation to the cops and as a result we were raided. I told you not to cross the Boss. You knew the price of betrayal when we started our partnership, so we're here to collect. Doug, hold him down while we kill her." Annie's grasp on the bat slackened as the reality set in. They weren't here to rough up Cade, they were here to kill her in retribution for the raid.

A beast of a man came forward and easily took a large step over the still moaning Larry pinned down by an unconscious Curly. He went right for Cade, but before she could take a swing at him, the last of the triplets came at her. He stood easily at six feet and was nothing but hulking muscle.

"Get her, but just hold her. I want to have this pleasure." Trevor Gaylen stepped forward into the room. He was handsome in a dangerous way in his black suit, his red hair slicked back, but it was the cold of his eyes that worried her.

Annie had seen enough to know she was in trouble. She didn't dare take her eyes off of them, but heard Cade in a battle with Doug the Beast. She tightened her grip on the wood bat. Her slick palms slid over the smooth wood as she brought the bat up and swung with all she had at one huge, shiny, bald head.

It was a great swing. She felt it arching through the air, the momentum of the bat twisting her body. Suddenly she was yanked off her feet. The bat had made contact, but not with his head as she had hoped. He had grabbed the bat with his bare hand and jerked it forward. She was powerless to stop herself from falling forward as he pulled the bat towards him. She lost her balance and fell forward, right into his muscle-bound chest. Strong arms wrapped around her, crushing her to the point of not being able to even shout to Cade. One of the vices called an arm moved from around her back to grip her hair as she was thrown to the ground.

"Annie!" Cade screamed. She heard the smack of a punch hitting the mark and then Cade cursing.

"Well, now we get to be properly introduced. My name is Trevor Gaylen, and I will be your executioner tonight," he purred in his Scottish brogue. He pulled out a knife from behind his back.

Annie fought for all she had. She pulled until she felt her hair tearing out of her scalp. She tried to kick, punch, bite, anything, but was held unmercifully by Baldy. Pain shot down her shoulder as he kept her on her knees. Trevor walked forward, the knife held casually and confidently at his side until he stood before her.

Annie couldn't hear Cade struggling to get free as the cold knife blade was brought to her neck. It tickled as he slowly ran it along her throat, the hot blood warming the blade as it trickled from the shallow cut across her throat.

"No need to look so terrified, at least not yet. That was just me saying hello," Gaylen laughed as he wiped the bloodied blade across her white t-shirt.

Her head swam as her stomach flipped. Her heart was beating loudly, blocking out almost all other sound. All other sound except heavy panting? She strained her ears to block out Gaylen's threats. There! She heard it again, this time accompanied with a low growl. It was coming from the corner of the room behind her. The sound of large paws running across the hardwood reached her as she saw Gaylen's eyes widen.

She pulled with all her strength against Baldy. He held tight and twisted his hand around her hair, tightening it even more and pulling her to her feet. She was jerked back against him and spotted Cade for one brief moment. He was pinned on the ground by the Beast, fighting to get free. She may just be able to save him yet.

The growl that came from behind her was now near. Baldy finally noticed it and twisted around, sending her crashing to the floor. Her head was yanked violently back as Baldy raised his arms to shield off the imminent attack. Justin, teeth bared, purple bow bobbing, leapt into the air. His hairy jowls were pulled back to show an impressive amount of teeth, his hair flowing behind him as he sailed through the air.

Annie felt the moment Baldy released her hair. His arms came up defensively as Justin bit down on his arm. His momentum sent Baldy sprawling to the ground, screaming as Justin continued his assault. Annie didn't waste any time. She vaulted forward and tackled Gaylen in the midsection.

The knife flew out of his hand and slid along the floor until it bounced off the baseboard as they crashed into the door and landed on the floor. Annie fought to gain the upper hand, but Gaylen beat her to it. She clawed at anything she could and was rewarded with cursing in Gaelic when she raked her nails down the side of his face. The sound only motivated her to continue fighting.

She kicked, bit, and hit anything she could. He managed to roll her so he was straddling her. She felt his full weight on her hips as he brought back his hand to punch her. She lifted her bottom off the floor as fast as she could. It wasn't enough to toss Gaylen off of her, but it was enough to cause him to fall forward. She wrapped her arms around his chest and rolled to her left until they rolled into the wall, neither of them willing to give up control.

She was aware of noise behind her but didn't have time to focus on it. Arms were tangled and legs were intertwined as they fought. Annie felt his breath on her neck and the smooth material of his suit on her legs as she tried to get on top of him.

Suddenly she was free, warm hands were under her arms pulling her off the ground. Baldy! She lashed out with her legs and connected with his knee. "Ow, I'm trying to save you here."

"Cade!" Annie finally let the blinding rage die down and took a look around the room that was now filled with people.

Noodle was cuffing a battered and bloody Gaylen. EMT's were seeing to Larry, Moe, Curly and one of the steroidasaurus men. Justin was lying on the bed, his back legs stretched behind him, his head resting on his front paws, his purple bow dangling off to the side of his head as he watched the action going on around the room.

Annie looked around and found that Baldy was backed in the corner, begging Dinky to get him away from that dog. Justin raised his head and cocked it to one side. "Woof!"

"That's it. I'll tell you whatever you want, just get me out of here safely. That dog is the devil!" Justin grinned, his pink tongue licking his lips before laying his head back down on his paws.

"Where's that beast of a man you were fighting with?"

"He's already loaded up in the cruiser. He was very conveniently tossed through a window. Landed right in front of my SUV," Cole said as he strutted into the room wearing his navy blue FBI jacket and black cowboy hat.

"Agent Parker? This isn't your jurisdiction, is it?" Annie asked. She felt her feathers become ruffled at the idea of him moving in on her case.

"No, I'm just helping out the Sheriff's department. The Sheriff is down with a kidney stone so when the 9-1-1 call came in, the switchboard operator called her grandmother Edna, who called Miss Lily who lives next door, who then called Marcy, who in turn called Paige, who told me to get over here, or she'd make the incident with the vacuum cleaner seem like a piece of cake.

"Oh, um, okay?" She had no idea about the vacuum cleaner, but Cade was nodding and clearly understanding the situation. At least he wasn't trying to take her case away from her.

"Excuse me," Cole said as his cell phone rang. He opened it and strode across the room. "Parker. Yes, sir. The FBI will be more than happy to provide any back-up you may need. Sure, I will tell them. Call if there is anything else you need." Cole shut off his phone and turned to the room. "Okay, men, all prisoners are to be read their rights and transported to the DEA offices in Lexington. There is to be no radio communication about this and no phone calls given. Ask for Special Agent in Charge Romero when you transfer the prisoners."

The Miranda warning started to echo throughout the room as the prisoners were cuffed and hauled off to various cruisers downstairs. "Miss Hill, if you don't mind getting dressed, I have been asked to escort you and Cade to the DEA's office as well." Cole looked over to Cade and grinned. "Now, aren't those cute boxers? A big smiling dog face right on your...wait! Is that a tail on the backside?" Cole laughed as a red faced Cade pulled on a pair of jeans.

"Oh shut up or I'll tell my sister you are thinking of giving her an iron for Christmas." The remaining men in the room gasped and Cole went white.

"That's not funny. Get in the car, Davies."

Cade stood next to Romero and some federal prosecutor who thought way too much of himself. He looked through the two-way mirrored glass at a very calm and collected Trevor Gaylen who was chained to a gray metal table. The door opened and Annie walked in. Cade got a lot of pleasure seeing the confusion on Gaylen's face.

"Hello, Trevor. It's nice to see you again. We were so busy the last time we saw each other that I didn't get to properly introduce myself. I am Agent Blake with the DEA's office."

"Agent? Well, bugger me."

"No thanks, I think I'll just send you to jail and let someone else have that pleasure."

Annie walked in and took a seat across from him. She was all confidence and Cade couldn't take his eyes off of her. She came to life in the interrogation room. "Strangest thing, Trevor, Devon Ross was found in a diabetic coma in his cell a little while ago. Luckily he was able to pull through. He told us a lot, Trevor. Funny thing, he wasn't cooperating until you all decided to try to kill him."

"What does this have to do with me?"

"I'm glad you asked. See, he told us who tried to kill him. We talked to him, and he gave up one of the men arrested with you tonight. Seems Jeremy was the guy holding me down so you could kill me. I talked to him for a bit, and he told me quite a story about you and your boss."

"I want a lawyer." Trevor didn't look so calm anymore. Sweat was beading on his forehead, and he had turned a ghostly shade of white. Annie, on the other hand, practically glowed.

"That's fine. You don't have to talk. I'll do all the talking. You just sit back and listen while I tell you a story. It's a story of an immigrant who is wanted for murder in his home country. Even though his home country hasn't had an execution since the 1960's, apparently he managed to piss off all the major gangs and has basically signed his own death certificate if he goes back home. Of course, committing such a crime in the U.S. could result in his deportation if it were brought to the Scottish Ambassador's attention."

"In this story, what does the poor immigrant need to do to stay out of his home country?" Cade watched as she slowly smiled as if she were a cat who had just eaten the canary.

"I'm so glad you asked! You're a perfect listener. If the immigrant writes down everything he knows about all the players in his organization, especially his boss, and agrees to testify, we can see about keeping him on American soil."

"But as you pointed out, the homeland doesn't have the death penalty, but you all do."

"We'll take it off the table if and when he chooses to cooperate. The offer expires in thirty minutes." Annie placed a pad and a pen in front of him as she got up from her chair. "I'll see you in thirty minutes, and if that pad isn't full, I'll call the embassy myself." Annie stood up straight and walked out the door.

"I don't think I'm going to send her back to Miami. I think I'll keep her," Romero joked.

"I think I will too." Cade smiled.

Annie read over the statement one more time. Damn, damn, damn. He didn't know the identity of the boss. He did give up the entire organization though and all the other major and minor players across the country. He gave her drop dates and times, dealers, middlemen and even explained that the boss used the teenagers as guinea pigs.

"This doesn't make sense. He wasn't at the games and neither were any of his people," Annie told Romero and Cade.

"Then the boss must have been at the game." Cade saw Annie look to Romero whose brow creased in concentration.

"He's right. Agent Jones!" Romero yelled into the cubicles outside his office. "Call a judge, any judge and get us a warrant for additional surveillance equipment to be put up in and around Commonwealth Stadium. Then call Commonwealth and get this set up. The boss will be there, and we need a picture of every single person who goes in or out. Also, we need everyone held for 48 hours. No paperwork on them, no phone calls. Get the judge to sign off on that too."

Annie watched as Romero went over to his desk and shuffled through the file. "Good job, you two. Go home. Get some rest. Good luck at that game tomorrow, Coach."

"Thank you. I assume the 9-1-1 call should be covered up?" Cade asked.

"I've already taken care of it."

"No disrespect, sir, but gossip travels at an amazing rate in Keeneston. It will take more than the DEA's office threatening the local cops to quiet this down."

"I know. I called John Wolfe as soon as I got the call. He's helping us out with a cover story."

"That's, well, that's just brilliant." Annie was in awe. She would never have thought about that.

"I'm from Paris, Kentucky. It's just a little bigger than Keeneston so I know the ropes of small town gossip." Romero actually cracked a smile as he pointed them out the door.

"Come on, let's go home."

Annie's heart warmed at the thought. She was becoming part of a town with the old guard looking out for her, a man who loved her, and a dog that had saved her.

"Sounds great. But, let's pick up a burger for Justin. I think he deserves it." They headed out to the parking lot and to the car waiting to take them home.

Chapter Twenty-Two

Annie was sure she had never felt such pain. Ow! There it was again. She had been trying to casually check out everyone in attendance, but it was proving to be very difficult with so many people there.

"Did you see that? I have never seen Trey or Austin so in tune with each other!" Paige hit her arm again and Annie cringed. She had been bruised before the first quarter was over. Now that the game was almost over, she was pretty sure one more hit would snap her arm in two.

"They are playing really well," Annie said absently as she looked around again.

"Playing well? What's the matter with you? They have led this team to beat the top school in Louisville with an unstoppable offense," Paige squealed as she hit Annie's arm again.

The game had been close until the third quarter, but then Trey and Austin had found their groove and never looked back. The Keeneston crowd gave the team a standing ovation as the clock reached zero.

Cade shook the hand of the opposing coach and headed for the locker room to celebrate with his team. He looked into the stands and caught Annie's eye. She shook her head slightly and he grimaced.

They hadn't found anything yet. It would be a long night for Annie, but he'd be waiting for her when she got home.

Annie paced the small, dark control room in frustration. They had been in there for three hours looking over security footage. By now she could name every person in the town who had showed up to the game. None of them shouted "Drug Kingpin." They were all the guy or girl next door.

"These are all my neighbors. It's none of them. This is pointless," she growled in frustration.

"I think you may be right. It's time to ruffle his feathers. Book the goons, put Gaylen in protective custody, and see if we can't get the boss to feel a little desperate knowing his organization is all in jail," Romero ordered. "Go home, Blake. Keep me posted."

Annie pulled into St. Frances' parking lot and found two trucks parked in front of her house. Warm light lit up her porch as she climbed the steps. She recognized Cade's farm truck, but the other truck was not known to her.

She cautiously opened the door and stuck her head into her house. She took a whiff and started to drool a little. It smelled warm and yummy. Cade was sitting on the couch with his dad, watching *SportsCenter*. She looked around her small house and found Marcy in the kitchen. She was pulling the casserole out of the oven and Annie's stomach rumbled. There was the source of the great smell.

"Welcome home, dear! Cade said you had a meeting that would run late. I also know you don't cook, so I thought I would bring this chicken pot pie over so you have something good to eat before bed." Annie bit the inside of her cheek to prevent from tearing up. No one had ever thought to make sure she had a good meal before bed.

"Thank you, Marcy. Maybe someday I will learn to cook that. It smells great."

"Well, to each her own. If you don't like cooking, then don't. Cooking is made with love after all."

"It's not that I don't like it. I just don't know how. I never had anyone to teach me," she said quietly.

"Well! Why didn't you say so? I'll teach you. Now, it's late and you need your rest. Jake! It's time to go." Marcy leaned forward and gave her a motherly kiss on the cheek and a squeeze of her hand before herding her husband out the door.

Cade came to stand beside her and slipped his arm around her waist. "I take it, it didn't go well?"

"No, we got nowhere. I knew every person there and have no reason to suspect any of them. So, we booked the ones we're holding and will just hope that the boss will get nervous and slip up. But, your mom's cooking is making me feel better." She walked into the kitchen and got down a plate. "I must admit. I'm getting spoiled being around her. It gives me a feeling of family I never had."

"You could have the family you want now." Annie thought about what he said as she ate a late dinner. Could she have it all?

Annie sat at her home computer and stared at the old email. Cade was at practice at Commonwealth Stadium for the championship game Saturday evening, and here she was, sitting alone at home on a Sunday night. She forced her thoughts back to the old email from her cousin Chrystal. Cade and his family were stirring up feelings she never knew she had or wanted. All she could think about was wanting to share the love and closeness the Davies shared. But, was Keeneston just one more stop in a life of constant moves and let-downs?

She hit reply and typed a short message to her cousin. She did not agree to meet, but it was enough that the feeling of being alone in the world abated. The knock at the door brought her out of her thoughts.

"Hiya!" Paige pushed her way through the door with bags of food, heading straight for the kitchen.

"Hello, dear. We're here to teach you how to cook. I brought all the makings for Cade's favorite and easy dinner. And," Marcy pulled out a white box with a green ribbon tied on it and handed it to her, "this is for you. Every cook needs one."

Annie opened the box and pulled out a light-green apron lined with a white ribbon. Her name was embroidered across the chest. It was the most beautiful thing she had ever seen. "Thank you so much. This is lovely." It was also a sign. She was putting down roots. She had love and friendship. This wasn't just another stopover. This was home.

Annie smiled and asked old Mr. Fowler how his hip was doing as she walked with him to the cafeteria for lunch. Mrs. Bentley waved hello as she hurried to her next class. Ms. Lopez stood by the big double doors waiting for their lunch date. Ever since yesterday when Paige and Marcy spent the afternoon with her, she realized how much she had become integrated into Keeneston in the months since her arrival.

"Nervous about tonight?"

"You know I am, Margaret," Annie told her friend as she sat at one of the teacher tables in the brightly lit cafeteria.

"There's always a first time and it's always the worst. But, I promise, it does get better."

"Really?"

"Sure. I remember the first meal I cooked Randy and it was horrible. I had to throw out the pan. Now I can cook a meal for ten with my eyes closed."

"That makes me feel better. I'm going to leave a little early and get fresh groceries for dinner. Cade's coming over at seven, or whenever practice in Lexington ends. I'm going to need all the time I can get in case I ruin it the first time and have to start over."

"Call me if you need anything and good luck!"

"Thanks, I'll need it." Annie tossed her garbage into the trash can and headed back to her office to look over the recipe just one more time.

Cade ran his finger down the column and checked it off. Austin's grades were improving. He had three more tests to grade, and then he could head over to Commonwealth Stadium. School had let out, and everyone was on their way to Lexington for practice. He wanted them to get used to the stadium and the facilities so nothing would take their focus away on the big day.

Coach Parks had driven the bus over, and they had section meetings first and then they would warm up. That gave Cade enough time to get the quizzes graded and submitted. Cade put the graded papers in his finished pile and recorded the grades in his book before he reached for his mug filled with water. He absently took a gulp of water before starting to grade the next paper.

Cade closed his eyes and then opened them again. He had read the same answer five times and still couldn't finish reading it because it was moving around the page. Something wasn't right. He was sweating and very dizzy. He took another drink of water and tried to focus on the far wall. It blurred as his vision tunneled. Something was really wrong.

He tried to stay calm and assess the situation. He had taken a drink of water and then gotten dizzy and light headed. He had drunk more water to try to feel better and that's when he started sweating and getting tunnel vision. He tried to reach for the phone to call 9-1-1, but his arms wouldn't move. He was positive now, he had been poisoned.

He took a deep breath and focused on his cell phone sitting on the edge of the desk. As he exhaled, he lunged for the phone only to fall out of his seat and onto the ground completely paralyzed. His eyes blurred and everything started to fade to black. He tried to focus his eyes but could only see a shadow of a figure come to stand over him. It had to be the boss. He was making his move.

He felt hands grab under his arms. He willed himself to fight, to kick, to punch, but nothing would work. He tried to open his mouth, but no sound came out. He wasn't even sure his mouth opened. He was trapped in his own body as he watched the blurry lights pass by him as he was dragged down the hall. He had to fight. He had to try. With one last effort, he felt his finger move before the tunnel collapsed and everything went black.

Annie placed the groceries on the counter and reached for the ringing phone. "Hello."

"Annie? It's Al Parks. I know Cade was planning on coming over there for dinner, but I have some questions about practice I need to ask him. I thought he was coming after he got done grading papers, but I guess I was wrong."

"Cade's not here. He was supposed to be at practice." Annie felt a chill dance down her spine.

"Well, if he's not there and he's not here, then he must be at school. I tried his office, and I tried his cell, but he's not answering. If you see him, will you tell him to give me a call?"

"Sure, Al. Look, I gotta go." She hung up the phone and raced into her bedroom. She pulled out her underwear drawer and lifted the hidden compartment to get her DEA-issued 9 millimeter and badge. She had a boyfriend to save...again.

Chapter Twenty-Three

Cade felt like he was swimming in caramel. Everything was moving slowly and his memories were sticky. Only years of training kept him from opening his eyes. He knew he had no strength or balance so he focused on controlling his breathing and listening. If he could just figure out where he was and who took him, he could develop a plan for escape.

Shuffling sounds came from behind him and then the sound of a furnace kicking on. He knew he was sitting in a chair and hoped no one was in front of him. He cracked his eyes and peered out through his eyelashes, right into the face of a skeleton. He looked past the skeleton and saw shelving full of old beakers, test tubes, and Bunsen burners. He knew where he was. He was in the science storage room in the basement of the high school.

He tried to move his arms but found both wrists were duct taped to an old, wooden teacher's chair. He knew the answer but tested his legs anyway. He wasn't surprised to find them bound to the chair as well. From behind him, a cell phone rang and was quickly picked up.

"Yes?" He knew that voice. If his mind would just focus he could place it. "No, Mr. Klaus, everything is fine. The shipment will be sent out on time. It's just a simple matter of reorganization of management. You know how hard good help is to find." The voice laughed, and it clicked in his head who it was. "I look forward to many years of partnership. Please tell the others the organization is strong and all contracts will be met on time with quality product. Yes. Thank you."

The cell phone was clicked shut, and Cade gave up trying to pretend to be asleep. For years he had known that voice, for years they had been friends, and the whole time his friend was the boss of a major drug operation.

"I see you are awake. Surprised it turned out to be me? I bet I never crossed your mind," the Boss practically spat out at him.

"Why?" Cade still couldn't process the betrayal.

"Money, of course."

"What about all those kids who were killed because of the bad product you made?"

"That was merely a bonus. I can't stand all those sniveling brats. They were the perfect lab rats." The Boss stood directly in front of him now, and he could hardly believe it, but the evidence was right there before his eyes. Unable to stand the sight, he looked away. A small movement behind the Boss caught his eyes. The tip of a gun slid through the door. He was being rescued.

"Why are you doing this to me? After all we've been through? I don't understand."

"You wouldn't. You were too focused on that slut. Do you know how many times I could have killed you? I could have killed you any time of any day, but because of our relationship, I gave you the courtesy of keeping you alive. I gave you the courtesy of only hurting you a little when you went against our partnership and turned Devon over to the police. I ordered that slut to be killed and for you to be spared. What is the thanks I get? My whole organization gone! And right when I have my biggest shipment ever to make."

Cade saw Annie's jean clad leg appear, along with the steady arm holding the gun. He just needed to keep talking to keep the attention away from the door. "Because your men were inept you're going to kill me?"

"I thought I would give you the respect you deserve and let you die while you were with those who cared for you. I know you military type. I'm going to give you the respect of knowing you are going to die and who is responsible for it. I wanted you to know it was me." Cade's eyes fell to a large needle in the Boss's hand. He watched as the plunger was pressed slightly down, liquid spewing out the sharp tip of the needle.

The sound of the gun being cocked drew his attention back to the door.

"It's over, Stephanie, put the needle down." Annie saw her back go rigid.

"Annie?" Stephanie slowly turned around on the balls of her feet and stared icily at her. Annie saw the needle still in her hand. What worried her was that Stephanie's hands weren't shaking.

"You can call me Agent Blake. I'm with the DEA. Put the needle down or I'll shoot you." Annie took a couple steps forward and leveled the gun at Stephanie's cold heart hidden under her pale blue sweater set.

With no warning, Stephanie lunged forward. Annie shot off a round, but it went wide. Stephanie went after her gun. She felt the needle jab into her hand and she screamed. The gun dropped to the ground, and Stephanie went after it. Annie ripped the needle out and tackled Stephanie.

"I won't let you win this time. You may be smarter than those expendables I hired, but you're not smarter than me." Stephanie stretched for the gun, her fingers crawling along the floor to reach it.

"It's not about being smart. It's about being strong." Annie grabbed her own hand and used the force to slam her elbow into Stephanie's back.

Stephanie reared up, screaming in pain and Annie grabbed the only thing she could get a hold of. She wrapped her hand around Stephanie's perfect hair and pulled with all her strength. Baldy had taught her this move. Steph was stronger than she gave her credit for. The elbow she threw caught Annie right in the ribs and sent her falling back. Not letting go of Stephanie's hair, Stephanie rolled with her as they both landed on their sides and scrambled up to their feet.

Annie grabbed more hair to pull Stephanie closer, and Stephanie kicked out at her. Pain shot up her lower leg where Steph's heel caught her. Okay, enough playing around. Annie pulled harder on the clump of hair in her hand while sliding her other arm around Stephanie's throat and squeezed. Stephanie dug her nails into Annie's arm. She felt warm blood bubbling up from the claw marks and screamed, but didn't let go. She squeezed tighter as Stephanie fought more frantically.

Annie released Steph's hair and put her in a proper choke hold. Stephanie dug her nails in again and slammed her heel onto Annie's foot. Annie saw spots in her vision but held on. Her foot was on fire, and she was sure it was broken. Through the pain, she realized that Stephanie's struggles were weakening. If she could just hold on a little longer.

Annie shifted her weight to her good foot and applied more pressure. Stephanie clawed again, but it wasn't as strong. She tried to reach behind her but never could reach Annie. Annie felt when Stephanie lost consciousness and let go. They both collapsed to the ground. Annie sucked in ragged breaths as she crawled toward Cade.

"Here we are, back at the beginning," she mumbled as she found an old scalpel to cut the tape tying Cade down.

"How so?"

"I'm saving you again."

"There's no one else I'd rather be saved by." Cade opened his freed arms, and she managed to climb into his lap before her foot gave out. Cade stroked her hair and held onto her for dear life.

"Freeze!"

"It's okay, Noodle," Cade called out as Annie raised her head from his chest to look at the room filling with the local sheriff's department and Cole Parker. "It was Stephanie. Call an ambulance, Annie's foot is probably broken, and she has some nasty cuts on her face and arms from Stephanie." Cade held on tightly to her until the EMT's arrived. If he had things his way, he'd never let her go again.

Annie hated what she was about to do, but she had no choice. She left the warmth and comfort of Cade's arms and struggled to stand on one foot. She had a crime scene to control.

"Cole, can you call Special Agent Romero at the DEA's office and tell him to get down here with a prisoner transport?" She reached into the back of her jeans pocket for her badge, but Cole stopped her.

"Already done, Agent Blake."

"You know who I am?"

Cole looked slightly embarrassed. "I figured you for a cop the second we met. I ran you through the system and figured it out. When you put in place enough cover identities as I have, you can spot one from a mile away. Would you care to have the honors?" Cole gestured to a now cuffed and waking up Stephanie being held by Noodle and Dinky.

"Nothing would give me more pleasure. Stephanie Long, you have the right to remain silent." Annie grinned down at the once spotless and perfectly perky Stephanie. "Agent Blake, we can now call you that, right?" Dinky looked to Noodle who shrugged.

"Wait. What do you mean now? Did you both know who I was too?" Dinky looked nervous but kept his back straight and his eyes on hers.

"Yes, ma'am. We knew who you were the night we arrested all those guys at your house. Between the two of us, we've dated or tried to date all the school teachers around here, and none of them could beat up three men. So, we looked into it, put two and two together and came up with fed. A little more digging and we came up with your name down in Miami."

"Why didn't you say anything?" Unbelievable. She had a topnotch, undercover identity, and now here were all these people who had known who she was the whole time.

"We may work in a small town, but we both graduated top of our class from Eastern Kentucky University. It has a great criminal justice program. We may seem laid back, but we keep our eyes and ears open."

"I'm really impressed. But, you don't need to call me Agent Blake. Annie is fine. Thank you, all of you, for having my back. Is that how you got here so quickly?"

"I saw you race out of the house while I was on patrol. Your gun was attached to your hip so I knew it wasn't good. I called Noodle and Cole as I followed you. I lost you once inside the school though, or I would have been here sooner to help you." Dinky shifted his weight slightly but stood firm.

"That was a great job, Dinky." Static sounded, and he excused himself to radio in. "DEA is here. I directed them down here. What do you need us to do?"

"Crowd control?" She laughed. She stopped laughing though as everyone cringed. "What?"

"I'll rock, paper, scissors you for it," Dinky told Noodle.

"Crowd control? Seriously?"

"You ever try to keep the Rose sisters or John Wolfe from a crime scene? And this is a BIG crime scene," Dinky explained.

"I better check the batteries on the taser," Noodle drawled.

"Oh, that's horrible! Stop joking."

"If she's going to be hanging around, she'll learn," Dinky said to Noodle as they went out the door.

Was she going to be hanging around? She loved Keeneston. But, with her job at the DEA she didn't have a real say in where she was going to live. She could be transferred at any time. Suddenly the prospect of moving again didn't sound nearly as fun and exciting as it used to.

Annie and Cade took a seat at the Blossom Café later that night. Her foot was fractured and in a large air cast. She had wanted to go home, but Cade had sworn up and down that they wouldn't be able to hide. If they didn't tell the story, the town would hunt them down and they wouldn't get any rest. Better to go to the hot spot and tell the story once.

"Miss Blake, I'm so glad we can finally call you that. I was terrified I would slip up and call you the wrong name and get you shot," Miss Daisy said as she whipped out her notepad to take their order.

Annie stared at her dumbfounded. "You knew too?"

"Of course. See, Edna told my sister Lily that she had heard from her brother's, wife's, second cousin's third son that you were DEA. She was real careful who she told though so we wouldn't blow your cover."

"Well, thank you for keeping it quiet." Annie suspected Stephanie was maybe the only person in town who didn't know who she was.

"Of course, what do you take us for, a bunch of old gossips? We protect our own." Miss Daisy headed over to another table to fill them in. Annie looked over at Cade who just raised an eyebrow. This seemed all very normal to him. What scared her was the fact that she wasn't upset about her blown cover. Instead, it felt good to have a whole town looking out for her while she did her job.

"Psst." Annie looked past Cade's shoulder to the plump face of Miss Violet sticking out from the kitchen. "January is still a great time to get married you know."

Chapter Twenty-Four

Annie gasped and brought her hands to her mouth to cover her surprise. "I'm so sorry, Paige."

"It's okay. After a season of sitting next to me you should know I don't mind." Paige shook out her arm and smiled.

"Actually, it's only fair someone hit her for once. You notice I'm only sitting down here with my daughter when you're the one next to me." Marcy handed her a cup of hot cocoa and took the seat to her left.

Commonwealth Stadium was packed for the high school state championship game. They were playing a great team from Danville, but Austin and Trey had found that magic groove again. Now in the fourth quarter, they were pulling away. Trey had just run in a thirty-eight yard touchdown.

Cade was pacing the sidelines, yelling out defensive plays, pulling players aside to pump them up and teach them what to do when on the field. Even though they had the lead, she could tell he was nervous. He had told her he had never expected to make it to the playoffs, let alone the championship game.

Annie jumped up and screamed as J.T. King leaped into the air and intercepted a pass. He fell to the ground and came up with the ball still in his hands. The townspeople were on their feet cheering. Flashes from cameras lit up the stadium as J.T. collapsed underneath the weight of his team jumping on him in celebration.

Cade stood on the sidelines and closed his eyes for just a moment. He knew it was coming, but there was no way he'd move. The cold water still took his breath away as his team dumped the water cooler on him in victory. Cold water ran down his back as his winter coat soaked a lot of it up.

His team was around him then. The cheers were deafening. Music blared in the stadium as he shook hands with the opposing coach before the field was stormed by his friends, family and neighbors. Parents and friends embraced each other, his back was slapped, and he was hugged and high fived. Tonight was the best night of his life, and he just wanted Annie by his side.

"Cade!" He turned his head and saw her red hair peeking out from behind a wall of players all giving her hugs. He pushed himself through the crowd towards her.

His players, seeing him trying to get to Annie, grabbed her and hefted her up onto their shoulders. She squealed like a little girl, and Cade couldn't help but laugh. He'd never seen her have so much fun. Her hair was blowing in the breeze, her cheeks rosy from the cold winter weather, and her eyes alight with happiness. God, she was perfect. He watched with a huge smile on his face as she was placed in front of him. His players backed away to form a small circle around them and cheered as he pulled her against him for a victory kiss.

His heart beat so loudly he thought everyone in the whole city of Lexington could hear it. He tightened his arms around her and knew he wanted her right there with him for the rest of his life. He forgot he was cold and wet. He forgot the whole town was pressing in on them, trying to see what was going on. All he knew was her laugh, the feel of her lips on his, and the way she fit so perfectly against him.

Now was the time. Come on, Cade, you can do it. He removed one hand from around her waist, slid it into the pocket of his coat and felt what he was looking for. It may be a little wet, but he didn't think that mattered. His hand slid down her arm to her hand as he went down on one knee. With how loudly his heart was beating, he didn't notice that everyone on the field had grown quiet.

He looked up into Annie's eyes and knew it would be all right. Her answer was there for him to see. "Annie Blake, I love you with all my heart and soul. I wish to spend the rest of my days making you as happy as you make me." He pulled out the damp, red velvet ring box and opened it. "Will you marry me?"

Annie gaped at the large emerald sitting on a diamond band, and tears filled her eyes. She looked to the man she loved and fell to her knees. She wrapped her arms around him and kissed him. In him she had found herself, her family, and happiness. What she knew was that they would be spending the rest of their days together, surrounded by the love and family she thought were beyond her reach.

"Did she say 'yes' yet?" Miss Lily's voice floated over the shoulders of the players holding people back.

"YES! I'll marry you, Cade." The tears escaped and she laughed as he slipped the ring onto her finger. The players lost their battle and Marcy broke through, followed quickly by Paige and the Rose sisters.

"I couldn't ask for a better daughter-in-law," Marcy croaked between sobs. "Two weddings, honey. Can you believe it?" Jake put his arm around his wife and pulled Annie in for a hug.

"We're glad to welcome you to the family."

"Thank you, Mr. Davies."

"I think you can start calling me Dad now." The floodgates broke as the tears streamed down her face. Marcy sobbed again and pulled her in for another hug as Jake went to congratulate his son.

The Blossom Café was packed for an impromptu victory celebration and engagement party. The Rose sisters were in their zone. Miss

Daisy flitted from table to table passing out food, Miss Lily used a heavy hand as she mixed her special ice tea, and Miss Violet was talking to people through the window as she put food on large plates.

"I don't know if I should have another. You know, I hold a very prominent position in the town and I wouldn't want anyone to think I'm a lush." Pam Gilbert said as Miss Lily pushed another glass of special ice tea into her hand.

"Oh lighten up, Pam. Even the PTA President can celebrate tonight. Go wild, undo that top button by your collar and no one will recognize you!"

Annie tried to contain the bark of laughter threatening to erupt at the scandalized look on Pam's face. All of Keeneston had turned out. Summer had cornered Henry, who looked petrified at her advances. The Davies family was all around her and the feeling of belonging swelled inside of her.

"Hmm. So, someone finally landed one of the famous Davies brothers. What are you, knocked up?" A snippy voice said from behind her.

Annie heard Paige's gasp and then hiss. She turned around and got an eyeful of bottled blonde hair and boob.

"Lord love ya, are you carrying a small child up there?" Annie asked as she pointed to what could only be described as a bump-it on steroids. She had never seen hair teased and piled up so high before. And she even knew women from Texas!

"Kandi Chase-Rawlings, meet my new sister, Annie Blake." Paige slung her arm around Annie's shoulder and just smiled as Kandi stomped off in a huff towards an even more terrified looking Henry.

"Someone should go rescue Henry. He was scared before when Summer mentioned always wanting to marry a lawyer, but I'm afraid he may keel over when Kandi gets her fake nails into him," Paige told her brothers.

Everyone looked at each other. No one wanted to deal with Kandi.

"Oh fine, I'll do it. Y'all are a bunch of wimps," Peirce said as he bravely went forth to rescue Henry.

"I can't believe how many people are here. The whole courthouse showed up. I'm sure the rumor of the two of you deciding to tie the knot tonight helped. Congratulations to you both! Will and I are so happy for you!" Kenna squealed as she gave Annie a hug and as Will shook Cade's hand.

"Oh! Oh! Sit yourself down right now. A pregnant lady shouldn't be on her feet too long or those ankles will swell as big as balloons. And heels! You're wearing heels! Don't you know those will give you ugly looking veins. Bless your heart! Don't you dare grab that drink!"

Kenna rolled her eyes and allowed herself to be pushed into a chair as Miss Lily clucked over her.

Annie stepped back and watched the town interact. People laughed and teased each other. Kids and parents alike were reliving the game, and a sprite of a girl was shooting daggers at Kandi and Summer as they fawned over Pierce. Henry had taken the shift in attention to his advantage and snuck off to talk to Judge Cooper. But, unlike Henry, Peirce seemed completely at ease with the women vying for his attention.

"Hey, Kenna, who is that?" Annie asked as she pointed out the blonde pixie with a couple bright blue streaks in her hair.

"Who? Oh, that's Tammy. She's the secretary at our law offices." Kenna looked to where Tammy had started walking and cringed. "For once I feel sorry for Kandi."

"I wish I had Tammy on my security team. She is a force of nature." Ahmed turned to Annie and gave her a kiss on her cheek. "Congratulations. Cade is a very lucky man. Never let him forget you are too good for him."

"Gee, thanks man." Cade moaned, all the while smiling.

"Well, he is right on all accounts." A smooth silky voice said from behind her.

Annie glanced behind her as Mo and Dani approached. He had his fiancée's hand tucked into the crook of his elbow as he guided her through the crowd to stand in a circle next to her and Cade.

"Congratulations you two! I couldn't be more excited!" Dani gave her a warm hug and Annie couldn't be happier. She had a wonderful fiancé, a new family, and friends. Actual friends.

"Excuse me. I hate to interrupt the celebration, but there is someone looking for you, Annie" Annie turned to where Dinky was standing with a young woman in her early twenties.

She was about her height with curly dark red hair standing nervously in front of her. Dinky stood up very straight and it looked like he was trying to impress whoever this girl was.

"Yes? Can I help you?" Annie felt the circle break apart and all turn towards the newcomer. Cade came to stand next to her, and she was comforted by the feel of his reassuring hand on her back. Marcy and Jake stood on either side of them, as she waited to find out who this woman was.

"I'm Chrystal Sharp, your cousin. I got your e-mail and I just had to meet you," the girl said hesitantly.

All conversation stopped in the Café. Everyone wanted to know who this new person was. After finding out Annie was undercover, they all assumed the story of a cousin in Louisville was just a cover and Annie hadn't corrected them. Annie just stared at the girl who looked somewhat like her. She didn't know exactly what to say.

"I had to come find you. I looked all over town, but couldn't find anyone. I guess they were all at the game. Then I came across this nice man who said he knew where you'd be. Is there someplace we can go talk?" She asked as Dinky seemed to stand even straighter with the compliment.

"What did she say?" Someone in the back of the Café asked.

"She wants to go someplace to talk to our Annie," another person answered before being shushed by the onlookers.

"We'll just all find out anyway. Why don't you speak your mind? We'll be quiet. Besides, Annie's here with family," Miss Lily told her as she shoved a glass of ice tea into Chrystal's hand and took a seat so she could be the first to hear what this newcomer wanted.

"She's right. They will find out. What do you want?" Annie stood rigid as she watched the woman fidget with her hands.

"I had to find you to tell you that I didn't know. I didn't know what my mother had done. See, I was only three when your mother died. My mom had moved up in the world. She had married my father who was much older than she was. He was a surgeon in Indianapolis and then moved to head up the department at the University of Louisville. He passed away three years ago at the age of eighty-three."

"I'm sorry to hear that, hon," Marcy put in when Annie didn't say anything. Cade gave her a reassuring touch and she focused back on her cousin.

"Well, my mother had been furious when she heard I had contacted you. I didn't understand why. She said you were just like your mother, looking for a handout and that you would see how well off we were and try to steal from us. I knew that wouldn't be so. I had done a lot of research and knew you were with the DEA's office. Anyway, my mother just lost her battle with breast cancer six months ago. I was going through all her things when I found the letters from Children Services in Florida, begging her to take you or you would end up in foster care." Annie saw tears start to glisten in her cousin's eyes and softened a little. She had been just a child. She couldn't have protected her.

"When I got your email, I had to come see you. You're the only family I have left, and I would love nothing more than to become a family." Chrystal dug a tissue out of her purse and dabbed her eyes.

Annie didn't know if she could speak, so she just nodded. Her little cousin looked so relieved. Color came back to her face, and when she smiled, Annie felt it in her heart. Cade gave her a hug, and for the first time in her life Annie didn't feel bitter. The chip that had sat on her shoulder for almost twenty years was lifted.

"Welcome to the family. I'm sure when my fiancée can talk, she'll let you know you now have a rather large extended family," Cade said as he rubbed his hand up and down Annie's back.

"Really, a large family?" Chrystal asked excitedly.

"Yes, Cade has five brothers and a sister. And this is my future mother-in-law Marcy Davies and her husband Jake Davies," Annie finally said.

"This is my oldest son Miles, and that one is Marshall, and the younger one there is Pierce. Cy is out of town at the moment. And this is my daughter Paige." Marcy introduced Annie's new family to her cousin.

She hadn't heard them come to stand behind her, but they were all there now shaking hands with her cousin. The Café erupted with introductions and people came to embrace the newest extended member of the Keeneston community.

"You know, I never got to thank you."

"What for, Peirce?" Annie asked.

"It's pretty cool that you saved my brother. It finally gives me something to hang over his head. He had to be rescued by a girl. That's the best gift anyone could give me." Pierce gave her a bear hug and went to torture his brother. She had never been happier in her life. She was finally at peace.

Annie came downstairs early the next morning. She and Chrystal were going to go shopping together later today before Chrystal had to get back to college on Monday. She opened the sliding glass door and called for Justin.

She heard him run down the stairs. She heard when he slid around the corner, his feet clawing madly to get traction on the hardwood floor. He appeared then, hair blown back as he sped toward the door. Annie could see the instant he remembered that last time he had done this he went head first into the glass door. Justin tried to back pedal, but when that didn't work he sat down. His hair slid across the polished hardwood floor, and his eyes grew round as he neared the door. He ducked his head in preparation for impact but went sailing through the open door and stopped on the patio. Annie shook her head and laughed as Justin stared at the now closed door in confusion.

"You have a sick sense of humor. You realize since you closed the door so fast he now thinks he just slid through glass." Cade leaned against the kitchen island in nothing but some low hung jeans. "What got you up early?"

"I got a phone call this morning from Noodle," she told him.

"Noodle?"

"It seems that the sheriff is on medical leave and they need more help. He offered me a job as a deputy and the head of the rural drug education program. Twice a week I would have office hours at the high school."

"What did you tell him?"

"That I could start in two weeks," she said as she smiled.

"Are you sure?" She could hear Cade trying to contain his excitement at the idea of having her working in Keeneston.

"I'm positive. I don't want to do undercover work anymore. I loved working with the kids, and maybe I can make a difference in some of their lives. I want to be near you, to have the kind of family I never thought I would have." Annie ran her hand up his bare chest and wrapped her fingers around his neck, bringing his head down for a kiss.

The doorbell rang and Annie reluctantly pulled away. Justin jumped onto the sliding glass door and fell sideways, opening the door enough for him to nuzzle it open and slip through. He ran ahead of her to the front door and barked.

Annie opened the door and was surprised to see Chrystal, Paige, Marcy, Kenna and Danielle standing there. "Um, not to sound rude, but what is everyone doing here?"

Marcy stepped forward, "I talked to Chrystal some after the game, and we thought it would be fun to do some wedding shopping. Well, I told Paige...."

"And I insisted I come too. You're going to be my sister after all," Paige cut in.

Kenna walked forward with her rounded belly and Danielle by her side, "And when Paige told us what you all were up to, we also invited ourselves."

"But, we come bearing gifts." Danielle handed over two binders to Annie who stared at them in awe. "That's right. All the wedding planning details, names, colors, locations, you could ever imagine. I had to steal it from the royal wedding committee to make a copy. I like keeping those folks on their toes."

"So, I thought it would be fun for us to all get together and start planning your wedding," Chrystal said.

"Have you all decided on a date? If not, can I suggest April?" Kenna asked with a grin. Annie rolled her eyes. God, she loved this town.

Epilogue

A nnie set the patio table with the china she had received for her wedding three months ago to the day. She and Cade had a beautiful ceremony at St. Francis the week after Valentine's Day. Cade had told everyone it was her birthday, and there would be a party at the farm that afternoon. Birthday invitations had gone out to the whole town. The Rose sisters were in charge of keeping it a surprise.

While the Rose sisters and others were putting final touches on cakes, gifts, and so on, she and Cade had quietly gotten married with just their family present. Marcy had cried alongside Chrystal, whom she had become very close to in the last six months. Paige had been her maid of honor while Marshall had been Cade's best man. Justin had looked very handsome in his black tuxedo and tie as he walked her down the aisle. She had worn a beautiful white lace dress that had belonged to Marcy. Paige had added a red satin sash that flowed down the train. It had been perfect. Kenna and Will were even able to attend with their perfect, two-week-old baby girl Sienna. Will and Kenna were beaming with pride as they showed off the cute baby with strawberry blonde hair. With her chubby cheeks and her mommy's mischievous glint to her eye, Sienna was the life of the party.

Cy even made a brief appearance to welcome her to the family. She had been taken aback by the similarities in all the brothers, but the cold, fierce distance behind Cy's eyes had her feeling an instant connection to him. After all, she had once been like that. Although no one seemed to realize it, Miles had the same look. He just hid it better. They were determined to conquer some enemy in their past, and if she was a betting woman, she'd put her money on them.

After the ceremony, they had entered the "surprise" birthday party and surprised their guests instead. The Rose sisters cried and hugged them after playfully hitting Cade for fooling them. Trey had stared at them in awe as he pulled out a little piece of paper from his pocket.

Put $50 on February 21st for the Cade/Annie wedding. The winnings should cover the gap in tuition and scholarship you received from Miami of Ohio.

Annie lifted her finger to her lips and gave him a wink from across the room. Trey was the only person in town to bet on the correct month and day. He won the pot of over $5,000.00 and could now afford to attend his first choice college.

Annie smiled to herself as she filled the glasses with sweet tea. She had another secret, but this one she'd share with the family. After all, the new deputy sheriff shouldn't be accused of rigging illegal gambling pools. It just wouldn't look right.

"Cuz?"

"Back here, Chrystal!" Her little cousin had just graduated from the University of Louisville and was moving to Lexington to start her first job.

"Look at all this food. Did Marcy come over again?"

"Nope. She cooked it all by herself," Marcy answered as she came out of the kitchen with a platter of food.

Within minutes, her family was around her, talking, laughing, and teasing. Her cousin had been adopted by the whole family and was being interrogated by Miles about her latest boyfriend. Cade stood behind her and slipped his arms around her waist. He nuzzled her neck and whispered something dirty in her ear that had her laughing out loud.

Cole and Paige came around the house and joined the party. They had just returned from their honeymoon. They had been married on some large rocks, in the middle of a stream, in the woods on her parents' property. Wild flowers had surrounded the natural alter as most of the town formed a semi-circle around the couple on the banks of the stream.

"Hello, everyone!" Paige bounded up the stairs as Cole hurried after her. He looked slightly ill. His face was pale and he looked nervous. "I know it's Annie's dinner, and thank you for hosting it tonight, but I just can't wait until after dinner to make an announcement."

Annie watched as Paige clasped Cole's hand, and by the way she was glowing and the way Marcy was tearing up, there was no doubt what the announcement was going to be.

"We're going to have a baby!" Paige couldn't contain the smile on her face. Her mother started crying and even Jake got misty eyed when he hugged her. Cole started looking better the longer they were there, but he still looked terrified until Jake gave him a hug. When he had gotten Jake's approval, he visibly relaxed.

"Oh! A grandchild, oh Jake, we're going to have a grandchild." Marcy hugged her husband as tears trickled down her face.

"Ma, I'm sorry to tell you, but you're not going to have a grandchild." At Cade's statement, the patio went quiet. "You're going to have grand*children*." The patio remained silent as they stared at Cade, trying to figure out his meaning.

Cade squeezed her hand and took in the moment. Justin came bounding up with his yellow bow pulling back the hair from his eyes and stopped before Annie. He placed his nose on her belly and thumped his tail. Marcy gasped and pulled Paige and her into a tight hug.

"My daughters are having babies together. Jake, I can die now."

"Why don't you wait to die until after you meet the babies? You may then wish to re-evaluate the time of your death, dear."

"Congratulations, brother!" Cade shook Marshall's hand and gave him a hug.

"You better be careful. You might be next," he teased.

"I wouldn't bet on that." Even as Marshall said it, the unwelcome picture of a tall, angry, blonde crossed his mind.

Cade caught Annie's eye and they shared a secret smile. She was pretty sure they'd be taking Marshall up on that bet. They'd visit the Blossom Café tomorrow to do just that.

About the Author

Kathleen Brooks is the bestselling author of the Bluegrass Series. She has garnered attention as a new voice in romance with a warm Southern feel. Her books feature quirky small town characters you'll feel like you've known forever, romance, humor, and mystery all mixed into one perfect glass of sweet tea.

Kathleen is an animal lover who supports rescue organizations and other non-profit organizations whose goals are to protect and save our four-legged family members.

Kathleen lives in Central Kentucky with her husband, daughter, two dogs, and a cat who thinks he's a dog. She loves to hear from readers and can be reached at Kathleen@Kathleen-Brooks.com.

Check out the Website, http://www.Kathleen-Brooks.com for updates on in the Bluegrass Series. You can also "Like" Kathleen on Facebook (facebook.com/KathleenBrooksAuthor) and follow her on Twitter @BluegrassBrooks.

Bluegrass Series News

Love Keeneston? Don't want to say good-bye? Then don't! The next book in the Bluegrass Brothers Series will be Marshall's story. All of Keeneston will make an appearance and you can once again slip into the story of the town we all love.

So, make a pitcher of special iced tea, cut a slice of pecan pie, and get ready for some more Southern charm from your favorite town!

Want to know when the next book is published? Go to http://www.Kathleen-Brooks.com and sign up on the contact form. I will email you as soon as the next book is published.

See you real soon!

32888021R00145

Made in the USA
Lexington, KY
06 June 2014